A BOND OF WORDS

Published by Scout Media
Copyright 2019
ISBN: 978-1-7330740-6-3

Cover and story header designs by Amy Hunter

Visit: www.ScoutMediaBooksMusic.com
For more information on each author and all volumes
in the *Of Words* series.

Table of Contents

"COME MOONSHINE
OR FOG"
BRIAN PAONE

Stanley shifted on the log, trying to revive feeling in his buttocks, and flipped the page of his Mead composition notebook. His favorite blue BIC pen scribbled words faster, trying to keep up with his brain. He stopped midsentence and tuned his ears to a faraway sound. He strained through the birds' chirping and the natural ambiance of the rows and rows of trees enveloping him.

Stanley lowered his head and placed his pen to the paper but did not scribe the next word in his story. He trained his gaze down the small dusty pathway that led from the cluster of trees to the fallen log where he sat.

Shuffling. Feet shuffling—not the padding of animal hooves. He recognized the distinct sound of sneakers on his trail. One set of footfalls. And they sounded light. Quick. Dainty even.

Stanley swallowed hard and rested the pen in the gutter of the composition book, so he could scratch at yet another pimple breakout. He glanced around, contemplating whether to hide in the thicket behind him and let the hiker pass by or to stay put on his log and subject himself to the possibility of making chitchat with a stranger.

And then he heard singing—from a female.

Stanley snatched his pen and began writing again. The words didn't even form complete sentences. He wrote random nouns and verbs just so whoever was about to crest the top of the trail would see how busy he was and would hopefully continue their journey onward through the woods.

Movement from his peripheral vision. She had entered his sight line.

Just walk on past, like I'm part of this log. Don't make eye contact. Don't stop to chat. Don't—

The dusty soil crunching underneath her sneakers grew louder.

Just keep writing … His pen skittered left to right, then down again on the page: *Tree, ball, run, Stephen King, The Muppets, jet packs, moonbugs, ground, red, hyena, clouds, Uncle Dave, hair bow, Godzilla …*

A list of stream-of-conscious words filled each line. He scribbled faster as her footsteps approached.

Walk by … Walk by … Walk by.

His heartbeat pounded in his cheeks, his ears, his brain … He didn't have to strain his eyeballs far left to see her anymore. She bounded along the trail, headphones covering her ears and a large Walkman clasped in one hand. He knew she saw him now—his log was in direct sight of her—but, instead of slowing her speed or indicating she saw someone sitting all alone out here in the woods, Stanley noticed how she dug deep to inhale and then belted the lyrics to whatever song must be playing through her headphones—offkey and way louder than the serene silence of the woods deserved.

A handful of birds took flight.

She removed her headphones and let them fall around her neck—the distant and tinny sounds of Hank Williams still emanating from the foam-covered earpieces now resting on her collarbones—when she stopped in front of Stanley and his log. When he didn't look up from his composition book and kept scribbling, she placed her hands on her hips.

Nintendo, football, ice cream, mayonnaise, pool parties, mountain ranges, guitars, Luke Skywalker, Ireland, Phil Collins …

"Hey, Ponyboy. You gonna say hi or just keep acting weird?"

Stanley didn't really put down the pen inasmuch as it toppled when his grip relaxed. "Why'd you call me *Ponyboy*?" he asked and looked up at her.

"You, all solitary, sitting out here with your wrinkled journal, writing away with furious abandon."

Stanley immediately liked the way she talked. Her words felt poetic, lyrical. He stood from the log and folded the composition book into his back pocket. "But who's Ponyboy?"

She squealed and bent over to slap her jeaned thighs right above the threadbare holes in the knees. Her headphones slid from around her neck, and she caught them by the wire before they hit the dirt.

"You're weird," Stanley said.

"And you're unworldly." She secured the headphones around her neck again and stood upright. "What'cha doin'?"

"Writing …" Stanley mumbled and shot a look toward the way home. "I should get going."

"Poems? Monster stories? Comic strips? *Ooh*, … love letters!"

Stanley chortled. "Look. I don't know who you are or what you're doing in my part of the woods, but I'd like to be left alone."

The girl clicked Stop on her Walkman and shoved it into her back pocket. "Name's Angel. Moved in this morning with my aunt"—she glanced over her shoulder at the way she had come—"into the Council Towers. Needed to take a break from the chaos and found this trail."

Stanley placed a hand on top of the notebook sticking out of his back pocket and sighed. "Short stories. Fiction mostly."

"I didn't peg you for a serious author, Ponyboy. Had you more of the comic-book superhero type." She scanned his attire. "Or maybe penning sappy poems."

"Why do you keep calling me Ponyboy?"

"*The Outsiders*, silly!"

"Never heard of it."

Angel placed a palm to her forehead and held it there. "*Hoe-ley shite!* You've never read *The Outsiders*? Like, it hasn't even been on your required reading list for school yet?"

He shook his head. "Maybe in senior year?"

"That's it." She reached behind him and snatched his notebook from his pocket. "You're not allowed to write another word until you read that book."

"Hey! Gimme that!" Stanley jumped to grab his journal, but she held it behind her head.

Angel studied him with a stoic expression and tossed his journal at his face, the sprawled pages hitting his nose and cheeks before falling to the ground. "You're no fun."

Stanley bent to retrieve his composition book, and she turned to leave the way she had come, slipping her padded headphones over her ears.

"Wait!" he said, startling himself that he had spoken at all.

Angel stopped but did not turn to face him.

"I'm Stanley. I live at the end of the trail. I come up here to write and to be alone. It's the only place I can go to think. I'm not used to anyone coming by, never mind talking to me."

Angel kicked a small pebble, and they both watched as it bounced off a root protruding from the center of the pathway.

Stanley cleared his throat and hoped they wouldn't stand here in silence for too long before she decided either to continue walking home or to stay a bit.

"I don't know if I'm living here permanently or going back home when school starts. My mom said it would be safer for me to stay with my aunt for the summer, while Daddy gets help." She turned but kept her gaze on the scattered yet dense maze of trees. "And I'm dreadful at making new friends."

Stanley sat down on the log and patted the empty space next to him. "You got one up on me. I don't even *have* any friends."

Angel chuckled and accepted his invitation. "So, are all these woods yours?"

"I like to pretend so, but I'm sure the mayor would have something different to say. It's my favorite spot to write. Coming here makes me feel like I've stepped into—"

"Narnia!" she finished.

"Well, I wasn't going to say that, but I guess it'll do."

"Please tell me that you've heard of it."

Stanley snickered. "Well, duh!"

"I dunno, Mr. Bigshot Author Who Has Never Heard of *The Outsiders*."

"Why does your dad need help?"

"What kind of stuff do you write about?" she asked in reply.

"It-It's personal."

"Mine too," she said.

"I see what you did there." Stanley handed her the journal. "Then I'll go first."

Angel took the notebook from Stanley's trembling hands and cuddled it to her lap. "What do you want to be when you grow up, Ponyboy Stan?"

"Super Mario's brother, Luigi."

She kicked his sneakers with her Converse Chuck Taylors. "No, seriously."

"You're pretty much holding evidence of my dreams. All I've ever wanted to do was write. What about you?"

"I just wanna get the heck out of this crummy state. It's not so much what I want to be but *where* I want to be when I grow up."

"And where's that?"

She scratched the back of her ear, then placed both palms on her thighs. "Any-the-fuck-where but here. Paris. London, Munich, Tokyo. Fucking Mars for all I care."

Stanley pursed his lips and focused on the path, breaking his uncomfortable eye contact with her. "It's because of your dad, huh?"

Angel looked at her hands and wrung them together. "You here every day?"

Stanley nodded. "As many days as I can."

"Maybe I'll see you here again tomorrow. I'll make sure I head up that path at the same time." She returned the composition book to him and looked at her watch. "Two o'clock?"

Stanley gave her a single thumbs-up.

"Stay gold, Ponyboy."

"Just because you keep calling me that, it doesn't mean I'll magically get the reference. It doesn't make you look smarter than me. It just—"

Stanley stopped talking when he realized she had already pressed Play on her Walkman and was bebopping toward civilization.

Stanley shoveled spoonfuls of Chef Boyardee into his mouth, glancing at the ticking clock in ten-second intervals as the hour hand hovered right at the two-o'clock mark.

"Have somewhere to be?" his mother asked, elbow deep in suds and hot water.

"Wanna finish the story I'm writing," he replied with bits of Beefaroni falling from his mouth and glanced at the clock again. He stood from the table, dipping his chin to meet the spoon in the bowl, scooping the last pile of pasta into his mouth, and dropped the dish into the sink. "Gotta go."

His mother started to say something but stopped as she ran the sauce-stained bowl and spoon under the hot water.

Stanley burst through his back door, climbed the small incline to catch the entrance to the trail, and jogged the curves and small hills leading to his writing spot. As he crested the top of a slope, he saw her Chucks and jeaned legs already sitting on his log. He reached for his back pocket, and his fingers grasped at nothing. He slowed to a meandering pace and cursed himself for forgetting to grab his composition book in his haste to leave the house on time.

"'Nother day, 'nother dollar. Ain't that right, Ponyboy Stan?" she called from the log.

"You're so weird," he mumbled and trucked toward the log.

"I heard that!" She waited for him to sit beside her.

He hoped she didn't notice he was panting, out of breath.

"I brought you a present."

He furrowed his brows and cocked his head. "Oh?"

"But first you gotta let me read one of your Ponyboy Stan specials."

"I-I left my notebook in my room."

Angel leaped off the log, her hands behind her back, and stood in front of him. "So, let me get this straight. You *still* came up here, at the right time, but didn't bring your journal? Knowing there was a chance I would be here too?"

"Jeez, when you put it like that, it sounds like—"

"That you like me, Ponyboy Stan. Well, I'm gonna give you your present anyway. Because I'm a proper lady." Angel moved her hands in front of her and held out a shopworn paperback. "No rush to get it back. Read it at your leisure."

Stanley took the book and chuckled. "Is that Ponyboy on the cover?" He flipped the book over and scanned the back-cover blurb.

"I want a full book report when you're finished. Introductory statement and conclusion *must* be included!"

"You really crack the whip," he said, shoving the paperback into the pocket that should be holding his composition book.

"I take *The Outsiders* very seriously." She closed one eye and pointed at him. "And you should too, bucko! Or I'll be comin' for ya. I might not know where you live, but I know where you hide, my pretty." She threw back her head and cackled. "And your little dog too!"

"You're demented."

"Please tell me that you know what that's from, or we seriously can't be friends anymore."

"I'm not a complete doofus. Of course I know that's from *Willy Wonka*!"

Angel punched him in the arm. "You're so lame. Indubitably."

"So, we're friends now, are we?" Stanley rubbed where she had hit him.

"You wish. Just proves you can't believe everything I say!" Angel brushed off some dust from the trail on her jeans. "I guess we can just hang here and listen to music and daydream about greener pastures." She flipped her headphones over her head. "Please tell me that you at least came with some tunes?"

Stanley shook his head. "Got a Walkman for my birthday, but I don't like music all that much."

"Why do I feel like, if you looked up 'pathetic' in the dictionary, there'd be a picture of you?"

He returned the playful punch to her arm, and she giggled.

"What's farther down this path?" she asked.

He shrugged. "Never been past this log."

"You mean, you don't know?" Her eyes lit up. "Master Explorer Stan became a literal bump on the log?"

"I found my perfect writing place and just—"

"You just stopped looking. No desire to find something better."

"You don't know me," Stanley said and slid off the log.

"Oh, I know *exactly* who you are." Angel stood to meet his gaze. "And someone like you will never change. Enjoy the book. See ya when I see ya."

Stanley stood, mouth agape, as she disappeared from sight back down the trail.

Stanley's mother knocked on his bedroom door before opening it. "Lights out, kiddo."

He glanced at her over the top of the dog-eared pages. "Just let me finish this chapter."

She shifted her weight and put a hand on her hip. "I must've read that three times when I was in college. It was one of your dad's favorites too."

Stanley used his thumb as a bookmark and lowered the book. "I had never heard of it until some new girl let me borrow it. She moved into the Council Towers a couple days ago and is staying with her aunt for the summer."

"Oh? A girl? I *knew* you were acting funny today." His mother stepped into his room. "How did you meet?" She elongated the *E* sound, as if asking a child if they wanted ice cream.

"We ran into each other on the trail."

"After you finish the book, you should invite her over. Your dad recorded the movie from HBO. I'd just need to figure out where he left the tape."

"I dunno, Mom. I think I may have messed it up already." Stanley crisscrossed his legs underneath him. "I'm not really sure what I said, but it offended her, and she took off today, when we were hanging out."

"Girls can be finicky, kiddo. She's the new kid on the block and probably being very guarded, until she feels more comfortable."

"You don't know Angel."

"And, after two days, you do?" She winked at him. "Give her some time. She's obviously just nervous and being cautious. Ten more minutes and I want this light turned off."

Stanley nodded and opened *The Outsiders* again. He awoke the next morning with his light still on and the book resting like a pitched tent on his chest.

Stanley paced in front of his writing log, glancing at his wristwatch for the umpteenth time—2:35.

She's really not coming, he thought and kicked a rock into the shrubbery. He sat in his spot and opened his composition book. Gnawing the end of his BIC pen, he shook his foot to expel some nervous anxiety. He reviewed the string of nonsense words he had written that first day Angel had come up the trail. He ran his fingers over the letters and felt a pang of longing— longing for someone he had only met twice. He flipped through the journal and scanned the story he had been working on prior to meeting Angel, and it felt inconsequential—everything felt like the color had been stripped from it.

Sigh. Already 2:50 p.m.

Any further hope that she would arrive for their scheduled rendezvous dwindled. Stanley collected his notebook and Angel's copy of *The Outsiders* and took a step toward home.

Then stopped.

He glanced behind him at the path continuing deeper into woods, past his writing log. His feet seemed to itch to investigate what lay beyond his safe spot. His body was drawn, like a magnet, to the unknown dark depths.

Stanley turned and stared down the trail, then took a step past the log and around the first bend. As the trail straightened, he saw the familiar Chucks swinging back and forth a few inches off the ground.

"I thought you'd never get here, Ponyboy." She scooted off the stump she was sitting on. "See? Ya took a chance, and you got"—she spun around like she was on a catwalk—"me!"

"You've been here this whole time?" Stanley quickened his pace toward her.

"Made sure I got here early, so you wouldn't catch me on the trail."

"How long would you've stayed here?"

"Until you left your log. And I would return every day until you found me."

He slapped her on her back with her own paperback. "You're bonkers. You know that, right?"

"But I'm irresistible!"

Stanley looked at his sneakers.

"Did you …?" She pointed at his face and took a step backward. "You did! I saw you blush!"

Stanley touched his cheek. "Did not."

"All right, hot stuff. This is your only free pass from me. I won't tease you about it. But don't let it happen again, or I'll tell everyone."

"You don't know anyone but me!"

"Touché, monsieur. Now kiss me before I change my mind."

Stanley's gaze shot to meet her. "What?"

"Don't you think it's proper to kiss someone who was willing to wait for you, day in and day out, through the wind and rain, through the famine and plague …"

"Dramatic, are we?"

"Oh, stop stalling and being such a wuss and kiss me!"

Stanley dropped his head and kicked a stick into a small pool of mud.

"You've never kissed a girl before! Ponyboy Stan, you tell me the God's honest truth. Have you ever kissed anyone before? And the back of your hand don't count!"

He bit his bottom lip.

"And don't you blush again! I already warned you what would happen if you do that."

Stanley took a deep breath, closed his eyes and put his shaking hands on her waist.

Angel stepped backward. "You were really going to kiss me!"

"But I thought—"

"What kind of floozy do you think I am? We've only met three times, and you haven't even taken me out on a proper date yet. You should be ashamed of yourself, Stanley Winston."

"My last name isn't—"

"It is now. Because that's what I called you. I have a good mind to ask your mother what kind of boy she is raising."

Stanley pressed his open palm against his forehead to shield his eyes. His knees quaked, and he shivered.

"I'm just joshing ya." Angel punched him in the arm. "Lighten up."

Stanley exhaled—and didn't stop until his lungs were emptied of every molecule of breath—as adrenaline and lustful excitement coursed through his body "You know?" He shook his index finger at her. "I'm not sure if I want to kill you right now or give you that kiss after all."

"Make me a character in one of your stories. Then we can call it even."

"I got a better idea. Tomorrow we meet at my house instead and watch *The Outsiders*."

Angel reached for the paperback. "You ain't watching jack until you finish the book first. That's the law of the land here in Angel's world."

Stanley jerked backward, out of her reach. "Oh, I'll finish it tonight. You be ready to hang out at my house and meet my mom."

"And what about your pops?"

Stanley swallowed hard and picked at a pesky cuticle, dropping eye contact.

Angel nodded. "I'm sure your mom's lovely. And I promise not to call her Mrs. Winston."

Stanley shook his head, like warding spiders from his hair. "Well, I hope not, since that's not our last name!"

"Doesn't matter what it is, Ponyboy Stan. I like *Winston*." Angel slipped her headphones over her ears. "Now walk this unkissed girl home and point out your house along the way."

Stanley pushed the video cassette into the VCR and listened to the motor whirr.

"I was going to make cookies," his mother said. "What kind do you think she likes?"

"Mom, we're not ten. And she's coming to watch the movie. It's not a playdate."

The doorbell rang, and Stanley's heart pitter-pattered. He opened the door and invited Angel inside.

"You must be Angel," his mother said, approaching her with a doting smile.

"And you must be Mrs.—" Angel glanced at Stanley.

"Don't you do it," he said, laughing.

"Do what?" his mother asked.

"Inside joke, Mrs. … Stanley's mom," Angel answered. "And it's nice to meet you."

"I'll let you kids watch your flick. I'll be upstairs if you need anything."

Stanley pushed Play on the VCR remote and offered Angel a seat on the couch. Then he sat in his mother's recliner adjacent to the television.

"You not gonna sit next to me? I don't bite, you know. At least, not on the first date."

"This is a date?" Stanley asked, standing and approaching the couch.

"It is because I say it is. And, oh, I want my book back after the movie is done. Gotta make sure it's readily available for the next illiterate hunk I meet in the woods."

Hunk? He sat on the empty cushion next to Angel and locked his gaze straight ahead at the opening scene, not courageous enough to look at her. "Is that Ponyboy? I look nothing like him."

"But see? He writes in a composition book too. His is way cooler."

Stanley suddenly regretted inviting her; he didn't know if his blood pressure could take two hours of sitting next to her, staring forward at a screen, pretending that every second with her wasn't amazing and stressful all at the same time.

Just as Stevie Wonder finished singing over the opening credits, Angel's pinkie finger slipped into his hand and curled around his pinkie. Both of them stared at the film and neither flinched when he squeezed his pinkie around hers.

And they stayed like that until the end credits rolled.

Stanley held Angel's hand as they surveyed the thirty-foot drop to the water-filled quarry below.

"You're trembling," she said. "I've jumped from much higher than this. You'll be fine. C'mon. On three—"

"It's not the height."

She looked from the shimmering water's surface to his face. "What is it?"

The setting sunlight struck the quarry, so sparkles of reflections made the water appear as if it were dotted with shards of glass.

"School starts next week. And you haven't told me if you're staying with your aunt or going back home."

Angel squeezed his hand. "Let's just jump and say, *Damn the future!*"

Stanley slid his fingers from hers. "I need to know if I'm losing you or not."

She turned to face him. "Even if I go back home, you'll never lose me, Ponyboy Stan. You've been the bestest friend I've ever had. Ever."

He kicked a rock from the ledge into the open mouth of the quarry and glanced at her jeans. "Were you really going to jump into that water with your pants still on?" He placed a hand on his bare chest and stomach, self-conscious of his scrawny physique.

"I … I don't like bathing suits."

"But your clothes will be all wet and gross and stuck to you."

Angel pursed her lips and glanced skyward, avoiding eye contact. She wiped the first remnants of a tear from the bottom of her eyes.

"I'm sorry. I-I didn't mean to make you feel bad." Stanley took a step forward. "You okay?"

She nodded and smacked her lips open, saliva lines stretching like ropes as she took a deep breath.

"Don't go all Sodapop Curtis on me," he said.

She chortled. "You really need to brush up on your references."

"Maybe. But I got you to laugh."

"You always do." She paused and folded her lips into her mouth. "This is why I'm staying with my aunt for the summer." Angel reached down, grabbed her pant cuff, and lifted the fabric above her knee.

Stanley placed a hand over his mouth, and his eyes grew wide. He squatted to inspect her shin and knee closer. "Your … dad?"

Angel nodded and burst into tears. She placed her face into her open palms as her pant leg drooped to her ankle again.

Stanley stood and wrapped one hand around the back of her head and pulled her face into his chest.

"Don't go back home," he whispered.

"It's not up to me," she replied, sniffing through her words. "I'm scared what he may have done to my mom for letting me stay here, even just for the summer."

Stanley pushed Angel away at arm's length, keeping his hands on her shoulders. "We can call, like, social services or something."

"It'll only make it worse."

Stanley glanced into the quarry and watched the sunlight dance, like orange kisses upon the water. "Fuck it. Let's run away. Together. Right now. I-I'll go pack a bag, and we can be—"

"I don't want to drag you into my shit world. It's not fair to you."

Stanley swallowed hard. "You *are* my world. Even the shit that comes with it. Your shit is now my sh—"

Angel leaned forward and pressed her lips to his before he had the chance to close his eyes and react. Stanley felt her tongue intertwine with his, and he closed his eyes as her hands ran along his waistline.

"Never let me go," she said and guided him to the ground. Angel opened her eyes to focus first on Stanley and afterward at the evening sky.

Stanley followed her line of sight, sharing the beauty of their surroundings with her. They watched the moonshine replace the fading sunlight on the quarry water and smelled the fog rolling in from the depths of his woods.

Stanley's fingers peeled away her clothing and her defenses, one layer at a time, until she was naked and her soul bared. "Never let *me* go," he whispered.

"I promise."

Stanley crested the top of the incline that would reveal his writing log and removed his composition book from his back pocket. The corner of the journal tangled with the cord from his headphones and pulled the right pad off his ear. He adjusted the round foam and repositioned the metal headband atop his hair. Whistling to the Hank Williams song blaring from the Walkman, he skipped a single time and kicked a stick against a protruding root in the path.

And then he stopped. Stopped walking. Stopped moving. Stopped breathing. Hank Williams's voice seemed to now only exist faraway in some alternate universe.

A single sheet of paper, anchored by a large rock, flapped on his writing log.

Stanley willed his feet to move, and he approached the frayed paper that had been ripped from a paperback novel. He slid his headphones off his ears, and the sound of the trapped paper flapping in the breeze stabbed him with each flutter. He reached for the piece of paper and realized it was the copyright and title page to Angel's copy of *The Outsiders*—her half-cursive, half-printed scribbles graffitiing the page like black strokes of a teenager's fall from grace.

Stanley read the message, then crumpled it in his fist and screamed as he pitched the paper ball against a tree. The note rolled and landed in a small puddle of collected morning dew. He watched as the water ate the paper, changing its color to a darker brown and disintegrating.

Stanley cupped his tearstained face with his hands as Hank Williams's crooning of "Weary Blues from Waitin'" drifted from the nearby headphones into his ears. He removed the Walkman from his pocket and pressed Stop, then ejected the solid-white-colored cassette she had loaned him. The song titles were faded and smeared from being handled an exorbitant amount of times.

Stanley closed his eyes and traced his fingertips along the rough edge of the well-loved cassette—conjuring the memory of Angel handing him her favorite album a few weeks ago and ordering him to learn every word, while dusk had settled behind her in the woods. He tapped the tape against his thumb knuckle, took a deep breath and wiped the tears from his eyes.

He huffed and exhaled, long and slow. Then he sat on his log and opened his composition book to the most recent story—the one that remained unfinished, interrupted by the girl who had ushered in a summer of so many firsts. He tore out the handful of written pages to cleanse the notebook of any words he had penned before Angel had entered his life.

Everything before that moment felt meaningless and insignificant. And his writings needed to reflect that, or it would all be for naught. Stanley wrote furiously, drafting the first crumbs of a larger world onto the blank pages, with newfound courage to unleash his well-guarded musings into the world.

Stanley sat at his writing desk, tapping the chewed end of a blue BIC pen against his black-and-white spotted composition notebook still unopened in his lap. The glow from his lamp cast a reflection on each of the two windows on either side of the desk overlooking his front yard. He caught his reflection in the turned-off computer monitor and noticed a new batch of graying hair along his receding hairline. He sighed as he wiggled the pen with more vigor against the notebook's cover.

Taptaptaptaptaptaptap …

His gaze focused on his two sons as they took turns running at full steam across the lawn and jumping into the pile of rustic-colored leaves, raked together by Stanley's labors for most of the morning.

Taptaptaptaptaptaptap …

Stanley chuckled as his youngest son yelled, "Geronimo!" before leaping into the leaves, then he glanced again at the notebook in his lap and took a deep breath, holding it before exhaling.

"Empty-page demons still got you?"

Stanley dropped the notebook near his feet and turned to face his wife. "Been eating at me all day."

She picked up the blank notebook from the floor and set it on his writing desk, reading what he had scribbled on the front cover. "So, you're finally going to write about *her*."

Stanley snickered. "Still don't know if I'm ready yet."

His wife wrapped an arm around his neck and sat in his lap.

"What tipped you off?" he asked.

"That's not the most cryptic of titles you have there, bub." She leaned forward and rapped her finger on his sloppy handwriting inside the white rectangular box on the cover, then leaned against him. "You do know they think you spent all that time raking this morning just for them, right?"

Stanley followed his wife's gaze out the window at their boys. "What they don't know is that they'll be in charge of raking all of it together again."

She slapped his arm. "You're too much of a softy to carry out that threat. I know you love watching them destroy those piles. Probably reminds you of your own childhood or something."

He squeezed her to politely signal that he wanted some alone time to write … or to think. The anticipated outpouring of words seemed to diminish as the long bouts of silent introspection replaced any actual writing.

"Just remember you promised the boys to help them carve their jack-o'-lanterns before they go to bed." His wife slid off his lap and headed for the door of his writing office. She stopped as she reached the doorjamb, turning, facing him. "None of your books wrote themselves. And I know you'll never admit it to me, but every single one of them started with doubt and anxiety. And yet they all ended in magic for your readers. I'm sure this *Angel of Deception*—or whatever you eventually decide to name it—will be another opus. You just need to believe in yourself, Stan."

She closed the door behind her, and Stanley swallowed hard as he scanned the rows of framed covers of his best-selling, award-winning novels and also the magazine covers sporting his professional author photo, advertising exclusive interviews with the "new face of modern literary genius."

He flipped open his black-and-white spotted composition book to the first page again and drummed along with his pen to Hank Williams's "I Saw the Light" coming from his Bluetooth speaker.

Tap tap tap-tap tap …

The light-blue horizontal lines on the page turned into highway veins of failure, mocking him with every inch of empty space—a reminder of the courage he couldn't muster to transform his thoughts to paper.

"On Garth!"

Stanley squinted so he could see his sons better through the fading sunlight.

Like he was holding off an army, his youngest held a foam sword which Stanley's wife had won at the Parkview Fair last year.

"It's *On guard*, you dummy," said his eldest boy, pointing a bent stick in the same fashion toward the disheveled pile of leaves.

"Charge!"

Stanley sat back in his chair just as the two boys leaped into the air to defend the pile of leaves from some invisible enemy army of dragons or knights or aliens or samurais—or robots, for all Stanley knew.

He closed the notebook and danced his fingertips over his Sharpie strokes that formed the tentative title for what he had hoped would be his most unabashedly honest work to date, but … that's for later. He decided to invest his time carving pumpkins with his family—instead of wasting away the day, knowing he wasn't ready yet to do anything on this new project—other than think.

Maybe some words weren't meant for the rest of the world, he thought. *Maybe they're safer trapped inside.*

"DEAR PAIGE"
RAYONA LOVELY WILSON

She always wiped away my tears and held me when I couldn't stand.

Dear Paige,

As a little girl, poop was important to you. Every time I took a shower, there you were on the toilet going to the bathroom. I don't know how you'd get in, but you always managed to. I was annoyed, because you smelled so, so bad. You'd stare at me, and I'd get lost in those hazelnut eyes, unable to stay upset for even the shortest amount of time. Sometimes, I wasn't sure if you were staring at me or through me. Now that I think about it, you were probably concentrating on taking care of your business.

You are the prettiest girl I've ever seen, and no matter what I'd do, you were always there, your arms stretched out, waiting to trap me in your embrace. You smelled like our garden—roses and lavender. How I would much rather smell that than the times you "needed to poop" while I "needed to shower."

I'd always ask you the same thing, "Why do you always have to go when I'm in here?" I don't know why you changed your answer every time, but my favorite was, "'Cause poop is important."

Every time you spoke, I was amazed, because your answers or comments were so out of this world. How did a four-year-old figure out that poop is important? I don't know, but you did.

Paige,

I hope this finds you well. I haven't talked to you in a while, but I thought I'd let you know that I've been thinking about you constantly. You are the light of my life, and I miss you.

Do you remember when I couldn't go anywhere without you? Separation anxiety was a thing; you were attached to my hip. I didn't mind at all, but everyone else hated it. I couldn't go anywhere; maybe that's why I couldn't take a shower without your company.

I miss you. Why haven't you called me?

My dearest Paige,

There was a time when you'd wrap those tiny arms around me, and all my troubles went away. No matter what I did, you were there. Like the time I forgot the right cereal, and you gave me the silent treatment for a whole three minutes. You'd scrunch up that little nose you got from your dad, and your eyes would squint down, and it's like you were trying so hard to be angry. It never lasted long.

"Mommy, I'm hungry." You'd break your silence, and all was well again. You'd eat the wrong cereal then sit on the couch for a cuddle and some TV. Those were the moments I'd absolutely love. It was me and you in our own little world. Why couldn't we stay there forever? I love your sweet face, with all my heart. I'd give anything to hear from you.

Paige,

I'm not angry, but I'd like to hear from you, maybe a call or letter. It's been a while. Did I do something wrong? I don't understand. I've sent several letters, and I've tried calling. Why aren't you speaking to me? You've never gone this long without any communication. I know I wasn't always the best parent, but I always did my best by you. I've always given you what you wanted, because I love you with all my heart. You're the best thing that ever happened to me.

You remember that dollhouse that you saw at Walmart? It was $189. It was the only thing you had wanted for Christmas. I knew at the time I couldn't afford it, but seeing your face light up in that store was the reason I worked so hard for those next two months. I wanted you to have the best Christmas ever.

No matter what we went through, I had to give you the best I had. That's why I'm not upset that you haven't called. I know you may be busy with your life, but I'm your mom. I'll always be your mom. I'll always ALWAYS love you no matter what, baby girl.

Paige,

Have you seen those old photo albums we used to sit and go through? I'd love to see all the photos of us over the years. There's one specific picture I'd love to find. It's the one of you in your unicorn dress and that blue headband. You wore that dress for three days before you finally let me take it off to wash. It was always the sweetest thing. You'd gotten attached to that dress, and, no matter how dirty it got, you still wanted to wear it. "Unicorns are really real, Mom" is what you'd say to me. I never, and I mean never, told you any different. I wanted to let you experience the magic of childhood, because I didn't get to. Things were different when I was growing up. I'm not going to get into it, but know I did not want my childhood affecting yours in any way shape or form. I wasn't going to be like my parents.

Maybe you can call me and let me know where those albums are. I would love to see some photos of you as a little girl again.

Where are you? Paige, it's been several months since I've heard from you. Is there something you're not telling me? Is there something that I did? I feel like you don't want to speak to me, or maybe you want nothing to do with me, but there's no way I'm going to let you go. I was in labor with you for twelve and a half hours. Every ounce of pain I went through was worth it, because I got you. I never told you I nearly died giving birth, but I did. I would do it all over again if it meant you'd be there. I miss your hugs; I miss our late-night talks about unicorns and your favorite dolls. I miss your sloppy cheek kisses, those ones where you'd first give me an Eskimo kiss and then wrap your arms tightly around my neck and hold on for what felt like eternity. I don't know how much longer I can go without hearing from you, sweet daughter. Maybe you can come for a visit?

Paige,

Today I was singing and was reminded of the time I sang to you in the car. My voice was never good, but I always dreamed of singing to my children, singing to you. It's funny because you would—you'd hold your little finger to your lips and shush me. You never actually told me I couldn't sing, but I kinda got the idea when I'd look back, and your hands were over your ears, and those eyes were squinted shut. I would laugh so hard, because you adored me. Even those little things made me love you more. Thank you for never telling me to my face that I was horrible at singing.

Thank you for letting me think I was as good as those people we used to watch on TV.

Anyways, I was singing, and your face popped up in my head, and I thought I'd write you another letter in hopes that it reaches you well, and you know I love you and think about you every day.

Darling Paige,

I don't know if you know that I love you, and I'll do whatever I can for you. I always thought I'd live forever, but something is wrong. The doctor said I'm sick. Maybe you can come speak with her and help me understand what's going on. I don't quite know.

Paige,

I've always wanted to live forever, because I never want you to be without me. The doctor says I'm sick. I don't feel sick. I feel fine. Maybe she's wrong. I've always been healthy. I need you to call or come by the house, please. This is important. I wouldn't disturb you if it wasn't.

Sweet Paige,

I'm looking for pictures. I can't find my pictures of you when you were a little girl. I want the one of you in your favorite dress. Can you come by the house and help me find it? I need you, honey; it's been a while since I've seen you. I don't know how to contact you. I'm not angry that you broke my favorite vase. Accidents happen all the time. Remember I stepped on your doll? Things are replaceable. I want you to know everything is going to be okay. I'm not mad. Mommy could never be mad at you. You are the reason I get up every morning, the reason I work so hard. Nothing will ever come between us.

Oh, Paige,

The doctor says I'm sick. I need you to come speak to her for me. I don't remember what she said besides I'm sick. Maybe you can help me understand. I think they're lying to me. I've never been sick. Sweetie, I need somebody here with me. I need help. You're the only one who can help me. I cherish all those days we spent together and really wish you'd come by and spend some time with me.

Paige,

There was a strange girl here today. She hugged me so tight I thought I might die. Maybe that's an exaggeration, but it was as if she knew me. She sat with me for hours, holding my hands. She was warm and had the same dark hair as you. Oh, sweet girl, where are you? It's been forever since I've seen you. Each morning I sit at this table, writing to you, and I get nothing back. Have you forgotten about me? It's okay if you have, but I'll never forget you. I'm sure you're living your life, but it would be nice to get a visit from my favorite girl.

I believe the young lady who visited me said she was having a baby. I don't know the details, but I've always wanted to be a grandmother one day. Have you met anybody you thought about having children with?

I hope to hear back from you soon.

Paige,

I wrote down something I needed to tell you when you come to visit, but I cannot find it anywhere. It was here on my desk, and now it's gone. I'll try to find it, because I can't remember. I'm so sure it was important, and you needed to know.

Oh, honey,

Today was beautiful. I went to a wedding. I wore a dress; I can't recall the details of that or the wedding, but I was told it was beautiful. I wish I could remember something else. I can't wait to see the photos.

Paige,

Mommy has so much to do, and I don't want to forget, so I'm writing you this letter so you'll remember. Be sure to take the chicken out when you get home from school and please, please, please dice the vegetables that are in the bowl in the fridge. I know you might have tons of homework, but I'd like to have dinner ready by the time your father gets home. I shouldn't be too long running my errands, but I cannot wait to see you! I have a gift for you. I won't tell you what it is, but you're going to be so excited.

Love, Mom

Paige,

There was a young woman here today with a man. She cried. I don't know why, but it made me think of you when you came home from that dance at school because that boy broke up with you. I hated seeing you so sad, and I hated seeing this young woman so sad. I hugged her, like you used to hug me. I told her everything would be all right, like you used to say in high school when we were struggling.

My heart ached for this young woman. The man she was with seemed sad too. He kept saying, "She could get better," but I'm not sure who he was speaking of.

She told me she loved me and didn't want to go. She said she'd be back.

I wish I knew who she was, that way I could figure out our connection.

Paige,

Today I felt you kick for the first time. I thought I loved you already but feeling you inside me has made me realize that being your mother is all I want in life. Oh, sweet girl, I cannot wait to hold you in my arms and see if you look more like me or your father. He's excited too but a bit scared. I've told him we have nothing to worry about. He'll be a wonderful father.

Five more months and you'll be here. I cannot wait to dress you up and take you places. Every time I think about it, I get butterflies. Maybe I shouldn't assume you're a girl. You could also be a boy.

Today has been hard. I'm sick. I can't get out of bed. I remember seeing the doctor today but not sure of what she said. There was a young woman there with me today. She reminds me of you. She held my hand so tight it hurt. I think she's afraid but she never said of what. You should've been there with me. You're my daughter, not her. I would appreciate if you'd get in contact with me. You're so important to me.

A daughter is someone to always laugh with, to dream dreams with, and to love with all of one's heart. I love you with all my heart, and I would do anything for you.

Paige,

Today we held hands and walked through the park. You skipped quite a bit and pointed at all the flowers that caught your eye. I don't know why you love flowers so much. Yes, they are beautiful, but they also have bugs, which I absolutely hate. Remember that time that butterfly nearly made me fall running from it, and you giggled so hard you cried? It wasn't funny at the time, but I laugh now.

Our relationship has always been important to me. I wanted to always be better to you than my mother was to me. Aren't I doing that?

The way you look at me gives me my answer. Oh, Paige, I love spending all this time with you.

Daughter,

Somebody gave me a card that says, *Mothers and daughters share a special bond—whether they are near or apart— the words that describe it are written on the heart.* How true is this? I know you're out of state for college but thank you for calling and telling me about the classes you're taking and the friends you've made. I cannot believe my precious girl graduated high school and left for college. It's bittersweet. I miss you. I miss our late-night movie dates on the couch where we talked about boys and makeup. I cannot wait till you visit on break.

Don't worry about me. I'll be fine. I'm just in my feelings right now.

To my brave, strong daughter,

What happened to you shouldn't have happened, and I wish I had been there to protect you. I wish I would've told you that you couldn't go, but I didn't want to shelter you too much.

I want you to know it wasn't your fault, and you aren't to blame. You are innocent in this whole thing, and there's NO EXCUSE for his actions.

I'm here when you're ready to talk. Mommy will always be here, no matter what.

Please don't ever blame yourself for his stupid actions.

Hey, Paige,

I can't walk today. My legs aren't working. I'm lonely. Maybe if you were here, I'd be able to get out of bed. I can't remember the last time I saw you. I can't remember the last time I hugged you or even smelled you. I don't want to forget you.

Maybe you can send me some photos to help.

Paige,

I NEVER WANT TO SPEAK TO YOU AGAIN!!! You've had all this time to come see me and you haven't, not once. I'm your mother, and you don't care about me. This is disrespectful. Everything I've ever done has been for you. I knew you were a spoiled brat. I shouldn't have given you everything you wanted growing up. I shouldn't have had you.

Paige,

Dearest daughter,
   Hello.

Paige,
   I'm hurting today. I'm sorry for

Paige,
   Today I saw a young lady. She's pregnant. I'm not sure why she came to visit. She showed me sonogram photos. A baby girl. She cried in excitement. Said she couldn't wait to see her baby, and I was reminded of when I was pregnant with you. Feeling those kicks and punches was the best feeling until it started to hurt.
   "I want to be as good as you were." That's what the young woman said. I don't understand why she'd want to be like me. She doesn't know me. She doesn't know I struggled or went through some things. She doesn't know sometimes I'd go without so you could have. Why does she want to be like me?

Oh, Paige,
   I cannot do this anymore. I've not seen you in so long.

Paige,
   My heart hurts. Things don't seem right anymore. I'm not sure what's wrong.

I got up today.
My name is …

I got up and walked to the mirror to see a face I don't recognize. The sticker on the mirror says, *My name is Stacey*, but I don't look like a Stacey. Who am I? What's wrong with me?

I am not addressing this letter, but it's for the young woman who came and sat at my bedside today. You kicked up your feet and laid your head in my shoulder. I wasn't lonely today, so thank you. I appreciate the company.

"You are the best mom in the world." Is what you said. I almost wish I was your mom after that. You then grabbed my hand and held it to your belly. Oh, how amazing that was. Congratulations on your bundle of joy. I bet you'll be a great mom.

My hands hurt. My body aches. I'm tired. Part of me is missing but I don't know what's the missing part. I want to say goodbye, but who do I say goodbye to? I love you whomever or whatever you are. I'm ready to go.

I saw a few faces today, but I don't recognize them. The young lady said I can go if I'm ready. She said she doesn't want me to hurt any longer …

"If you knew her, you would've loved her as much as I did. I just hope I have a relationship with you, like I did with her." I lean down and place my lips against my mother's head—a goodbye kiss. "She was the best mom a girl could ask for." I stand up straight and kiss my own daughter on the head, matting her hair down.

"Mommy, can I say goodbye too?"

"You sure can, sweet face." I pick her up, hold her over the coffin that my mother's lifeless body lies in and try to force a smile.

"Bye-bye, Grandmother." Her little voice is so sweet that I can't help but remember Mom describing my voice the same.

She always wiped away my tears and held me when I couldn't stand. I hope she knows I did the same for her.

"THE HEART OF
THE MATTER"
K.M. REYNOLDS

I saw him again today. He was pacing in the window of the coffee shop, scowling into his phone. I nearly went inside, just for the chance to be near him, but instead I fled the scene. Even a glimpse of him through a window is enough to send my heart skittering up my throat; I don't know what I would do if he actually spoke to me. He has no idea who I am, but I know his heart. The heart of the man I love.

The muffled sounds of city traffic float by on the breeze. I sit on my usual bench at the park, watching the vibrant scenes unfolding before me—children flying kites, young lovers on a picnic, a few women jogging together. I collect my thoughts as I sit alone in this city teeming with life. I haven't always been alone. Once, there was David.

David was, to put it simply, the great love of my life. Since childhood we were inseparable, and, as we grew, so did our relationship. From friends, to lovers, to a happily married couple, we were the shining example of true love. All of that changed on August 16, 2016. It was an average Tuesday with the world proceeding as normal … until suddenly, it wasn't. I'll never forget the voice of the paramedic that called to tell me that David had been in an accident and that I needed to go to the hospital. I'll never forget the faces of the doctors who worked tirelessly to find signs of life in the man I loved. And I'll never forget the arms of the nurse who held me as I wept while I wrestled with the decision to let him go. That day, a gaping hole had been torn in my very soul, and I was certain that nothing could ever fix it. I lived day to day, surviving in the black haze of grief that threatened to swallow me whole. I was drowning in paperwork, decisions, and the bleak realization that I was alone.

The funeral came and went quickly before I had a chance to fully catch my breath. Condolences and casseroles came pouring in from every corner, and, for a time, I was able to wrap myself up in my grief, like a blanket on a cold winter's night. But time ticked on, and the calls stopped. Ready-made meals no longer arrived in the arms of friends, and the silence became deafening. The burning in my chest dulled to an ache that became my new normal. I moved through life like a robot, completing my days with a monotony that seemed endless. Then, that day in the hospital counseling room, I found Martin.

I'll never forget the first time I saw his face. In the cold, brightly lit hospital room, his face stared up at me from a photograph on the table. My tear-blurred gaze traced the worn lines in his expression—the sunken eyes, the greying temples. It was a bleak, hopeless photograph, but that in and of itself filled me with hope. I could hear the counselor talking behind me, but her words were muffled by the sound of my own heartbeat. I knew, in that moment, that I needed to find him. My gaze flitted to his name typed in bold across the top of the page—Martin Harris. The compulsive need to know him was like a bright light burning through the fog that had recently enveloped my life. I scanned the other names and photographs quickly before returning my focus to Martin. Martin was the key to moving forward with my life, I was sure of it.

Days later, after working up every ounce of courage in my body, I made an appointment with his office. I didn't know what I was going to say to him or how I would feel to see him in the flesh, but I knew I had to at least try. As I rode the elevator up to his office, my stomach churned, and my knees grew weak. By the time I reached the waiting area, I was hyperventilating and on the verge of tears. I turned right around and rode the elevator all the way back down. I wasn't ready to face him yet.

A few more months went by, and I found myself wandering near his office building with growing frequency. I'd linger nearby, hoping to catch a glimpse of the business tycoon that consumed my thoughts. I'd often spot him coming from meetings, his phone always in hand, a scowl nearly always darkening his square features. Each time I saw him, I would feel conflicting waves of happiness and heartbreak wash over me. I longed to approach him, but that little voice in my head always warned me, "Not yet!" So, I waited.

And now, sitting here in the crisp fall air, my heart still racing, I've finally made up my mind. Come Hell or high water, I'm going to do it. I am going to talk to Martin.

My hands tremble as I dial, my breath coming in short gasps. I hesitate, my thumb hovering over the green call button. *It's now or never, Jen. Just do it.* I close my eyes and allow my thumb to fall. The phone rings once, twice.

"Thank you for calling Harris and Hart, how can I help you?"

I exhale, realizing that I've been holding my breath. "Hi, my name is Jennifer Standridge, and I'm on the chair for the Philharmonic. I was hoping to secure a meeting with Mr. Harris to talk about a fundraising opportunity."

The voice on the other end doesn't reply immediately, and I can hear papers shuffling in the background. The seconds feel like hours, and I can feel myself growing lightheaded.

"Hi, Ms. Standridge? Sorry about the delay."

"Oh, it's no trouble," I reply, chewing my lip.

"Mr. Harris has a forty-five-minute window between appointments on Tuesday, and I can squeeze you in. Does two fifteen work for you?"

"Yes! Yes, that will be just fine. Thank you so much. You are a lifesaver!" My words rush out in a jumble as my heart begins to pound. "I'll be there. Tuesday at two fifteen."

"See you then, Ms. Standridge. Goodbye."

I slowly lower the phone, my pulse now a deafening roar in my ears. I did it. I made the appointment. *Now you just have to show up,* the little voice in my head whispered. I clench my fists, willing away the negative thoughts. *I will,* I promise myself. *I will do this.*

I glance at the clock on my bedside table again, turning over restlessly in the dark. 5:17 a.m. I sigh deeply, pulling the blanket over my head. My alarm isn't set to go off for another hour and thirteen minutes, but I can't sleep. Today is the day I'll finally meet Martin.

I sit up in bed, stifling a yawn as I brush my tousled hair away from my face. It's no use fighting it—I'm up for the day whether I like it or not. I swing my legs over the side of my bed, my feet tingling as they touch the cold floor. I shuffle to the kitchen and begin to make some coffee. Once the pot is percolating happily on the counter, I turn my attention to Fergus, my cat, who is winding himself around my ankles impatiently.

"I see you, fuzzball. Your breakfast will be ready in a minute."

Fergus meows in response and continues to march about underfoot in an attempt to kill me, I'm sure.

"Fergus, if you trip me and I die, who will feed you then, eh? You'll be all alone. Knock it off."

He looks at me with his big yellow eyes and struts off, his attitude oozing all over the place. I pour myself a giant mug of coffee and open the cat food. With a heavy sigh, I begin to carefully arrange Fergus' breakfast on the tiny porcelain plate. This is something I have to do every morning, because if I don't, I'll come home to a mess all over my kitchen floor. King Fergus is picky about his meals and petty if he is displeased.

"Asshole cat," I mutter as I straighten myself up, my back cracking as I do. "He's lucky he belonged to David."

I grab my coffee and settle down on my couch to catch the morning news and wake myself up. I sip slowly, savoring the bitter beverage as it warms me from the inside out. My mind wanders away from the weather report to my meeting with Martin. *What will I wear? How will he sound? Should I tell him who I am? Who he is to me?* Butterflies flutter in my gut as my anxious thoughts create a dogpile in my head. I set my mug down and draw a deep breath, making note of my trembling hands. *Maybe I don't need the caffeine today.*

The morning flies by as I try to bury myself in busywork. Before I know it, the clock is singing that one o'clock has arrived. Panic begins to rise in my throat as I stare at my closet. *I have nothing to wear.* After a few more precious minutes of internal struggle, I grab my navy skirt suit. *This will have to do.*

The elevator dings softly and the doors hiss open. The portly man to my left steps off, leaving me alone in the cold metal box as I continue my ascent. With each floor that falls away beneath my feet, I can feel the familiar fist of dread squeezing me tighter and tighter. I'm a little early for my meeting, but that was an intentional choice. I know I'll need all the time I can get to calm my nerves before I'm called in.

Ding. My stomach lurches as the elevator comes to a stop on the forty-second floor. I have arrived.

My legs are lead as I step into the lobby, the familiar sign above the reception desk welcoming me to Harris and Hart Advisory Co. I inhale deeply, forcing one foot in front of the other, a smile that doesn't reach my eyes glued to my face. I reach the desk and steady myself against it. My tongue is sandpaper in my mouth, and I swallow, desperate for relief.

"Hi," I manage to croak out. "My name is Jennifer Standridge, I have a two fifteen with Mr. Harris."

The secretary doesn't look up from her computer screen. "Have a seat, I'll call you when he's ready. He's not finished with his other appointment yet." She waves dismissively toward the chairs against the wall, her neon pink claws glistening in the fluorescent light.

I turn stiffly and make my way toward the chairs, my pulse roaring in my ears. I make it over to the one closest to the desk, but, instead of sitting, I lose control. My legs seem to have a mind of their own as I whirl and shuffle toward the elevators, head down. *I can't do this. I can't, I can't.* I'm so engrossed in my flight that I don't hear the elevator doors until it's too late.

With a jolt, I crash full force into someone exiting the elevator. I cry out as hot coffee scalds my skin through my blouse, and I stumble backward, arms flailing. One step, two step, stumble, and fall. I cry out again as my ass connects with the tile floor, my carefully coiffed hair now flying in disarray around my beet-red face. My flustered apology sticks in my throat as I lift my gaze to see who I had so ungraciously bowled into. It's him.

Standing over me, a concerned scowl on his face, is none other than Mr. Martin Harris. I can feel my blush deepening, and my mouth flaps like a fish out of water as I struggle for words. Thankfully, he speaks first, extending a large hand to help me up.

"I am so sorry, ma'am! Are you hurt?"

I hear him, but his question doesn't quite register in my shell-shocked brain. I accept his hand, and, as I stand to my feet, I hear him begin to repeat his question.

"Are you all r—"

"I'm fine," I fumble, cutting him off. "I'm okay, really."

He exhales in what appears to be relief. "I'm glad to hear it. I'm so sorry. I wasn't watching where I was going."

My gaze is glued to the floor, and I'm willing the extra blood to leave my cheeks. "I wasn't paying attention either. It's not your fault."

"I still feel terrible about it, I ..." his voice trails off, and I look up, surprised to see him studying me. That familiar scowl has returned to his face as he takes me in from head to toe.

"What's wrong?"

"You ... You just seem so familiar to me. Have we met? I feel like I know you, but I can't quite place how."

My breath hitches as I meet his gaze. There's a rushing sound in my ears, drowning out the rest of the world as I stare at him. I open my mouth, ready to tell him everything.

"She's your two fifteen." The long pink claws wave in my direction. "The lady from the Philharmonic."

Realization dawns in Martin's eyes, and he extends his hand again, this time offering a firm shake. "Of course, how could I have forgotten. I'm Martin Harris." He pauses, looking slightly uncomfortable. "Would you like to reschedule? I can't have made the best impression."

I close my eyes, deciding that the moment is now or never. "Mr. Harris, I do work for the Philharmonic, but that's not the only reason I've come to see you." I pause, my lips trembling. "My name is Jennifer Standridge. I am the widow of David Standridge, the man whose heart is beating in your chest." I exhale sharply, opening my eyes.

To my surprise, Martin's own eyes are misting, and a smile has settled on his face. He takes both of my hands gently and brings them to his lips.

"It is an honor, Ms. Standridge. I'm so glad you've come." He glances at the perfectly polished blonde behind the desk. "Karen, cancel all my appointments for the afternoon. Ms. Standridge and I have much to discuss."

Martin's laugh fills his office, and I shake my head, chuckling. "No, it's true! David really would hide his veggies, no matter where we were or what company we were with. He hated them."

Outside, the sky has turned a dusky purple, and the lights of the city are twinkling below us. We've been talking for hours, sequestered in Martin's lavish office, undisturbed by the outside world. Martin had even turned off his cellphone, a move that had surprised me. Surely a businessman with such a heavy workload couldn't afford to just drop off the map. He had been quick to assure me that he could, and he would, because our time together was the priority. We had spent the better part of our time together talking about David, about Martin's heart failure, and about how the transplant had given him a renewed sense of life and self. It was cathartic for me, and I sensed it was for Martin as well.

As our laughter dies down, I bite my lip, reluctant to bring our time to an end. "Martin, this has been absolutely lovely, but I do need to get going."

He stood, nodding somberly. "I understand. But before you go, I must say—I'm so thankful you came by. I've been wanting to make contact with you for months, but I didn't want to rip open any old wounds. But you've been on my mind constantly."

"I'll admit, it took every ounce of courage I had to make this appointment today. I almost left! In fact, that's what I was doing when you came out of the elevator."

Martin chuckled. "It would seem the universe felt it was time we meet."

"Indeed. This has been so good for me. I feel like after years of anguish, my heart can truly begin to heal now. I needed this."

Martin comes out from behind his desk and takes my hands. "I want you to know that this has been healing for me too. I feel like a part of me that was missing is now whole."

Tears sting my eyes as I look up at Martin. "If it's not too much trouble, could I—" My voice cracks and I stop, feeling a hot tear snake down my cheek.

"What is it, Jen?"

"Could I hear his heart beating, one more time?" I stifle a sob, terrified of the answer. I know what I'm asking is intimate, and we are practically strangers. I steel myself for rejection.

Instead, I'm wrapped in a warm embrace, my head cradled against his chest. "Of course, you can," he whispers.

I close my eyes and listen. *Thump-thump. Thump-thump.* There it is. Tears pour freely from my eyes and I cling to Martin's shirt, dampening his chest. The sound of David's heart echoes through me, cutting like a sword while also healing like a salve.

We stand there in our tight embrace for several long minutes, frozen in time. When we finally pull apart, we are both wiping tears from our cheeks.

"Thank you for that," I gasp, every nerve in my body on fire. "I know it was a lot to ask of you."

"As far as I'm concerned, Jen, this heart still belongs to you. David's heart beat for you for decades, and it hasn't stopped." He leaned over his desk, scrawling on a note pad. "Here's my personal cell number. I'm at your disposal, day or night. If you ever want to talk, or grieve, or just listen to his heart, I will make myself available to you. Without David, I wouldn't be here today. I can't thank him, but I absolutely can thank you." He hands me the paper and leans forward, placing a tender kiss on my forehead. "I mean it with all my heart. Whatever you need, I'm there."

I nod and accept the paper, incapable of forming a response. I turn to leave when Martin's voice stops me.

"Oh, Jen, one more thing. Do you have a black cat?"

I turn back to Martin, eyes wide. "Yes, why do you ask?"

"Well, I keep having dreams about this black cat, and I can't figure it out. He's a real asshole of a cat, but, for some reason in the dream, I love the darn thing."

A sharp laugh comes bursting from my throat, and I shake my head. "That's David's cat, Fergus. He's a real piece of work, but David adored him."

Martin shakes his head, smiling. "Well, give him a pat for me, would you? I feel like I owe him one too."

I smile and nod before exiting the office and making my way to the elevator. As the doors slide closed and I begin my descent, I can't help but dissolve into a fit of uncontrollable laughter.

"That damn cat!"

The kitchen smelled remarkable. Bo was nearly finished with supper. Today was the first time in eight years that she'd been able to make a homecooked meal for her boy James. He would be leaving soon, and his mother refused to lose an opportunity to feed her child, especially when he had asked for her specialty.

Black bean and white corn chili—Bo had transformed it into an art. The woman had been cooking since she could pick up a spoon, and Bo's chili was the culmination of years of culinary practice. She had found a way to perfectly blend the right amount of heat with the right amount of savory, making her chili a to-die-for dish. Every cook or chef who tried it had asked Bo for her recipe, but she never gave it to anyone. She told them the recipe had been given to her as a family secret, and it would stay a family secret. The only hint she ever gave regarding the mystery of her chili was that none of it came from a can, box, or packet; it was the love she put into it that made it good. To date, the highest compliment Bo could recall about her chili had come from James' Scout leader.

"Bo, this is like camping out underneath the stars on the Fourth of July," he had said.

Bo wanted this supper to be perfect. She remembered how overjoyed she had been when she got the news that James would be available and had specially requested her cooking. She had barely seen her boy for the better part of a decade and rarely ever got so much as a phone call from him, so for her, this supper was a treat for them both.

She dipped her long wooden spoon into the crockpot she'd started tending the night before and gave it a taste. The breathtaking blend of spices and heat washed over her tongue and down the back of her throat. She felt the tingle of her chili all the way in the bottom of her belly. *Perfect*, Bo thought. Now the only ingredient this pot still needed was time—time to sit and let the flavors fully intertwine with each other.

With the chili taken care of for the time being, Bo turned her attention to the kitchen's double oven. It was time to pull out the cornbread. She slid on her oven mitts and opened the top oven door to be greeted with the rush of her cornbread's sweet and creamy aroma. She recalled her grandmother's words as she removed the cast-iron baking pan from the appliance.

"Cornbread doesn't need to bake as long as you think it does. Good cornbread should be light and fluffy but also moist and chewy. Nobody likes their cornbread dry as a bone."

Bo set the baking pan on the kitchen counter and grabbed a toothpick. This she stuck in the center of the perfectly golden crust and quickly withdrew to inspect it. Precisely as she had hoped, a little bit of the cornbread stuck to the toothpick, but it was not soggy or wet. *This is just the way my James loves it,* she thought. She quickly laid a fresh white dishtowel over the top of the cast-iron pan to stop the cornbread from cooling too quickly. Then she took a moment for herself to wipe a few fresh beads of sweat from her brow and take a long sip from her glass of sweet tea.

Refreshed, Bo focused on the sizzling pot of grease on the stovetop and the sliced wedges of eggplant on the counter. She grabbed a fistful of eggplant and proceeded to batter the slices in a bowl of flower, milk, cornmeal, and pepper before dropping them in the hot grease. Leaving the eggplant to fry, Bo rubbed her sore, worn hands at the flare of arthritis in her knuckles. *That smarts like the dickens, girl,* she thought. *I should have taken my pills this morning. I'm certainly no spring chicken.* Then the flash of pain subsided.

After a few minutes, Bo skimmed out the beautifully crispy brown wedges of eggplant and placed them on a plate covered in paper towels. She had just finished sprinkling them with a dash of salt when the telltale ping of her favorite egg timer struck her ear.

Dessert was ready. Bo opened the bottom oven and pulled out a picture-perfect apple pie. She had to admit she was proud of herself for this pie. The apples were at the height of the season; this batch had been a good one. She had picked the apples herself from the tree growing outside James' window. She relished in the scent of cinnamon and vanilla subtly hidden underneath the robust fragrance of mounds of warm apples. The latticework on the pie's crust had come out splendidly. Bo felt a sense of victory for battling through the pain in her arthritic hands when she saw how exquisitely the flakey strips of dough sat atop the pie.

It was suppertime now, and Bo couldn't wait to feed her boy. She gave one last quick polish to her grandmother's silver serving tray then put together the meal for her James. Starting with a small dish of the fried eggplant wedges, she then placed a hunk of warm cornbread on the tray. These were joined by a few small cups—one with soft butter for the cornbread and the other with a dollop of sour cream for the chili. Bo ladled out a steaming bowl of her black bean and white corn chili and sprinkled a little grated cheddar cheese on top. Then she served up a thick slice of warm apple pie, finished with a spoonful of homemade whipped cream. Before leaving the kitchen, she went to the ice box and retrieved her son's favorite beverage—an ice-cold can of ginger ale.

Bo carried the silver tray with her boy's supper on it down the long hall as quickly as her aging knees would allow. When she finally got to his room, a lump appeared in her throat so quickly she nearly sent the tray crashing to the ground. After the door opened, she stepped inside and felt her eyes burning at the sight of her darling baby boy.

"Mama," James said, true love in his voice amidst the biggest smile Bo had seen in years.

"My sweet baby," said Bo. "I made your favorite, just like you asked." She raised the tray as if to petition for her son's approval.

"Oh, Mama, it looks grand for sure." James eyed the feast his mother had prepared for him. "It's okay if you stay with me for a while."

"I would love to sit with you for supper," Bo said, fighting tears of joy.

The mother and her son sat and talked. They laughed and they cried. They embraced time and time again as they recounted past happy moments and celebrations. Bo watched James consume the meal she had prepared for him down to the last morsel. They sat for an hour, trying to make up for eight years of separation in sixty minutes. Finally, it came time for them to say goodbye yet again.

"James, baby, I have to go now," Bo said, her joy from the last hour disappearing from her voice.

"I know, Mama. I know."

"When it happens, I don't think I can be there," Bo said.

"It's okay, Mama. I don't want you to see me like that anyway," James replied.

Bo stood and so did James.

"If I don't go now, I don't think I'll be able to." She hugged her son one last time then kissed him on the cheek and held his hands. "I love you, my beautiful baby boy."

"I love you too, Mama," James said, his voice cracking.

Bo turned and left James' room. She felt she needed to get out before she fell to pieces. She hurriedly made the trip down the long hallway, and, just before the door closed behind her, she heard the saddest three words of her entire life.

"Dead man walking."

Bo started crying and didn't stop.

"ABIGAIL JONES"
LAURIE GARDINER

Abigail Jones had just settled into the recliner with her fourth beer and a bag of chips when the racket started again. It was the third day in a row, and Abigail had about run out of patience—not that she'd had much to begin with. She cranked up the volume on the TV, but even Steve Harvey and the roar of the *Family Feud* audience could not drown out the noise from above.

"Damn kids. I knew they'd be trouble." She muted the volume and bellowed, "Shut up," at the ceiling.

The racket stopped.

With a satisfied *humph*, Abigail unmuted the volume and took a swig of beer. Just as she shoved a handful of chips into her mouth, a scream and a loud crash came from above, followed by more screaming and the pounding of small footsteps.

Abigail chugged the last half of her beer and tossed the can onto the floor beside the case of empties. She reached down the side of the chair and pulled the lever to lower the footrest. With a grunt, she heaved herself forward and struggled to her feet. She stood for a moment with a hand on the wall, catching her breath, then lumbered into the hallway to get the broom from the closet.

Back in the living room, she steadied herself against the doorframe, held the broom with both hands and pounded the end of the handle into the ceiling. "Stop that racket! You hear me? Stop it now! Or I'm callin' the police!"

The noise stopped. She pounded the broom a few times more for good measure then let it clatter to the floor as she sagged against the wall, her chest heaving. Once she caught her breath, she headed into the bathroom to mop the sweat from her face.

A few moments later, Abigail turned off the faucet and heard a soft tapping. She froze, listening.

Tap, tap, tap.

She quickly dried her face, walked down the hallway into the foyer and stood in front of the door. The knocking came again, louder and more insistent. She peered through the peephole but saw no one. "Who's there?"

Silence.

Abigail turned to walk away when a small voice said, "It's Grace."

"I don't know any Grace."

"Grace, your neighbour. I live upstairs."

There were three apartments in the triplex: Abigail on the main floor, Grace's family—who had just moved into the second-floor apartment about a week ago—and one in the basement, along with the mailboxes, utility room, and storage units.

Abigail pulled the door open and sized up the girl. She looked about eight or nine, wore bright multi-coloured leggings and a long T-shirt, and had dark braids pulled so tight against her head Abigail wondered how her face stayed where it should.

"What the hell do you want?"

The girl put a hand on one hip and raised a brow. "Mama says it's rude to curse."

"Is that right? You know what I think is rude? Disturbing your neighbours by makin' a racket."

Grace looked down and shuffled her feet. "Mama says I should 'pologize for that. I don't understand why, since it was mostly Moses making noise, and she didn't make him come with me."

"Moses? That your brother?"

"Yeah, he's only five."

"Who the hell names their kid Moses? Just asking for him to be teased." Abigail mimicked a child's voice: "Hey, Moses, can you part the sea? Talk to any burnin' bushes lately?"

Grace's hand returned to her hip. "It's my grampa's name. Why are you being so mean?"

"Honey, I just tell it like it is. If that comes across to some people as mean, that ain't my fault."

"Mama says ain't's not a real word."

"Your mama sure has a lot to say about things. Look, because of you I'm missin' my show. You came to apologize, so get it over with and get out of here."

Grace squinched her face as though in pain and muttered, "Sorry."

"Fine. Keep the noise down, will ya?" Abigail swung the door shut in the girl's face and shambled back to her chair.

Two days later, there was another knock at the door. Abigail pulled it open to see Grace standing there. "You again. What do you want this time?"

The girl held out a cookie tin. "Me and Mama made cookies today after school, and she told me to bring you some."

Abigail reached for the tin. "What for?"

"'Cause she feels bad for all the noise me and my brother make."

"*Humph.* Well, she should. Never had any trouble with noise until you folks moved in." She opened the tin and sniffed the cookies. "Chocolate chip, huh?"

"Yes, ma'am."

"Well, as you can see, I ain't one to turn down free food."

Grace raised a brow but bit her bottom lip and said nothing.

"Smart girl," Abigail mumbled around a bite of cookie.

"Mama says, 'If you don't have anything nice to say, you shouldn't say anything at all.'"

"Hmm. Guess my mama never taught me that." Abigail squinted at the girl. "Say, you interested in a job?"

"A job? I'm only nine years old. Mama says I can't get a job until I'm in high school. She says school is my number-one job besides being a kid."

"Mama says, Mama says. It ain't all about what Mama says, you know. You gotta think for yourself sometimes. I'll give you a dollar to run down and fetch my mail twice a week. A dollar total, mind you. Fifty cents each time."

Grace wrung her hands. "I—I don't know if Mama will let me."

"Well, run on home and ask permission then."

Abigail sat at the kitchen table and dug into the cookies while she waited for the girl to return. They were damn good cookies, and it had been a long time since she'd had anything homemade.

"Come in," she yelled when she heard a knock.

Grace entered.

"Well, what'd she say?" asked Abigail.

"She said I can if I want."

"You want to?"

Grace shrugged. "Depends … You gonna keep being mean?"

Abigail nearly choked. When she finished coughing, she tilted her head and gazed at the girl through watery eyes. "You're awfully cheeky for your age, ain't ya? I suppose I can try to hold my tongue when I'm in a mood. But I won't tolerate no sass, you understand?"

"Yes, ma'am."

"You want the job then?"

"Okay, but Mama says I shouldn't take money for it. I should just do it 'cause that's what good neighbours do."

"I ain't no charity case. I'll pay you to do it, and that's final."

"Yes, ma'am. I'll tell Mama you said so."

"Every Tuesday and Friday work for you?"

Grace nodded.

"You might as well start today then, since it's Friday." Abigail motioned to a key hanging on the wall behind the door. "Key's right there, and it's mailbox number two."

Abigail unlocked the door at 3:55 p.m. Grace had been collecting the mail for a few weeks now and always arrived right on time. Abigail would never admit it to anyone, but she was starting to look forward to the brief visits. She got a beer from the fridge then shuffled to the living room and settled into her recliner to wait.

At four o'clock on the dot, Grace rapped twice on the door and entered the foyer. "I'm here, Mrs. Jones!"

"I heard. You come see me when you get back, and I'll give you your money."

A few moments later, Abigail heard the door open again, and Grace entered the living room with a bundle of letters and flyers in one hand and a plastic container in the other. "Mama sent leftover spaghetti."

Abigail took the mail and nodded at the container. "Go on and put that in the fridge for me, and I'll eat it later for supper." She sorted through the letters, mumbling about all the junk mail.

When she looked up again, the girl was standing beside the chair. "Huh, I guess you're waitin' to be paid. Go on into my bedroom and bring me my purse. It's on the floor in the closet."

Grace returned a moment later, handed over the purse and stood by waiting while Abigail dug through it. "Mrs. Jones, do you have a family?"

Abigail's hand stilled. "What kind of question is that?"

"I saw a picture in your closet of a woman who looks like you, only younger, and a man and a baby."

"Didn't your mama teach you not to snoop?" Abigail snapped as she withdrew a dollar and slapped it onto the end table.

"Yes, ma'am, but I wasn't snooping. It was right there on the floor beside your purse."

"Still ain't nice to ask nosy questions about things that are none of your business. Besides, you ever seen anybody else here? Be like me askin' you questions 'bout your daddy when I know full well you probably don't even know who he is."

"I do too!"

"That right? How come I've never heard a man upstairs? How come all you ever talk about is your mama?"

Grace's eyes shone with tears. "'Cause my daddy's dead. He got shot."

Abigail shook her head and heaved a sigh. "That's a damn shame. You people have a real problem with violence, killin' each other like you're in the middle of a civil war."

"Don't you talk like that! Mama says Daddy was a hero. You can get your own mail from now on. And keep your damn money. I don't want it," Grace retorted before running out the door.

An hour later, Abigail stood in the kitchen reheating her spaghetti when she heard three loud knocks. Thinking it was Grace again, she flipped the lock and opened the door.

A woman stood there, one hand on her enormous belly, glowering like she was about to commit murder. "Are you Mrs. Jones?"

"I am."

The woman took a step closer and pointed at Abigail's chest. "How dare you? You have no right saying the things you did to my daughter."

"I didn't say nothin' that ain't true."

The woman gave a one quick shout of laughter and stepped closer. "Every word that comes out of your uneducated, racist mouth is a damn lie, and you're too ignorant to know it. You want to know how Grace's father died? I'm sure you heard about the shooting at Columbia a couple months ago? My husband was a professor at that school, and he died trying to protect his students from a white man with a gun. Now you tell me who you think is killing who. You tell me who you think has a problem with violence, when my children's father is dead, and I'm about to have a baby who'll never know his daddy because of some crazy white man who hates 'my people' enough to kill us." She stood so close to Abigail that their bellies brushed, and she jabbed her finger into the older woman's chest. "You leave my daughter alone. Don't talk to her. Don't even look at her. Because if she comes home again crying because of you, there'll be hell to pay."

Grace's mother didn't wait for answers, explanations, or apologies; she turned on her heel and left Abigail standing in the doorway, covered in a cold, nervous sweat with her mouth agape.

Nearly a month had passed since Grace had stopped coming. Abigail felt the loneliness right down to her aching bones. She felt tired and lethargic, and yet she tossed and turned for hours in bed. It was the girl's fault; before Grace had showed up at her door, Abigail hadn't even realised she was lonely.

And now, she had to get her own mail, which meant navigating her massive body down and back up a flight of stairs. After each trip, she returned to her apartment drenched in sweat and had to lie down just to get her breathing back to normal.

Sleep did not come easy that night. Abigail lay awake for hours and finally drifted off fitfully. The dream hit fast and hard, so vivid it was like reliving the nightmare that had changed her life thirty-four years earlier.

Frank had been away on business that night, leaving her home alone with the baby. She had always liked to drink, but, after Jack was born, she developed a bad case of the blues and often drank heavily, even though Frank disapproved. Taking advantage of her night of freedom, Abigail put baby Jack to bed early and cracked a beer. She had finished a twelve-pack and moved on to vodka when she decided she was hungry.

There was next to nothing in the fridge. She opened the cupboard and spotted a lone box of macaroni and cheese. There was nothing better, in her opinion, than a bowl of hot cheesy pasta to soak up the alcohol before bed. She half-filled a pot with water, dumped in the noodles, turned the burner to High and staggered to the couch to wait for the water to boil.

The next thing she remembered was waking up in an ambulance on a gurney, lungs burning and lights flashing all around. She sat up, ripped the oxygen mask off her face and tried to yell, but a coughing fit seized her. "M—My b—baby. My baby's in there!"

Abigail woke in a panic and struggled to sit up, wheezing as she gasped for air. It had been a long time since she'd dreamt about that night. Still disoriented, she took a few deep, steadying breaths. The fog lifted from her brain enough to register the smell of smoke.

The panic returned full force. Had she done it again? She was certain she hadn't used the stove before bed, and she'd only had five or six beers—barely enough to feel a buzz. Her nose twitched again. It was smoke all right. She swung her legs over the side of the bed and fumbled in the dark for the lamp.

She shuffled to the kitchen, flicking on lights as she went. The stove was off. The smell of smoke was stronger, but it was not coming from her apartment. In the foyer, she placed a hand on the door to be sure it wasn't hot then opened it a crack and peeked into the lobby. A ribbon of smoke drifted below the ceiling.

Abigail pushed the door shut and leaned against it, trying to calm her mind enough to think. Where was the fire—upstairs or down? And why wasn't the smoke alarm going off?

She opened the door again and scanned the stairwells, looking for flames. There were none in sight. The smoke seemed to be drifting up the stairs from below and was visibly thicker than it had been a moment ago.

Abigail closed the door and pushed away the panic as memories of that night came flooding back. Did she have time to go to the bedroom and get her purse? She took a step in that direction then paused when the image of Grace popped into her head. It was three o'clock in the morning, and they were all up there sound asleep with no smoke alarms to wake them.

911. She needed to call and get the fire department here. They'd get Grace and her family out. She hurried into the living room and picked up the phone.

By the time Abigail hung up, a thin haze of smoke had seeped into her apartment, burning her eyes and throat. She grabbed a sweater off the arm of the couch and held it over her mouth and nose as she stepped into the lobby.

Thick clouds of dark smoke billowed from the basement and streamed along the ceiling, obscuring the lights and leaving the lobby in eerie semi-darkness.

Abigail watched the smoke creep up the stairwell to the second floor. She was certain the firefighters would be here any minute. All she had to do to get to safety was walk across the lobby, down a few steps and out the main entrance.

But what if the fire department was too late? They could all die in their sleep from smoke inhalation—Grace, her little brother, their mama, and her unborn baby.

Abigail hesitated then yanked the sweater sleeves around her head and tied them at the back of her neck. With one hand on the wall to guide and steady her, she climbed the stairs.

Halfway up, the smoke thickened, and she fell to her knees, coughing. As she knelt on the step gasping for air, it occurred to her that the smoke was thinner down here. With her hands on one step and her knees on another, she crawled upward. Her lungs burned, and her muscles screamed, but she trudged onward until, finally, her hands searched for the next step and instead found the cold tile floor of the landing.

Abigail dragged herself across the tile, keeping one hand on the wall until she felt a doorframe. She raised a fist and pounded then pulled the sweater off her face and yelled, "Fire!" over and over until her throat was raw.

Abigail felt weightless. She floated high above the city, high above the clouds, above even the stars, to a place filled with nothing but golden light. She heard his laughter, and her heart filled with a joy like none she had ever felt. He appeared before her, all chubby cheeks and smiles, and the smell … Oh, how she had missed that indescribably sweet baby smell. She inhaled deeply, and it filled her senses.

She opened her arms. "Come to Mama, Jack."

His smile faded. Flames danced around his head and licked at his cheeks. He whimpered and reached for Abigail, but, when she held out her hands, the fire blazed to life, engulfing him.

Abigail woke with tears on her face and Jack's screams in her head. A slight breeze left goosebumps on her skin. Engines rumbled, people yelled, water gushed. She opened her eyes, lifted her head and looked around.

It was like déjà vu waking up in an ambulance on a gurney, lungs burning and lights flashing all around. This time, Abigail was too exhausted to sit up. She couldn't even muster the strength to pull the oxygen mask from her face.

Someone squeezed her hand, and a small voice beside her called out, "She's awake!"

Abigail turned her head to see Grace's face beaming down at her. "Mama says you're a hero, just like Daddy."

Abigail closed her eyes and shook her head, remembering the screams. "No, I ain't."

"ETERNALLY MINE"
AUSTIN P. SHEEHAN

It was the morning of a scorching day last summer when God first spoke to me. I was waiting at the lights in my beat-up Pontiac Phoenix when it happened. Of course, it sounds silly now, but, back then, I was doubting if He had a plan for me at all. So, there I was, sitting in my car, when a brunette crossed the road. Her dark wavy hair cascaded over her shoulders and bounced with every step. She wore a pink mesh singlet top, revealing her toned arms and stomach, with skintight black and grey ankle-length pants showing off her legs. Our eyes met, and the silver crucifix on her chest reflected the bright sunshine into my eyes. Watching her lycra-clad backside as she took off jogging around the park, a heavenly trumpeting overwhelmed me. It was an angelic choir, wedding bells; it was the Metatron proclaiming, "That's her, the meaning of your life. Make her yours."

I had to obey. I mean, when you think about the billions of people on Earth, the chance of finding the one who makes you whole, the one God has made just for you, is infinitely miniscule. But it happens. By some miracle, our paths crossed, and I received His message. I parked the Phoenix and watched her complete a lap of the lake, my hand resting on the wooden cross in the centre console, a prayer of thanks on my parched lips. Like an angel she ran, weaving between the other joggers, dog walkers, and cyclists. My heart leapt as I realised she was coming back towards me. I climbed out of the car and walked to the footpath, excited and full of joy, hardly believing my luck. As she approached, her soft hazel eyes concentrated on the path, and her crucifix bounced against her chest in time with her steps, giving me courage. With a soft, rhythmic *thud, thud, thud*, her footsteps brought her to me.

Stepping into her path with the confidence of a man hand-picked by the Lord, I locked my eyes with hers, holding out my hand with a welcoming smile.

"It's funny to run into you like this!" I said, full of hope and happiness.

She danced around me with grace and poise, not breaking stride. "Get lost, creep!" Her first words to me echoed through the park and through my aching heart.

Head bowed, I looked down in confusion at my hand, still waiting for hers. *That's not how it should have happened,* I thought. She should have shaken my hand, smiled up at me and given me her number. Full of anger, feeling betrayed, I clenched my hand into a fist and stormed back to the car. She mustn't have got the message that God had destined us to be together. *How could I make her understand?* I asked myself. *How could I show her that I was the one for her?* Catching my reflection in the rear-view mirror, I found my answer. Hard grey eyes stared back framed by a mop of greasy matted hair and a scraggly beard barely concealing acne-covered cheeks.

I changed my life—I ditched crap food; I took out a gym membership and promised the Lord that I would make her mine. I read the Bible with renewed vigour, morning and night. My angel always ran through my mind and danced in my dreams. Each morning, I cruised by the park just to make sure she was okay. I didn't approach her again, but I did follow her back to her Richmond home once or twice just to make sure nothing happened to her; we're living in dangerous times these days, after all.

After six months of studying the Bible, eating right, working out, a proper skincare routine and prayer, I was unrecognisable. I'd dropped a lot of weight, built up muscle, lost the beard, and splurged on new clothes and a proper haircut. I was a new man, made in God's image. And I felt so much better about myself too, not only from looking after myself but because I had a purpose. Because God had spoken to me, had given me this angel. The bond between us was so strong and true that I'd transformed myself into the man she'd like, and we'd only spoken once.

In the middle of winter, I began running in the park every morning the same time she did. I knew her routine. Two laps of the lake, a drink at the fountain and one lap back the other way. I knew the scripture. For forty days, Jesus wandered the desert resisting temptation. So, for forty days, I ran, from the dead of winter to the start of spring, watching the flowers bud and start to bloom. Some days I ran ahead of her; some days I followed her, and not once did I speak to her. But I couldn't stop myself from smiling at her or from thinking of our life together and the surprise God had in store for her.

On the forty-first day, I waited for her at the fountain. I'd had months to plan this moment, and it was obvious. The good book says, *To the thirsty, I will give from the spring of the water of life without payment,* and I was parched. So, I waited at our fountain, heart pumping with a nervous excitement, full of hope and longing, and, with a *thud, thud, thud,* her footsteps brought her back to me.

"We've gotta stop running into each other like this," I joked as she approached me.

Looking me up and down, she took in my expensive Reebok shoes, shaved legs, Nike running shorts and singlet, my tanned muscular arms and unblemished, clean-shaven, friendly face.

"Do I know you?" she asked, her voice angelic, looking up into my eyes with curiosity just like I knew she would. "My name's Karen," she said and, after a moment's hesitation, reached out to shake my hand.

It started like any other relationship. We had coffee after our morning runs, flirted over text messages and phone calls and went on dates to dinner and the movies. Yet, at the same time, it was unlike any other relationship, because, from the beginning, I knew that we were destined for each other, that we would be together forever.

Forty-one days after our meeting at the fountain, I'd booked a table for us at an expensive restaurant. It was wonderful; we were drinking champagne, and the conversation flowed. We flirted, laughed and made eyes at each other. I wore my best suit, and she was in a stunning low-cut black dress, her hair soft and shiny, her eyes glowing. Over our candlelit dinner, I told her that we were meant to be together. Her face erupted with laughter, her hazel eyes beaming, her smile infectious. I was overcome with elation—finally God's truth had been spoken, and my Karen was happy. To celebrate, I ordered a decadent, exquisite dessert to share, not caring about the stains the chocolate sauce would leave on my suit. It was one of those heavenly nights at the end of spring—the warm air infused with the delicate aroma of life and love—and we walked all the way home, hand in hand, our footsteps in sync, *thud, thud, thud.*

By a stroke of luck, perhaps even divine intervention, Karen's housemate soon moved out. I had been given an opportunity and had to take it. When I first suggested I move in, she was uncertain, saying that we barely knew each other and had only just started dating. But as weeks passed and the room remained empty, she was concerned how she'd cover the rent. After offering to pay half that month's rent and the next month's when the room was still vacant, Karen soon saw the sense in us living together, and I moved in, adding my name to the lease and the bills. Those months we were both the happiest we'd ever been. She had talked about her former boyfriends that no matter how nice, handsome, or successful they were, it had never felt like it was meant to be. How nice it was, knowing she wouldn't ever have to worry about that again. We fitted into each other's lives seamlessly—we woke together, ran around the lake together, returned home and made love. Afterwards, as she showered and went to work, I thanked the Lord for seeing fit to give me the perfect wife. Everything was perfect. Only … Only she wasn't my wife yet. But surely it was just a matter of time.

In the evening of a long day at the end of summer, I had a feeling in my gut that it was time. Karen and I were together, but the promise I'd made would not be fulfilled until we were husband and wife in the eyes of the Lord. I'd left work early, my heart racing with anticipation as I drove the Phoenix home and sat on the doorstep. There I waited for her, a smile on my face and a prayer in my heart. When she arrived, she looked more beautiful than ever, her hair tied in a tight bun, a sweet smile on her face.

"Karen my love, when will we get married?"

"What?" She dropped her bags in surprise. "We barely know each other. Where's the flowers? Where's the ring?" she asked, looking down at me in disbelief. "And you have to ask *will* you marry me."

"What do you mean?" I asked, my mind a whir of confusion, a sudden knot in my stomach. "You only ask when you don't know the answer, surely?"

"This is crazy. We've only known each other for a few months!" she said, her usually sweet voice now strained as she shook her head. "And on top of that, you just assume it's going to be a *yes*?" she continued with a laugh, looking me in the eyes.

"Of course," I said, flashing her a confident smile. "It's our destiny."

Rolling her eyes, Karen pushed past me into the house and went upstairs, her leather shoes *thud, thud, thud* on the floorboards.

Why didn't she say yes? I asked myself, cutting up the vegetables with swift strong strokes. *Hasn't she learned that she's mine?* I asked, working on the lamb, the knife cutting cleanly to the bone. We ate dinner in an awkward silence. My irritation grew every time her foot tapped under the table, every time her eyes darted around the room, looking everywhere except in my direction.

After dinner, Karen apologised for how she'd reacted, saying she'd just heard that her uncle was sick, and one of her friends was having trouble at work. I'd surprised her on a bad day and with an unexpected proposal which lacked the traditional ring and roses. That was it, of course! She was upset that I hadn't got her a ring or flowers. She would have wanted to show it off to her friends. But still, it concerned me that she was so distracted by her friends and family. I was all she needed, after all. I didn't sleep well that night, and the next morning she had gone for her run and left for work without waking me.

Forty days later, on a breezy early autumn day with the leaves just starting to turn a beautiful golden colour, Karen's uncle died. His sickness had developed unexpectedly fast, and his death shattered my angel. While she sat sobbing in my arms and as I comforted her, I couldn't help wonder if she was being punished for not accepting my offer of marriage, for not accepting her place in God's world. For her sake, I couldn't allow her to make any more mistakes.

The few days before the funeral, things went from bad to worse. Karen was moping, distant, and inattentive to my needs, as if her dead uncle was more important than me. Troubled by her behaviour and not knowing where else to go, I turned back to the Bible, and a passage I was familiar with took on a new meaning. *When we are absent from the body, we are present with the Lord.* Again, God was there for me when I needed Him, guiding me. My resolve grew. I decided upon my plan. Well, God's plan, surely.

I had to keep Karen away from her uncle's body and home with me. That was what God had told me, so, the night before the funeral, I poisoned myself with holly berries. The next morning's episode of vomiting and diarrhea ensured Karen stayed home. How could she choose her family over me when I clearly needed her? Shaking with grief, she called her family to make her apologies. Someone else was going to have to do a reading, but that was of no concern. I couldn't understand why she was so distraught, but, after a few hours, she was satisfactorily resigned to looking after me. I felt content, safe in the knowledge that I'd done the right thing.

Even after the success of the funeral, with the added reward of her family meddling in her life less, Karen was still spending too much time with her friends. I stopped passing on any messages or letters that were left for her and encouraged her to come straight home from work. When she was home on time, I was extra nice to her. When she was late, I let my displeasure be known. She got the message, and, after the bruises healed, well, everything was perfect. Her family and friends hardly bothered us anymore, and we were together all the time. We ran together every morning; we read the Bible; we went to the zoo; we went to ball games; we went to the movies, just her and me, like we were meant to be. She had learned not to raise her voice at me or talk back. She was calm, quiet and compliant in all things. I felt like she was finally mine, like she finally understood.

After forty-one days of this paradise of her and I living in a state of bliss and our bond never being stronger, I decided it was time. Honestly, Karen herself showed me it was time, for the Bible says, *"Wives, submit yourselves to your own husbands as you submit yourself to the Lord,* and she was behaving just like a good wife should. She sat on my lap, her unfocused eyes directed towards the television, as we filled up the hours after dinner watching some mind-numbing game show.

"My Karen, my love," I began, my voice shaking with excitement, making her look at me. "It's time, surely?" I continued, answering the question in her eyes and handed her the box containing a bespoke diamond ring, resting on a bed of rose petals.

"What's this?" she asked, concern creeping into her voice. Her hands shook as she opened the box then looked at me with a sweet smile fixed to her face.

"It's your destiny," I answered, crushing her in my embrace. I felt tears of joy streaming down my face as she squirmed in my arms before going limp with acceptance. Finally, she accepted her place, understood that God had made her for me.

The next morning, Karen's hazel eyes looked up into mine. With her voice full of respect and apprehension, she asked if she could look at bridal stores after work. Karen wanted our wedding to be perfect, and, still elated from our engagement last night, I agreed to her request. What harm could it do? She was mine now. And after we were married, she could quit her job and stay home all day looking after the house. But I hadn't told her that part yet. I wanted it to be a surprise.

Before long, she started returning home late. Not every day, just once or twice a week. She said she was looking for the right wedding dress, visiting jewelry stores and wedding venues. And I believed her. But one late autumn day, I stumbled upon the truth. I was driving the Phoenix around town when I saw her at a crowded cafe. With another man. Someone was trying to steal her from me. That could not be allowed to happen. I drove home, shaking in outrage and disbelief. Something had to be done.

I was jealous, of course. Who wouldn't be? But it was more than jealousy; it was a righteous anger and fear. How could she even talk to another man when she knew God had made her for me?

When she came home, I flung her onto the couch, demanding answers. And the stupid thing is that the more I asked, begged, pleaded and threatened her, the more defensive and reserved she became. At first, she said it was just a friend who was helping her with the wedding. I didn't buy that for a second, and she soon stopped responding to my threats and accusations. After I had spent all my anger and frustration, I cleansed and soothed my aching fists in the sink before going to bed, leaving her on the couch. The poor girl still didn't know the truth. She didn't know that ignoring and betraying me was angering God.

The next day, I tried to explain it to her, but she just laughed in my face. I was only trying to help, but she just lay there laughing at me with her dishevelled hair, her eyes bruised and swollen, her clothes still covered in blood.

The day after that, she wasn't there when I came home.

I wanted to forgive her. It was the Christian thing to do. I tried calling her, but she didn't answer. I left messages on her phone saying that all would be forgiven if she'd just come home and marry me. I gave her forty days. But she never answered or replied to my messages. She never even came home to grab the clothes she'd left. It was as if she'd been dragged out of my life by her own evil desires and had been captured by the devil who tempted her. Oh, my poor Karen, if only she was strong enough to resist!

On the forty-first night, with the first blast of chill winter air filling the bedroom, God told me what needed to be done. The next morning, I called the gas company about our account, and they gave me her new address.

"God bless you!" I said, hanging up the phone.

Watching the house all day, I waited until they were home, until the lights were off, until they were in bed. My heart was thumping, betraying my eagerness to do whatever the Lord commanded. After sliding through the open laundry window, I crept down the hallway to the kitchen. On the counter, bathed in a halo of moonlight, was an eight-inch kitchen knife. *And the Lord will continually guide you,* the good book tells us. Isn't that the truth? I went upstairs, praying for strength with every step, my chest bursting with God's love. Karen's captor must have heard me, his bulky outline was illuminated by the light from the open doorway behind him.

As I reached the top step, he ran at me and leapt, trying to push me back down the stairs. He didn't see the knife. I sidestepped him, and his momentum buried the knife into his stomach. Silently praising the Lord, I listened to the cries of pain as Karen's tormentor fell—*thud, thud, thud*—down the stairs.

"What are you doing, you bastard?" screamed Karen, her body shaking in fear.

"You only ask when you don't know the answer, surely?" I replied with a laugh, full of love and the joy of seeing my angel again.

"You won't get away with this, you asshole!" she yelled, jumping out of bed and grabbing a phone off the bedside table.

I jumped onto the bed and kicked the phone out of her hands. She backed against the wall, inching her way towards the dresser as I watched from the bed, ready to chase her if she went for the door.

But she paused as her hands found something in the darkness. Karen took a steadying breath, then ran at me, *thud, thud, thud,* her delicate feet delivering her unto me one last time.

"You're mine, Karen. You can't fight it," I said, grabbing her wrist and driving my free fist into her stomach.

She stood firm until I smashed her face in with my forehead. Groaning, with dark red blood streaming out her perfect nose, she sank to the floor. The wine glass in her hand smashed on the floorboards, the stem snapping clean off.

I lifted her onto the bed, and, as she looked up into my eyes, I could see she finally understood.

"Okay," she whimpered. "I'm yours. I'll stay with you." Her voice broke as her tears and blood soaked her pillow. "I promise I'll never even look at another man again."

Picking up the stem of the broken glass, I made sure she kept her promise.

It's a sad, sorry tale. I did everything right, and I was betrayed and humiliated. But I learned something. I learned that God has a glorious plan for me. I just need to keep studying the Bible and keep following the path He has prepared. And I have good news! God has taken pity on me; he knows it wasn't my fault.

When I was driving my Phoenix today near the park, a honey-blonde girl ran across the road in front of me. As my eyes followed her tight shorts, I heard the same bells. I've been given another chance at love! And don't worry, I won't let anything go wrong this time. I'm coming for you soon, my angel. This time everything will be perfect.

"THE DUMPING TREE"
MIKA SPRUILL

Susan tapped her cigarette on the paint-chipped porch railing and wondered if the bastard would show his face again. She lived at the end of Baker Street, just before the undeveloped cul-de-sac with the path into the woods. An old white oak stood at the head of the leaf-lined trail, one of its roots looping up to form a handle in the dirt. She called it the Dumping Tree. It was the spot where heartless cowards tied up their dogs and drove away, leaving a family member lost and orphaned. They usually came at night, creeping along with headlights low, but this latest bastard had had no shame.

The sun was bright, and Susan's poop bag was heavy. She had almost finished picking up the backyard when a wretched howl rang through the neighborhood, sending a shiver through her body. *This can't be happening again*, she thought, dropping the bag and running for the gate.

The German shepherd leashed to the tree tugged and yelped desperately after his owner, who stood frozen just up the trail. The man was tall and thin and easy to spot in a bright orange shirt.

Susan watched him for a moment, wavering in his indecision. "Hey! Hey, you!" she called out, but, at the sound of her voice, he bolted into the woods.

Susan sprinted after him. Fueled by anger, she ignored the shooting pain from her spine and the deep burn creeping down her thighs. She chased him nearly a quarter mile around blind curves and across a creek, until he jumped from the trail and disappeared behind a boulder. Susan had to stop to catch her breath. She wheezed, clutched her chest and coughed violently, promising herself another go at the patch.

Back at the cul-de-sac, the German shepherd had forgotten its despondency. It sniffed a few bushes and lapped the rest of a puddle from yesterday's rain. When Susan reached for its collar, the dog pinned its ears and growled.

"So, that's how it's going to be?" she said breathlessly as she untied the leash from the root. Her lungs were on fire. "Let's go, dude. Wait … You are a dude, right?" With a quick bend, she nodded. "Definitely."

The house she rented must have been beautiful at some point before nature and neglect had taken their toll—before she had moved in. The little yellow cottage was half-hidden under a wild rose bush; green algae stained most of the visible siding; half the corbels were missing from the once-white porch, and her driveway was a mud pit. Still, Susan couldn't complain. The rent was low, and her landlord never bothered her. The only problem was that cursed tree.

Susan had rescued seven dogs since she'd moved in with Elvis three years ago. At first, she took pride in being their savior—that motley, misfit crew had become her mission amidst a lonely, unemployed existence—but her disability check only stretched so far, and, with every new dog, her grocery budget shrank. She was overwhelmingly close to the dreaded reality of rehoming.

With the shepherd tied up outside the gate, Susan flicked open the latch to the backyard. "Cinnamon, Barkley, Sweetie— get back!" she said, traversing a row of straw-lined dog houses.

Inside the last was a brindle pit bull snoring loudly with his big block head resting on crossed paws.

Susan crouched until her face met his. "Elvis," she whispered.

The dog's eyes drifted open like a lazy winter sunrise, but, once he recognized Susan, his tail twirled like a tornado. He slurped a wet tongue across her cheek and jumped to his feet, dancing. When Susan whispered low so only he could hear, he wiggled in a full circle and launched into her arms. Soon, the others piled on, licking and yelping with glee. It was a warm slobbery heap of love, and she might have stayed there all day if not for their visitor, but, with Elvis in tow and a head rub for the rest, Susan left the backyard to introduce her newest rescue to her oldest.

"Make friends, Elvis," Susan told him.

The German shepherd stood at high alert, hackles raised and ears pinned, but Elvis flashed a toothy grin and strutted forward. Elvis was Susan's tester dog—friendly and confident, usually putting other dogs at ease or in their place. He sniffed the nervous shepherd before offering his own hind end in return, and, with greetings completed, both dogs settled into the grass, fat tongues lolling from the side of their mouths.

Susan brought her bag from the garage and set to work examining her new charge. The shepherd's nails were too long, and he had a few fleas, but otherwise, he seemed healthier than the last few. The red highlights in his shiny russet coat sparkled in the sunlight, and his teeth were remarkably clean for the age in his eyes.

"At least someone took care of you. You're awfully handsome," she said, presenting a hand to sniff, but the shepherd snarled. "Kind of an ass though. Come meet the crew. They'll straighten you out."

Elvis led the way through the gate, splitting the pack with equal measures of authority and pizzazz. Each dog waited patiently for their alpha to pass before swarming the newcomer. It was Franklin, a small, placid cocker spaniel she had rescued last month, who lost his composure and jumped at the shepherd. Susan waited anxiously for bared teeth and snapping, but they surprised her by dancing like brothers. Just as the rest had begun their inspections, Franklin and the shepherd took off, racing the perimeter of the yard. They leaped and pounced on each other as they ran, and, when they reached the far end, they burrowed into the straw mound, kicking it into the air and batting it with their heads.

Susan's jaw hung as she watched the two cavorting. Despite her own best efforts, the spaniel had finally come to life.

A few weeks earlier, at the sound of Franklin's desperate cries, Susan had arrived at the tree to find a tumbleweed that barely resembled a dog. His body had been cocooned in a hardened shell of chocolate-colored fur, laced with thorns that dug in as Susan worked the clippers under the thick matts. His shave-down had taken hours, but, when she was done, he looked like a small, wiggly bear. Franklin, the bear. He was sweet and cooperative and demure—until now.

While the boys tussled in the grass, Susan left the yard to put away her things. Her mind had just drifted back to the man in the orange shirt when the shepherd catapulted from her four-foot fence like an Olympic gymnast. He landed on his front legs and rolled, then he stood up with a whimper and bolted for the woods.

Susan groaned and chased after him. She hated running, and she might have let him go, but it was obvious he was hurt. Just as they reached the tree, Susan caught up and grabbed hold of his collar.

"I'm trying to help you, you stupid beast," she muttered as she dragged the limping dog back to the house.

None of the other rescues had ever tried to flee. It wasn't that her fence was inescapable, but, in their worst moments, they'd all found a warm bed, a decent meal, and a reason to stay. Susan wondered if this one was just following his owner or if he knew his way home. In any case, she would have to get him to the vet in the morning.

Inside her garage, wire kennels and plastic dog crates lined the concrete floor while bowls, leashes, and dog hair covered every other surface. A utility sink sat along the far wall flanked waist-high with a dozen bags of kibble. Pushing the shepherd into the largest cage, Susan slammed the metal door behind him with a grunt. She straightened herself upright and reached for her back, stretching and massaging her knuckles into the spasms.

All this hustling had done her in. The last thing Susan would remember of her morning was the long walk into the kitchen for her painkillers and the shake in her hands as she fumbled with the lid and dropped two pills onto the counter. She swallowed both at once with a swig of cold coffee and waited for the wave of relief.

By the time Susan awoke on the couch, the sun was gone, but her body felt wonderful. She was immune to the pain in her back and was enveloped in a welcomed haze of intoxication. Her bladder, however, was about to burst.

Susan stopped at the bathroom mirror to smooth the wild spots from her short black hair. She yanked a few greys, pulled at the creases around her mouth and poked the furrow between her brows. *Not too bad for thirty-five,* she thought with complete disregard for her upcoming thirty-ninth birthday. Just as she'd perched atop the cracked toilet seat, a howl rang through the house, ruining her peaceful daze. She had forgotten about the shepherd in the garage.

"Calm down, buddy," Susan shushed as she ran for a bowl and threw in a scoop of kibble. "Here, take this. Just be quiet!"

Instantly, it worked. The shepherd gobbled the brown pellets and meandered to a bed, quieted but still gloomy. At least his gait looked better, Susan noted. She loaded her own dogs into their kennels for the night, popped two more pills and settled under her duvet for a peaceful night's sleep.

Susan had just boarded a gondola with a handsome Italian gondolier when the shepherd's sad yowling startled her awake. Try as she might, the sound was impossible to ignore. Susan groaned and rubbed her eyes as she staggered from the bedroom. She was beginning to regret this particular rescue.

With the flick of a switch, the garage's fluorescent lights buzzed into illuminance. Most of her dogs barely lifted an eye, but the shepherd whined and pawed at his cage door.

Susan cracked it open and sat on the concrete. "Dude, I was having a wonderful dream. What's wrong with you? Don't you know what time it is?"

The shepherd settled onto the ground next to her and rested the tip of his muzzle on her knee.

"I know you miss him. I could tell by your dramatic escape attempt earlier. I'm sure he had a reason, buddy."

She didn't believe it—the guy was probably just a schmuck—but the dog's sad, brown eyes had melted the frozen edges of her heart.

"Okay, fine. One night," she conceded. With the shepherd trailing behind her, Susan hauled a dog bed into the living room. "Tomorrow, it's back to the pen for you." She fluffed the round cushion and settled him in for the night.

Closing the bedroom door behind her, Susan nestled back into bed. A familiar dream quickly enveloped her, taking her back to her childhood where she could practically smell her mother's perfume. Only a few of her memories still had that power; they were all from another lifetime, before everyone she loved had died and left her in this cold world alone.

With her gentle mother's voice echoing in her mind, Susan woke again to loud whimpers. Sleep was the only time her pills couldn't control the sorrow and loneliness she'd buried inside, but, this time, the crying wasn't hers. She eyed the clock—3:30 a.m.

Susan grumbled and threw off her covers. Barreling into the living room with hard eyes and a wagging finger, she started to yell at the shepherd, but he cowered, and her temper softened.

"Listen," she said with a sigh. "You're all out of whack. I get that. Come lay in here with me, alright? Only for tonight though."

She yanked the dog bed into her room on the floor by her footboard. "Here …" She pointed.

He brushed against her leg and stepped on her feet.

"Yeah, yeah. Go to sleep."

Susan climbed under her covers and pulled the comforter around her neck, grateful to still have a few hours before sunrise. Her mind settled into soft, pink clouds that whisked her away like a magic carpet. She soared over mountains and rivers, oceans and islands, but just as they'd reached the heavens, a high-pitched whine broke through her dreams again and dissipated the cloud beneath her. Susan woke as she rolled off the bed, legs tangled in the sheets.

"Goddamn it, dog!" she yelled, pulling herself free. "Maybe he left you because you're so fucking annoying." She slapped a hand over her mouth. "I'm so sorry. I didn't mean it," she said through her fingers. Susan slowly lowered herself to the floor beside him and stroked the length of his silky fur. "You're a sweet boy. It's not your fault. I know this sucks, but it's going to be okay. If you want, this can be your home now. You can stay as long as you want." Susan leaned in and kissed his wet nose.

The only remnant of the shepherd's former life was his collar, which Susan had left on him in case of another escape. She removed it, scratching his neck and watching his leg shake. The red-woven band was threadbare and lined with fur. Just beside the clasp, a small metal plaque glimmered in the moonlight.

"Randolph," Susan read. "That's a terrible name for a dog—Randolph. Can I call you Randy?"

The shepherd grumbled.

"Okay. Not Randy." She laughed, rustling his ears.

Susan awoke three hours later with the sun tipping through her window. Even before she opened her eyes, she moaned and grabbed for her back. The shepherd's face rested inches from hers, and his hot breath stank.

"Good morning," she said to him.

Peeling herself from the floor took longer than Susan cared to admit. After a quick stop at the bathroom, she started the coffee pot and found her pills. Her back and head throbbed to the same rhythm while her heart hammered out of control. She was exhausted and angry, and she knew what she had to do. One way or another, Susan was going to find the man in the orange shirt. Just, not yet.

The best part of her mornings was taking coffee and cigarettes to the porch and watching the birds at the edge of the forest. Through the fog, she couldn't identify the songbirds, but Susan was a whiz with the larger ones, especially the hawks and vultures that soared overhead looking for roadkill. The one I'm searching for is dead meat too, she thought.

Two cigs and a half a cup of coffee later, Susan leashed the shepherd and went for a stroll. When they reached the tree, she patted his shoulder. "Let's go, buddy. Show me the way."

The shepherd bolted, tugging Susan down the trail, off the trail, over fallen trees and under natural rock bridges, until she forced him to stop.

"Where are we?" Susan asked, looking for anything familiar.

She stepped onto a large rock that teetered at the edge of a cliff overlooking a lush green valley. A thicket of rhododendron guarded the far side of a round grassy knoll situated at the buff's base. Several small makeshift lean-tos lined the border, and a larger hut dotted the center. It was the king's castle among elf shanties, and, judging by the smoke rising from the middle of the structures, the king was home.

Susan followed the shepherd from the precipice down the slope while her eyes scoured the opening for the orange-shirted man. She'd hoped to spot him first, maintaining her cover until she was ready, but he was already waiting for her.

"Hey there, Suzy. May I call you Suzy?" the man said, stepping from behind the hut. He had a deep southern drawl and a weathered face.

Susan bristled. "No, you may not."

"Ah. Well, I've been waiting for you."

"For me?"

He laughed. "Yes, you. I thought you'd come sooner, but I knew Randolph would bring you somehow." The man, still wearing orange, knelt and beckoned for his dog.

When Susan realized she'd been holding him back, she dropped the leash.

Randolph raced to his owner, bowling him into the grass. They tumbled and kissed and embraced. Susan swore she saw the shepherd smiling. Suddenly, a tiny but fierce bark rang out from the hut. Randolph's head sprang to attention, tracking the sound. Another bark and he sprinted off, leaving the man on the ground.

"He is a gorgeous dog," Susan said, still wary. She patted her pockets, angry at herself for not bringing her pills.

"Thank you. He's one of my favorites. Although, besides Bertha in there"—the man thumbed over his shoulder to the hut—"my all-time favorite would have to be Milhouse, the German shorthair I left you. He was my birddog for years."

Susan gasped. "Barkley was yours?"

"Barkley?" The man laughed again. "That's a dumb name."

"What kind of goddamn name is Randolph, you stupid—"

"Woah, woah! Calm your tits. My bad. I'm not good with people. Why do you think I live out here?" He raised him arms and face into the sunlight, and Susan noticed purple bruises on his neck.

"Are you sick?" she blurted, surprising herself.

The man's eyes twitched, but he ignored the question. Instead, he stood and bowed toward the hut. "Would you like to come in?"

From the tender age of five, Susan's mother had prepared her for scenarios just like this. Every cell in her body urged her to run. She knew this was how women got killed, or worse, so she couldn't possibly explain the compulsion of her voice when she said, "Sure," or her legs when they complied.

Susan followed the man around his homestead, staring at his back and willing it to give her answers, though she couldn't say why she should care. This strange man was cocky and rude and obviously unsocialized. "What's your name?" she asked.

"Clyde."

Speaking of dumb names. Susan rolled her eyes. "And how did you know mine?"

He stopped to face her. "Lots of people know about you, Dog Lady. I heard about ya from a man at the post office, but I've no idea where he learned it."

"Dog Lady?" She flinched. "Huh, and all this time I thought it had something to do with the tree. So, what? You just pawn off your pets on me, because you know I'll take them?"

Clyde didn't say anything. He stared, searching her face while she stared right back. His eyes were dark, yellowed in the whites and heavy with bruised bags, but everything beyond them was concealed.

Randolph nudged his owner's hand and broke their trance.

"I'm coming, man," he said to the dog.

Susan cleared her throat and followed him into the hut. It was larger than she'd expected—and warmer. A queen-size mattress took up most of the middle, with one side curtained off and two leather recliners opposite. The bed's headboard was made of interlocked deer antlers, and the blue comforter was pulled taut enough for a game of quarters. Two rough-cut tree stumps served as nightstands, topped with lanterns that sent dancing shadows up the walls. The room felt surprisingly comfortable for a branch house in the forest.

Susan startled from a low rumble behind her. A tiny white chihuahua lay bundled in a fleece blanket in one of the recliners.

"Don't mind her," Clyde said. "That's old Bertha. She's crotchety." He picked her up and settled the dog on his lap as he sat. "Please …" He gestured to the other chair. "It's not often I have company."

"Actually, I need to use … um, the facilities?"

"Behind the curtain." He pointed. "Familiar with a compost john?"

Susan nodded, hoping in vain that he might have a medicine cabinet.

When she returned, Clyde appeared dead. His head drooped backward against the chair, and his closed eyelids looked nearly translucent. The skin of his face had an obvious yellow pallor.

Susan leaned in to see if he was breathing. "Hello?" she whispered.

He popped upright, startling her backward into the other seat, and doubled over in belly-laughter. "Awfully sorry but that was funny."

"Damn it. You scared the shit out of me."

"Aww, you're all right." He stroked Bertha's chin, more comfortable with the silence than Susan.

"So, how many were yours?"

"Well, I suppose I've left you five, counting Randolph."

Susan wondered about the other three dogs. "What about the spaniel? He was in bad shape. My vet said his back had been broken at some point, and his teeth were severely infected. Most of them had to be pulled."

"That was Cody. He didn't start out as mine, but I knew he needed help. That's why I gave him to you."

"Well, it's a lot of freakin' work, you know—taking care of all of them. And I'm not exactly rich."

"I know that, and I commend you on what you've done. I'm mighty thankful, and I mean to show you that, but I've two more favors to ask of ya."

Susan shrugged with a mix of resentment and curiosity.

"This here is my late beloved's dog," Clyde said, pointing to the chihuahua in his lap. "She's paralyzed and needs some looking after, but she's the last one I've got, and I need you to take her."

"Like hell. I've already taken all the rest of your dogs, and you want to push another on me?"

"Let's not beat around the bush. We both know you're gonna do it, because you're soft on these critters. Now listen, she needs some medicine—"

"But why? Why're you getting rid of all of them?"

"Take a look at me, sweetheart. My liver is deader than a doornail. I can't leave 'em out here when I go."

Susan couldn't muster an ounce of sympathy for the dying man before her, but the helpless dog on his lap pulled at her heartstrings. "What's the second favor?"

He took a deep breath and then, teary-eyed, asked, "Can I see them all again?"

She considered the prudence of inviting this strange man to her house before remembering that he already knew where she lived. *I'm just doing it for the dogs,* she told herself. "Sure."

Throughout the walk out of the forest, Susan held her back with one arm and the chihuahua with her other.

Clyde watched. "Mind if I ask what happened to ya?"

"I guess not. It was a work injury."

"Were you a … dock loader?"

"What?"

"Well, you ain't giving me much to go on here."

Susan sighed. "I was in the Navy—a bosun on the USS Eisenhower. Four years ago, a cable snapped that caught me in the back and broke my spine."

"Damn."

"Yeah, it was pretty bad. Six surgeries and a year of physical therapy later, at least I can walk."

"You must be a strong woman to go through all that and come out so well." He gestured up and down her body.

Susan stopped in her tracks. "Don't you go getting any ideas now."

Clyde laughed. "None at all, darlin'."

By the time they made it to the tree, Clyde and Randolph were panting. The sunlight had faded into deep magentas and oranges, and the air was already heavy with a twilight mist.

Susan led Clyde through the backyard gate and told him to wait there. She disappeared into the garage and emerged a moment later with the pack yipping and jumping for her attention, until they saw Clyde.

The dogs swarmed him—all of them but Elvis. The entire brood carried on like wild monkeys full of piss and vinegar, but it was easy to tell which were his; they yelped above the rest with joy. Clyde lowered himself into the fray as Susan turned for the house. She needed her pills and a minute to rest.

When Susan awoke on the couch hours later, her stomach churned with hunger. She sat up, stretched lazily and searched her memory for the last time she had eaten. Suddenly, she remembered Clyde and the dogs. Susan jumped from the couch and ran to the backyard, but it was empty. The front yard too. Barely containing her panic, she turned for the house, kicking herself for falling asleep.

The garage was dark, but when she threw open the door, the shine of the hallway light illuminated a heap of dog and man limbs on an island of clustered beds. A chorus of grunts and snores sounded off at disjointed rhythms. Susan shook her head and closed the door behind her. *What's one night?*

The next morning, Susan awoke to Randolph's whining. She found Bertha under her comforter and padded to the kitchen in search of coffee and pills, but Randolph was relentless.

"What?" she yelled into the garage.

The dogs stood in a circle around the float of beds where Clyde was sprawled. Randolph whined again and moved to his owner's side, licking his face. Clyde didn't move.

"No, no, no, no …" Susan hurried to the man, feeling for his pulse or any sign of life. "Clyde? Clyde?" She pulled at his eyelids and put her cheek to his nose, but his skin was already cold.

Susan sat back. She wasn't a stranger to death, but she'd never seen it so close. Maybe if she'd known how sick he was, she could have gotten him help, but then, that wasn't what he'd asked for.

One by one, the dogs turned from the body to her, pressing and leaning into their new owner. She kissed each of them, their weight comforting her. As they sat together quietly in their collective pool of sadness, Susan noticed something in Clyde's hand. She leaned forward and removed a tiny slip of paper he'd been holding.

Tell Randolph to find the treasure.

Susan had no idea what it meant. Clyde hadn't been too forthcoming about the details of his forest life. She waved the paper in the shepherd's face. "Do you have any idea what this means? Huh? It says, 'Tell Randolph to find the treasure.'"

The shepherd's ears popped up. He ran to the door and jumped at it until Susan stood and leashed him. Barking excitedly, he led her through the yard and out the gate into the woods. It was easier going now that she knew the way.

When they arrived at the huts, Randolph aimlessly sniffed the ground. Susan had almost given up and yanked the dog home when he barked twice and sat pointedly in a pile of leaves.

She tugged the leash. "C'mon, boy. Let's go."

Again, he barked twice and pawed at the ground.

"Can we please go home? I have to go take care of the dead body in my garage."

Randolph didn't budge.

"Fine, what is it?" she relented, shooing the dog and sweeping the leaves where he sat with her foot. She kicked something hard that clanked like metal. "Well, well, what have we here?"

Susan cleared the debris from a large door built into the earth and lifted it. It was a poorly lit bunker, perfect for hiding any number of dangerous secrets. Overcome with curiosity, she eased down the first few stairs, but Randolph darted past her, knocking her to the bottom on her butt.

Suddenly, the room lit up. A large moose-antler chandelier hung from the center of the ceiling, a black bear loomed in the corner, and, except for walkways, metal shelves filled every remaining square foot of floor space, all lined to their limit in gold bars.

Susan's jaw dropped. "Holy shit."

Randolph whined from within the maze of shelves, and, when she found him, he was dancing in front of a pedestal with an old wooden box labeled TREASURE.

"What could be better than this?" She waved her arms around the room.

With stars in her eyes, Susan twisted the skeleton key in the metal lock and lifted the heavy lid of the old pirate-style treasure box filled to the brim with tennis balls.

"HOOKY"
R. ROY LUTZ

When I was a boy growing up, Al was my best friend. Al lived next door and was a year older than me. We did everything together. One week after my thirteenth birthday, Al talked me into skipping school to go fishing.

"It'll be like a late birthday gift to yourself," Al argued.

I didn't need that much convincing. I liked fishing a lot, and I didn't like school at all. But I thought I needed to justify the decision I'd already made. "Yeah, that's right, I didn't get that much this year, did I? I didn't even get a real teenage party like I wanted just that stupid *whipped cream* cake and some stupid underwear," I scoffed. "What's wrong with good old fashion chocolate icing? And what guy on Earth wants to get *underwear* for his birthday?"

I had sufficiently convinced myself that I was entitled to give myself a little well-deserved birthday present, but I pretended to mull it over before I shrugged my shoulders and pronounced, "Okay, sounds good to me."

My excitement was camouflaged with a sprinkling of righteous outrage. "You bring the worms, and I'll bring the poles." Al clapped, and we both laughed.

The day didn't go as I expected. We went down to the creek and found a hidden spot under an old oak tree. But Al forgot to bring the bait. It was a long walk back, and the chance that we might be spotted was a risk we didn't want to take.

Al said, "I guess we'll just have to think of something *else* fun to do all day."

We sat down on the blanket that Al had brought along. Al kept staring at me, waiting for *me* to think of a *fun* idea. Hey, I wasn't the one who forgot the bait. It was turning into a hot spring day.

Al suggested, "Why don't we go swimming?"

I don't know what Al was thinking. "We didn't bring our swimsuits," I scoffed.

"Well, we can just go skinny dipping," Al said quickly.

I reminded Al, "The water is a little muddy and way too cold this early in the year. Besides, we don't have any towels to dry off."

Al persisted, "We can just take a quick dip and lay out in the sun on the blanket until we get dry enough to put our clothes back on."

"Sure, and get sunburned? You know how easy I burn. No way, Al."

Al gave up with an exasperated sigh.

Since Al didn't seem to have any other *fun* ideas, I used the paper sandwich bag to make notes for my history theme paper that was due that Friday.

Al took a nap in the shade.

I never played hooky with Alice again. She just didn't know how to have *fun*.

That summer, my new friend, Pat, moved in down the street.

"DON'T MESS WITH IT"
KYLE LECHNER

Shiloh buried her face behind her hands. Her parents carried a birthday cake into the dining room while singing "Happy Birthday" with wide grins. Shiloh's cheeks flashed red with embarrassment despite it only being the three of them in the room.

Her parents placed the cake on the table in front of her. Two big wax candles spelling *18* sat slanted in the chocolate frosting.

Shiloh took a deep breath, made a wish and blew out the candles.

"What did you wish for, kiddo?" her dad asked while cutting the cake into slices.

Shiloh laughed and slapped him on the arm. "I can't tell you, Dad. It won't come true then."

"You can tell us, honey." Her mother smiled. "Parents are allowed."

Shiloh took a bite of her cake. "You're both liars. And terrible at it."

After dessert, Shiloh went to her room to call her best friend Julie. They talked for over an hour about their weekend plans for Shiloh's birthday. It was nearing midnight by the time they said their goodbyes and disconnected.

Shiloh walked down the hall to prepare for bed but stopped to look at herself in the mirror hanging beside a photograph of her as a baby. She examined her baby picture before leaning in closer to the mirror and touching her face. *I've changed so much,* she thought before continuing to the bathroom.

The sounds of sirens ripped Shiloh from her sleep. She stumbled down the hall in a dazed state as she rubbed her eyes and yawned.

Her father sat in the deep, leather sofa. He was painted shades of purple from the flashing lights of the police cars on the wall screen in front of him. He noticed her enter the living room and lowered the volume.

"What's going on, Dad?"

Her father chortled. "Just the news."

Shiloh sidled into the kitchen and returned moments later with a slice of chocolate cake and glass of orange juice. "What news?"

"It's always the same news, kiddo. Nothing you need to worry about."

"I'm not a kid anymore, Dad," she said with a mouthful of cake. "I can handle the bad, scary news."

Her father shrugged and raised the volume again.

"At least twelve children are left injured after a school bus ran a red light yesterday afternoon … and into oncoming traffic. Luckily, there have been no fatalities, but the children were rushed to ParaCelsus Hospital. So far, no other injuries have been reported. Police are under the impression that the cause of the accident is the result of an artificial intelligence … behind the wheel."

"You'd think—" Shiloh pressed the flat tines of her fork onto the chocolate crumbs on her plate until they stuck. She popped the fork into her mouth and used her lip to scrape off the crumbs. "You'd think that with all the advancements in technology we have made that we'd be able to get AI right by now."

Her dad plucked a strand of her hair that was dangling onto her plate and tucked it behind her ear. "Yeah, kiddo. You'd think."

She swung up her leg and tucked it underneath the other so she could turn to face her father. "I mean … I'm not saying we should have flying cars already or anything. Or teleporters. You know?"

Her father nodded.

"But I don't know, maybe robots or something. I mean real robots. Not these stupid robots that people program to say they're going to kill humanity."

The weather girl, rambling about how today was going to be an unseasonably warm day for early June, distracted her for a moment.

"Oh!" Shiloh clapped her hands together. "Julie showed me this video of a robot that keeps swearing at this guy. It's so funny, Dad. I have to show it to you. Let me get my phone."

She sprung off the sofa and pranced down the hallway.

"Don't you have school soon, kiddo?" her dad called after her.

Shiloh picked her phone off the nightstand and tilted it to wake it up. *He's right. I have to leave soon if I'm going to make it to school on time.* She shucked off her pajamas and squeezed into the same jeans she had worn yesterday. After throwing on a Daft Punk shirt, she bounded to the bathroom to brush her teeth and hair.

No time for makeup today, she thought as she made faces at herself in the mirror. She glanced at her phone again.

Her mother was standing in the kitchen pouring a bowl of cereal when she ran back down the hallway.

"Bye, Mom. Bye, Dad. Love you. See you tonight."

She didn't even stop to give her parents a hug as she ran through the house to her car in the driveway.

It would be cool if we had flying cars already. She pressed a fingertip on the door's sensor to open it. *It's almost 2100, after all.*

Something had been irritating Shiloh's back all day. At first, she thought it was the clasp of her bra, but it wasn't in the right place. Her teacher had reprimanded her three times for causing a scene when she was trying to reach the spot before she gave up and dealt with it until school ended.

When she got home, she found her dad asleep in the same spot on the couch, snoring lightly. His snoring ended in a loud snort when Shiloh jiggled his shoulder to wake him up.

"Hey, Dad. Is Mom home?"

"Mom?" He yawned and wiped crust from his eyes. "Shiloh? Your mom? Oh. Your mom." He looked around the room. "I … uh—I don't know. What's up?"

Shiloh slung her book bag off her shoulder and twisted her arms to gesture at her back. "It's … I don't know. Something has been bothering me all day."

"So, what do you need Mom for? I can check for you."

"Eww, Dad! No. That's weird."

"What's weird? I'm your father." He stood up and walked around the couch. "Let me take a look."

Shiloh grabbed her bag and slung it over her shoulder before starting down the hallway to her room. "No, Dad. It's gross. Just tell me when Mom gets home, okay?"

"What's weird? What's gross?" he called after her. "I used to wipe your butt, you know."

"Dad! Stop it!" she yelled over her shoulder.

"You know, you could've had your father look at this, honey."

"Don't be weird, Mom. What is it?" Shiloh asked with a heavy sigh and pulled her shirt back down before turning to look at her mom.

"It's nothing, honey. It's just a little spot."

"A spot! What? Like a pimple?" She twisted her head to look at her back in the full-length mirror. She couldn't rotate her eyes enough to get a clear view before the strain blurred her vision. "Do I have a big, nasty zit?"

"It's nothing, Shiloh. Just don't mess with it, and you'll be fine."

Shiloh huffed. "That's easy for you to say. You're not the one with zits popping up all over."

Her mom patted her shoulders. "Just don't mess with it. Dinner's in an hour."

"That sounds so gross. Is it, like, all red and sticky and covered with pus?"

"Eww! Julie. Knock it off. Don't be gross." Shiloh turned to look at her back again.

Julie's face beamed from the phone in her hand. "Let me see it, Shi."

Shiloh turned back to her phone. "What?"

"Yeah. Let me see it. Lift up your shirt."

"Yeah right, lezbo. You wish."

Julie rolled her eyes. "There's nothing I can see that I can't see better on myself."

Shiloh laughed. "You're such a bitch. Okay."

She propped up the phone, turned and lifted her shirt. "Do you see anything?"

Julie squinted until her eye almost filled the phone screen. "I don't think so. At least not through the phone."

Shiloh lowered her shirt and flopped onto the bed. "This is so stupid. How can you not see it? It itches so bad."

"Well, I'll look again tomorrow when we meet up, yeah?"

"Pervert."

Julie laughed. "Anyway, it's getting late. I'll see you tomorrow. We'll meet at the mall at around … ten?"

"Yeah." Shiloh scratched her head and yawned. "That sounds good."

"Goodnight, Shi. Love ya."

"Yeah. Love ya too, bitch."

Julie laughed again and flipped Shiloh the bird before ending the call.

Shiloh hardly noticed the moon starting its descent to morning as she thumbed news articles on her phone. She had been up all night trying to find out why she had an itchy spot in the most unreachable place on her back.

So, it's either all in my head, or I have cancer. That wasn't helpful. She sighed and glanced at her clock. She groaned in frustration. *At this point, if I fall asleep now, I can get about five hours of sleep before I have to wake up to get ready to meet Julie.* She sighed again and grabbed the remote control for her wall screen. *What's the point?*

The screen came to life with a blue glow and a warm hum. Shiloh flipped past countless channels of paid programming and home shopping before passing out to a repeat episode of *Small Wonder*.

The alarm was persisting into the tenth minute of chiming before Shiloh lifted her eyelids. She slid out of bed, pulling most of the blankets onto the floor with her, before traipsing to the bathroom to get ready.

Her parents were sipping coffee on the living room couch when she trudged in, mindlessly trying to scratch the itch on her back. She fixed herself a cup of coffee before dropping into the armchair adjacent to the couch.

"Morning, kiddo. Sleep well?"

Shiloh shook her head as she blew steam off the top of her mug.

"What's wrong, honey?"

"The internet says I have cancer, Mom."

Her mother disapprovingly clucked her tongue. "You shouldn't make jokes like that."

Shiloh sipped her coffee. "Sorry."

"What makes you say that anyway?" her dad asked.

"Nothing, Dad. Just the stupid itch on my back. It kept me up all night."

Her parents shared a glance.

"Your Mom says it's nothing, Shiloh. Just don't mess with it. It's probably a bug bite or something."

Shiloh gazed into her coffee cup. "Yeah. Maybe."

"Listen to your father, dear."

Shiloh finished her coffee and sighed. "I will, Mom. I need to get ready. I'm meeting Julie at the mall."

She slipped off the couch and put her mug in the kitchen sink before trudging to her room.

Julie was sitting in a coin-operated ride the shape of a NASA space shuttle when Shiloh arrived. The mechanics groaned from years of disuse. Julie lurched backward and had to brace against getting whiplash as the shuttle sprang forward with its nose pointing toward the ground.

Shiloh leaned against the coin slot and waited for the ride to finish. "I can't believe you wasted a dollar on this thing."

Julie smiled and shrugged. "Worth it. I like these old relics. Machines these days are too … sleek, you know?"

Shiloh nodded.

Julie hopped out of the shuttle. "You can tell these things are machines. Look at, like, TVs. Way back when, these rides were popular." She placed a hand on the shuttle. "TVs were big and clunky. Now everyone has a wall screen. It's hardly even a TV anymore."

"Yeah. I guess." Shiloh shook her head and looked at her feet.

"What's wrong with you?"

"I have cancer."

Julie shoved Shiloh in the arm. "You've had cancer about a thousand times since I've known you. Stop looking up every little thing on the internet. Let's go shopping."

The guy sitting behind the counter to the dressing room looked up when the girls approached with armfuls of clothes. He glanced at Shiloh before turning his attention to Julie. "You know, Jules, there's a limit what you can bring in."

Julie adjusted her items. "Shut up, Brandon."

"I might be able to make an exception if—" His gaze drifted to Julie's chest, and he nonchalantly licked his lips. "If you show me your tits."

"Piss off, Brandon. Come on, Shi." Julie grabbed Shiloh's hand and led her into a booth.

Brandon walked around the counter and knocked on the door. "You can't have two people in there."

"I said piss off, Brandon."

He slipped the toe of his shoe into the gap beneath the door and lifted his toe to rub it against the underside of the barrier. "I might be able to make an exception, you know."

Julie started to respond, but Shiloh grabbed her arm. She rolled her eyes and shook her head.

After a few minutes, the toe of Brandon's shoe disappeared from the booth. He kicked the door enough to rattle the lock. "Whatever, slut."

The girls waited until Brandon's shadow retreated down the hallway.

"I seriously can't stand that guy," Julie said.

"What was that all about?"

"We went on a couple dates, and he got all huffy that I wouldn't put out."

"I guess not having sex makes you a slut now."

Julie laughed. "I guess so. He was just kinda … freaky too. You know? He would get real angry for no reason. He tried to run over a cat on purpose on our way to the movies. Just because."

Shiloh shivered. "Why isn't he in jail or something?"

"Because he hasn't done anything, really. Yet, anyway. Let's make this quick before the blood drains back down and he tries to get in again."

They quickly tried on the clothes, deciding on nothing. Before Shiloh put her shirt back on, she had Julie look at her back.

"There's definitely something there, Shi. It's like, a little red bump with a hole in the middle."

"Ugh. I knew it. Why didn't Mom tell me that? Do you think it's a zit? Is it infected?"

Shiloh watched Julie's reflection in the mirror shake her head. "No. I don't think it's a zit. But it looks like … hold on—" Julie dug her phone from her pocket while Shiloh put on her shirt. She scrolled down the internet search until she found the image she was looking for. "It looks like this."

Shiloh took the phone and almost gagged. "What the hell is that?"

Julie took the phone back. "It's what happens when you get a bot fly in you."

"A bot fly?"

"It's like, a fly from South America that lays eggs in people."

Shiloh cringed. "How the hell do you know about this?"

"It was on some gross nature show I watched. I think the other guy had, like, ringworm or something."

Shiloh rubbed her arms. "I don't care about the other guy, Julie. How does a … a what? … a bot fly get to California from South America?"

Julie shrugged. "I'm not saying that's what it is. That's just what it looks like."

"Well, how do I get rid of—"

A loud knock interrupted them. Julie unhooked the latch and pushed the door open. A mall security guard stood in the hallway with Brandon behind him.

"That's them, officer." Brandon sneered at Julie. "Those are the sluts making out and trying to steal clothes. I told them. I told them both they can't be in there together and—"

The security guard looked from the girls to the stack of clothes hanging on the wall. "I'm going to have to ask you ladies to leave."

"Are we in trouble?" Shiloh asked.

Brandon nodded slowly as a malicious grin smeared his lips thin across his face.

The security guard shook his head and lifted his arm to show them the way to the exit. "It doesn't look like you're trying to hide anything. But you're breaking the rules, and you gotta leave."

The girls walked down the hallway with the security guard in-between them and Brandon. Their accuser dragged his feet all the way back to his counter.

The security guard slapped the back of Brandon's head. "This is the last time, Brandon. I'm tired of you calling me over here every time some little thing pisses you off."

Brandon rubbed the back of his head as the security guard walked deeper into the store.

As the girls made their way out into the mall, Brandon called to them. "Hey you, bitches."

They turned to face him.

"If I ever see either of you sluts again, I'll kill you." He dragged a finger across his throat.

Shiloh spent most of her evening researching bot flies on her phone. Hours' worth of videos left her pale. After a while, she decided to make sure what was happening on her back was, in fact, a bot fly larva before trying the list of remedies she had found.

She propped her phone on her desk and set the timer. *I should have thought of this before spending all night almost losing my dinner.*

The camera flash erupted around her. She turned and picked up the phone to look at the photograph. A light red bump sat in the center of her back just below her shoulder blades. In the middle of the bump was a small hole. For as irritating as it was, the bump was smaller than she had estimated.

I could probably fit a paperclip in there. She picked up a paperclip from her desk and twisted it straight. *Maybe if I poke it, I can feel the fly moving around. Then I'll know for sure before I start taping steaks to my back to try and lure it out.*

Shiloh maneuvered the paperclip to the bump. The tip found the lip of the hole. She held her breath and eased the thin piece of metal inside. The journey wasn't far. The clip met resistance only about quarter inch in. Shiloh bit her lip in hesitation before pressing on.

There was a barely audible click as the clip moved just a touch more. Then everything went black.

"I understand, sir. But—"

"No *but*. Don't *but* me, son. I want to know what happened to my daughter."

Shiloh's father paced around the bedroom. Her mother sat on Shiloh's bed, looking at her lifeless body standing slouched beside her desk.

"If you could just bear with me a second, I'd be more than happy to assist you," the customer service representative said. "How old is your model, and what is its number?"

Shiloh's father switched his phone to his other hand and wiped nervous sweat from his forehead. "Model?"

"Your 'daughter.'"

"I ... uh ... I'm not sure what the number is. She just turned eighteen a few days ago."

The customer service rep chirped in acknowledgement. "Just turned eighteen. Okay. That clears up a lot. Do you have your KeyTip?"

"The little ... thing ... whatever that came with the robot?"

"Mhmm. Yes, sir."

"Yes. My wife has it."

He covered the microphone on his phone and mouthed what he needed to his wife. She rummaged through her purse and produced a thin piece of haptic material that could stretch and fit over a fingertip. He tucked his phone between his shoulder and cheek as he fit the material over his forefinger. Gold wiring spread from the center like a fingerprint.

"Okay. I have it."

"Excellent, sir. Now, I need you to access the boot menu. On the android's back, you should see a reddish bump. That's the reset button. With your KeyTip, I'll need you to hold your finger just below the reset button for five seconds."

He did as instructed, and five seconds later, a screen illuminated from underneath the skin on Shiloh's back. The words Android Age Of Consent Deactivation: Initiated appeared below the Uncanny Robotics logo.

Shiloh's father read the screen's message to the customer service rep.

"Mhmm. Okay. That's what I thought. As you should be aware from reading the terms of service—"

He scoffed. "No one reads those things."

"Well … if you had read the terms of service, it would've informed you that when your android reaches the age of consent, it is given the option to deactivate itself. You cannot force something to live against its will, after all." The customer service rep paused to let the information sink in. "Could you press your KeyTip on the screen and hold it there for ten seconds? This'll grant me access to your model's data."

Shiloh's father complied. After ten seconds, Shiloh made a cheerful yet haunting humming noise.

"She … She just made a noise," he shouted in excitement.

Shiloh's mother bounced on the bed and clapped her hands together.

"Oh. That's nothing, sir. That's just the computer acknowledging the input. That's not your daughter."

His face fell. He turned to his wife and shook his head.

She lowered her head and folded her hands in her lap again. "I told her not to mess with it," she said under her breath. "I told her."

"Sir?"

"Yeah. I'm here."

"Great. I'm looking through the diagnostics and your account now. It seems you have one of our AgeX models and are under a … thirty-year warranty. Of which you're in your … eighteenth year."

"That sounds right. My wife and I—" He turned to look at Shiloh's mother. "My wife and I lost our daughter when she was a baby."

"I'm sorry to hear that, sir."

"And we just couldn't … you know?" A sob lodged itself in his throat. "We just couldn't deal with it. And then we found your company, and … and you gave her back to us. You let us watch our little girl grow up."

"I'm glad we were able to give that to you, sir."

The sob broke out. After a moment to compose himself, he continued. "But now she's gone again. You've got to help us."

"I'm doing the best I can," the customer service rep said.

Shiloh hummed again. Strings of code burst across the screen on her back.

"Sir?"

"Yes?"

"It appears that with our cloud storage service we'll be able to download your daughter to this android. However, the uploads to the cloud happen when the machine is in sleep mode, which it appears has not happened since yesterday. So, everything that has happened and along with anything she has learned or experienced will be missing."

Shiloh's father turned to his wife and smiled. He gave her a quick thumbs up. "That's fantastic news. All she did yesterday was spend time with her friend at the mall. I'm sure it won't be anything important."

"Okay, sir. I'll begin the download now. Since you've had this android for so long, it's going to take at least twenty-four hours for the download to complete."

"That's fine. That's absolutely fine."

"Also, once your android—your daughter—wakes up, you'll have to inform her what she is. You'll have to explain she's just a machine. A living, growing machine. And confirm it by pressing your KeyTip to her wrist. That'll initialize the free-will protocol and inform Uncanny Robotics that the terms have been agreed upon. Your warranty allows me to download your daughter only once in the event of an accidental reset after the age of consent is reached. If the android is lost or damaged beyond repair, then you'll be monetarily compensated under your warranty. There's no third chance at life."

Shiloh's father glanced toward his wife and exhaled a deep breath. "Okay. I understand."

Shiloh hummed warmly and softly. A progress bar appeared on her back.

"Is there anything else I can help you with today?"

"No. No. You've been a great help. Thank you."

"You're welcome. And thank you for choosing Uncanny Robotics. If you have any additional questions at a later time, please call again. If you feel that I provided exceptional service, I'd love to invite you to take a brief survey following the end of this call."

Shiloh hummed throughout the night. Her phone lit up as Julie repeatedly called her. The constant vibrating rattled the phone off the desk, and it bounced underneath her bed. The battery drained with each phone call and voicemail.

The progress bar on Shiloh's back reached seventy-five percent. She made a little singsong of accomplishment before resuming her humming.

The phone illuminated one final time before the battery drained completely. For a brief moment, a text message from an unknown number flashed across the screen.

"I know where you live."

"SOUL BONDS ARE A WITCH"
BETHANY HOEFLICH

As they dragged Elise's unconscious body from the clearing, one thing became clear—the high priestess had lied.

In all fairness, we knew it was risky. Awakening one's bonded wasn't exactly a tea party in a field of wildflowers, after all. But still, a basic heads up would have been nice. "Hey, just to let you know, you might die as a result of the ceremony. Sign this waiver please." Was that too much to ask?

But no, we were led to believe this would be quick and painless. One drop of blood and we'd be soul-bonded to an ancient magical being. No big deal, right?

I glanced around at my surroundings for the billionth time. Combined with the blood-red moon, the towering pine trees, and the swirling incense that made my nose itch, the high priestess's backyard looked like it had been ripped from a B-rated horror flick. Spooky, I could deal with, but, if a column of robed figures carrying torches marched through the trees, I was bolting. I hadn't signed up for the role of female victim number three, thank you very much. Magic be damned.

"Well, now that the unpleasantness has been dealt with, shall we proceed with the ceremony?" the high priestess called in a voice that was rich like chocolate and espresso. Wearing midnight-blue robes and an amulet that marked her as the matron of our coven, she stood, back straight, by an ancient stone table and beckoned to the next witch in line. "Chelsea O'Donnell, please step forward and claim your birthright."

Chelsea, red-haired and white as a tub of sour cream, walked up to the table, hands shaking while she played with the hem of her simple ivory dress. She looked even paler than usual. The other girls stood next to me, chewing on their lips and trying not to fidget. Some of them could trace their ancestry back to the survivors of the Salem witch trials. If they were this nervous, I was doomed for sure. I should be trembling, but I was too busy trying not to laugh at Donna Stile's ridiculous headdress, which boasted more stuffed ravens than an Alfred Hitchcock movie. These witches sure went overboard when it came to ceremony.

The high priestess cleared her throat, eyes narrowed, as she reached out to grab Chelsea's hand. With a precise flick of the stone knife, she drew a single drop of blood. Quick and efficient, but, then again, she'd probably done this hundreds of times. The blood dripped into a stone basin that held a candle and some herbs. She wouldn't tell us what they were, but I could just make out the faint scent of sage and rosemary. She acted as if it were some big secret—probably wanting people to think that she harvested them, naked, during the proper cycle of the moon and only after bathing in sacred waters. Naturally, the mystique was ruined for me when I ran into her at Whole Foods with a basket full of herbs, along with some organic avocados and overpriced coffee.

My skepticism was decidedly demolished by the sound of a cat being flattened by a steamroller when Chelsea clutched her chest, as if she'd been burned, and threw her head back with a piercing scream that nearly made me piss myself. Seconds later, a fox wearing a decidedly bored expression appeared next to her, licking its paws. Panting, Chelsea reached out a tentative hand and ran it down the fox's sleek body. Cool!

I leaned forward, now excited by the prospects of my bonded.

The high priestess smiled. "Well done! He is a fine addition to our coven, and I have no doubt that you will do well together. Now go and get to know your bonded." She waved her away, and Chelsea disappeared into the crowd of witches, accepting their congratulations with a smile that split her face in two.

My eyes roved along the ranks of witches, eagerly checking out their companions. Some had animals that could fit inside a pocket, like a frog or a sparrow, while others had enormous beasts, like the grizzly bear that was tearing into the coolers of refreshments meant for the after-ceremony party. That was unfortunate.

What would mine be? I hoped I would get something small, like a cat or a mouse. And preferably something that could fend for itself. I did *not* want to be the first witch who accidentally killed her bonded by forgetting to feed it.

"Victoria Blackwell."

My head snapped up at the sound of my name. The high priestess gave me an encouraging smile, and I stepped forward, insides churning. Keep it together, Vikki. Do *not* puke on her shoes. What if I got a lion? Or an alligator? Or worse, an owl. Those giant eyes always freaked me out. Bile clawed up my throat, and I wished I hadn't eaten before the ceremony. Yep, those extra-spicy enchiladas had been a terrible idea.

What if I couldn't bond at all?

The thought sent my knees shaking. Only two years had passed since the coven rescued me from my foster home, and no one knew who my parents were or where I came from. What if they'd made a mistake? What if I didn't have magic at all? Even though I was years older than the other girls, it wasn't like I was acing my studies. I could barely scrape by in potion making let alone spell casting. I was a magical fluke, and it would just be my luck if I failed at something that required zero effort on my part.

I barely felt the sharp bite of the knife as it sliced into my hand. My blood sizzled as it dripped onto the ravenous flame. The coven held their collective breath as the seconds ticked by.

Nothing.

I could feel the weight of my failure in the high priestess's gaze and the silence of the coven.

Would they send me back?

My insides twisted, and a raging inferno snapped inside my chest. I couldn't help the scream that tore its way from my throat as I dropped to my knees. I was burning! Why didn't anyone help me? Was I dying? Would they drag my body away like they had Elise's? Then, as quickly as it came, the fire vanished, replaced by a cool ice that flooded my veins. Note to self—schedule a root canal during the next ceremony. I never wanted to go through that again.

I shuddered and opened my eyes, eager to meet my bonded. A move I regretted immediately.

An albino cobra was coiled inches away from my face. Its tongue flicked out and brushed against my nose.

I shrieked, scrambling away like a person with ophidiophobia when confronted with a snake. Which I was. Any sane person would act the same when coming face to face with a disgusting, venomous beastie.

Not a snake! Anything but a snake!

The clearing filled with soft murmurs hid behind hands.

"Miss Blackwell! Compose yourself at once."

I rose slowly as anyone would do in the presence of a deadly predator. My once-white gown was now smeared with dirt.

Several of the girls giggled, and my face flamed. I would never live this down.

Keeping my eyes locked on the serpent, I cleared my throat. "Uh, High Priestess? I think there's been a mistake …"

"This is most unusual, but the Great Mother doesn't make mistakes. Go and become acquainted with your bonded." The tone of her voice brokered no argument as she dismissed me from the clearing.

Yeah, right. The only thing I was going to become acquainted with was a one-way bus ticket to Nopeville. I was *not* sharing any kind of magical bond with this danger noodle. No way.

The feeling is mutual, mortal.

I froze, heart pounding, and glanced down at the cobra that slithered along next to me—too close. I leapt away and asked, "Are you talking to me?"

No, I'm talking to the other human with whom I bonded.

"Sarcasm. Great. I'm bonded to a freaking sarcastic nope-rope. Could my life get any worse?"

Probably, if you don't watch where you're going.

"What?" I tripped over a log in the middle of the path, landing hard on my face. If snakes could laugh, I'd imagine he was laughing at me. Vile thing. I clutched my nose, hoping it wasn't broken. "What are you looking at?"

Absolutely nothing at all. Where is your dwelling? Call your servants to prepare my chambers and have them send up the plumpest rats they can find. I wish to be pampered.

I snorted. "Welcome to the twenty-first century, Rumplesnakeskin. We don't have things like servants or chambers. I only have one bedroom."

Ah, you're poor.

"I'm not poor! I'll have you know that I splurged on the twelve-pack of Ramen."

There's no shame in having little. Not all my witches were wealthy, after all. We'll just have to share.

My mouth went dry, and my palms began to sweat. "Share? Oh no. That's a hard limit right there. You are *not* sleeping in my room, and that's final!"

Thirty minutes and one extraordinarily uncomfortable taxi ride later, I sat plastered to the headboard of my bed, trying my hardest not to vomit as the cobra choked down a still-twitching rat two feet from me.

"Ugh, can't you do that somewhere else?" I pulled my violet covers up over my head to block out the disgusting sight. Come to think of it, if blankets were a failsafe against monsters and ghosts, would they work against other horrifying things?

Why shouldn't I eat in my chambers?

His voice came too close, and I peeked down to see his head threading its way beneath the sheets toward me.

Nope!

I screamed, practically flying across the room. What could I use as a weapon? A book? No. My aim was terrible. Could I trap him in a pillowcase? Pretty sure I saw an episode of the *Crocodile Hunter* where that Australian nutjob did that. But then I'd have to get close enough to grab him, and that was *never* going to happen. A bat? That would be perfect. I darted to my closet, wrenched open the door and grabbed my old softball bat. I whirled around, brandishing it before me like a sword.

Your overreaction is borderline offensive. You are warm, and the heat aids my digestion.

"It's *my* room. Look, just because we're bonded doesn't mean I need to share a bedroom with Satan's slimy brainchild!"

I am not slimy, and for your information, I have a name.

"Oh? What is it?"

David Hisslehoff.

I snorted and pressed my lips together, but I couldn't help the laugh that escaped before I could stop it. "Seriously?"

I'll have you know that my last witch was an avid Baywatch *fanatic.*

"Sure thing, William Snakespeare."

The cobra slithered off the bed and around my bedroom, pausing to examine every nook and cranny in sight. He seemed particularly amused by the book of Egyptian hieroglyphics that lay open on my desk.

One of my former witches was an Egyptian Queen, you know.

"And in a previous life, I was a Cherokee Princess," I deadpanned.

He twisted his head around, fluffing out his hood. *Really?*

I rolled my eyes. "What do you think?"

That's not funny.

"I think it was hilarious. And speaking of hilarious things, how about the idea of sleeping in an enclosed space with a legless death machine? Can't you just, I don't know, go away?"

You seem ignorant of the purpose of a soul bond. Can I suggest that you reference a dictionary? Didn't your masters instruct you in this?

"Uh, I might have been playing Candy Crush during my magical studies lessons."

Unbelievable. Of the thousands of available witches, the universe chose you.

"Well, I'm not exactly thrilled about this either, Severus Snake. If I could trade you for a magical tarantula, I'd do it in a heartbeat."

He jerked back as if I'd smacked him with the bat, and I could have sworn that he looked offended. Without another word, he disappeared out the door that I'd left cracked open.

"Wait, I shouldn't have said that. I'm sorry!" I called, dropping the bat and running after him.

Which was how I ended up stuck in the crawlspace beneath the house an hour later with scraped knees and dirt under my fingernails. I peered into a hole in the siding. A brief flash of white scales was my only confirmation that he was inside. Stupid, stubborn, irritating snake!

"David Hisslehoff, would you please come out? I'm sorry if I hurt your feelings."

No! You are rude and brash and far too undignified to be my witch. Good day!

"I'm in the dirty crawlspace under my house with spiderwebs in my hair, talking to a magic snake. How dignified do you expect me to be?"

Go away!

"Come out right now, you scaly asshole!" In a move that made me ninety-nine percent certain I was insane, I reached for the hole, preparing to grab him.

Without warning, his head shot out of the hole, and his fangs sank deep into my hand. I snatched it away with a scream as I retreated, my head slamming into an exposed beam with a thud. Did he just …? I glanced down. Blood trickled from two puncture marks in my palm.

That was it. I was going to figure out a way to severe this ridiculous bond if it was the last thing I did. Storming back into the house and slamming the door behind me, I stomped into the library. Rows of shelves lined the walls, while desks and chairs filled the center of the room. I tore through the books, flinging them from the shelves in a frantic bid to find one that could help. Then I spotted it—*The Encyclopedia of Soul Bonds*. I grabbed it and sank into a chair, flipping through the pages until I came to the one I needed.

A quick glance revealed that it was a complex spell which required several rare ingredients. It was far too complicated for me to mix—just my luck, I'd turn myself green—but I knew exactly who could help me. A rogue witch living in Boston was just my ticket to freedom. I could buy her help and her silence, for a price.

But first, I needed to fake my death. Otherwise, the coven would keep coming after me, and it would be a snowy day in Vegas before I went through this crap again. No, siree. I'd just disappear into the sunset like the hero in a cheesy western film. Maybe I'd get a perfectly respectable job as a cashier or a barista and pretend to be human for the rest of my life.

A quick glance at the clock told me it wasn't quite midnight, so all the witches were still at the ceremony. I should have at least an hour before they started trickling home. Perfect.

After gathering everything I needed from the basement apothecary, I ran back to my room. I threw my meager collection of belongings into a suitcase and tossed it out the window, along with the encyclopedia. Taking a deep breath, I proceeded to smash every piece of furniture I could. Would that be convincing enough? Eh, it would have to do. Then I doused my sheets, walls, and floor in lamb's blood. Satisfied, I crossed my arms and took in the view. My room looked like the prom scene from *Carrie*. That should fool them well enough, unless they tested the blood. Wait, I didn't have a body. Crap.

It was only a matter of time before they discovered my ruse, and I needed to be as far away from here as possible before they performed a tracking spell. I raced outside, grabbed my suitcase and disappeared into the trees beyond the house.

Needled branches clawed at my skin as I rushed through the evergreen forest. Dark shadows filled the path before me as I weaved through the thick undergrowth. How long had it been? I should have hit the road by now. When my legs seized and my side cramped, I slowed to a stop, hands on my knees as I gasped for breath. I could picture the headlines now—*Out of Shape Girl Dies from Running*. That was just my luck.

A twig snapped behind me, and I spun around, squinting into the darkness. Five figures stepped from the shadows, wearing the crimson cloaks of our rival coven. Heart racing, I took a step back. "Crap."

The tallest threw back her hood and glared at me. "You're in our territory, witch."

"I'm terribly sorry." I held out my hands in a placating gesture and offered them what I hoped was a smile rather than a grimace. "If you could just point me in the direction of the bus stop, I'll be on my way. No harm done."

"You know the laws. This is a slight against our coven, and our high priestess will demand retribution." She shook her hands out of her sleeves and began tracing runes in the air. Double crap.

I edged away, watching with growing trepidation as she formed a disabling spell. I couldn't disable a kitten let alone five fully-trained witches. Maybe I could still talk my way out of this? "Ladies, please. This was an honest mistake."

"I think not. Besides, we need some target practice," she said, her lips pulling back from her teeth in a sadistic smile.

I dropped my suitcase and ran, dodging their attacks. A fireball sailed by my head, and the smell of burning hair filled my nose. A spell hit my legs, freezing them to the ground. Triple crap. I was dead. I was so dead. The witches stalked forward, and ice filled my veins.

A glimmer of white flew through the undergrowth. One by one, the witches screamed and fell to the ground, clutching their ankles. What the hell?

My cobra slithered into view, looking rather pleased with himself. *Let's go, mortal.*

"You're insane if you think I'm going anywhere with you." The spell holding my legs in place vanished. Should I feel guilty that my soul-bonded just murdered five witches and probably guaranteed a decades-long blood war between their coven and mine? Probably. Was I? Nope. Not in the slightest. I set my hands on my hips and glared at the cobra, my gratitude at being rescued warring with my festering irritation. "You bit me!"

Are you dead?

"You literally bit me!"

ARE YOU DEAD?

I stopped, realization dawning. Had I imagined the bite? No. I could plainly see two puncture wounds in my palm. But cobras were venomous … "I'm not dead. Why am I not dead?"

We're bonded. If you had taken a second to bother learning what that means, you would know that you're immune to my venom.

That was a solid bonus. "Well, Merry Christmas to me!" I blinked and glanced at the repulsive reptile. "You saved me."

It wasn't entirely altruistic. What do you think happens when my witch dies?

Oh, right. I blinked at him. "I suppose that's reasonable."

So, are we fine?

"Yeah, we're cool. But if you ever bite me again, I'll you turned into a pair of snakeskin gloves!"

I accept your deal. Now, can we go home?

I turned slowly, eyeing the bodies that littered the forest floor. Thinking of the mess I'd left in my room, I had an idea. "I guess that depends."

On what?

"How do you feel about staging a crime scene?"

"DEATH, MY FRIEND MY PAL"
MARIA DELANEY

"How are you, today, Death?"

"I'm bored today, Riley. Been thinking of getting a new pet to keep me company. Day in, day out I transport loving souls to Heaven and damaged ones to Hell. It gets dull, Rye."

"Understandable, Death. What kind of pet did you have in mind?"

Death glared down and kicked the loose dust beneath him. An oversized black cloak engulfed the frame of the bony skeleton.

I have never seen his face, only two yellow deceitful eyes peering from behind a massive hood. Unsettling movements gave proof the harvester of souls was uncomfortable with his thoughts.

"Um, I'm toying with the idea of making you my pet, Riley," he answered with hesitation in his echoing demonic voice. "I believe that you'll cheer me up and take away some of this loneliness. What do you think?"

Well, as you can guess, I was completely taken aback by his answer—intrigued and a little worried. For a while now, Death has been visiting me at night. He arrives the same time every morning—three o'clock sharp. I would hear my name repetitively sung, long and eerie: "*R … I … L … E … Y.*" It wasn't until I rubbed the sleep from my eyes and gave an exaggerated stretch that the haunting sound of my name would cease.

"I gotta take a piss, okay, Death?"

"Yeah, yeah sure, Rye."

Whistling away at the foot of my bed, all scary eight feet of Death waited as I emptied my bladder. An odor of decomp always permeated off him. I had to keep reminding myself, he *is* Death after all. From there, we would ride my Harley over to the nearby graveyard together and just chew the fat. Every night the same routine. Why this was happening, I hadn't asked him. Now it became apparent what was brewing.

I parked my bike in the usual spot. That night, a dark fog hovered over the tombstones in the graveyard giving them an eerie reveal.

Swallowing hard before addressing the subject on hand, I asked, "As your pet, what do you think you and I should do together, Grimster?" I called him *Grimster* to lighten the moment. He seemed to like it.

Perched atop of a memorial bench the Macky family had donated, he placed that mighty scythe across his lap. Resting his chin on what would be the palm of a hand, he answered in a Peter Pan little-boy tone. "How about we play a game?"

"Game?" I answered.

Frantically rationalizing this could be the protocol with all souls before shipping them off for judgment, I asked myself if my number was up.

"Like hide and seek, tag, Monopoly?" I stuttered, following with some nervous laughter.

"Not that kinda game. How about something happy. All this doom and gloom can get to a guy after a while."

"Right, right, but don't you have work to do? Those souls aren't going to harvest themselves, ya know."

Jumping enthusiastically off the memorial bench, he slammed the scythe hard into the graveyard dirt then shouted, "They can wait! Let's have fun, Riley!"

So, we had fun. Well, at least for a while.

For the next several months, as the entire world slumbered, Death and I made the night our playground. Nothing was off limits—got matching BFF tattoos, hurt like a bitch. Death was surprised at all the likenesses of himself that adorned the walls in the filthy dump.

"Look at me here, Riley. Come see me in this one. There are so many of me! I'm so popular," he said while hugging himself like a teenage girl.

This went on for a while. Up till now, I never knew how many tattoos of Death existed; unfortunately, now I do. We put back shots of Jameson at McDougal's Pub until we were crazy, stinking drunk. Bouncer threw us out for disorderly conduct.

"Don't let me ever see you and your weird friend here again! You hear me!" he shouted while wildly waving his fist in the air.

"My goodness, he was rather rude," Death slurred.

"Who needs 'em? We'll find another bar to hang," I slurred back as we ripped out of the parking lot on my Harley.

We stumbled into a whorehouse to get laid. My god did that little lady wail when Death was finishing.

"Do you think she liked me, Riley?" he asked with a freshly fucked face.

"No doubt. She's crazy about you, buddy!"

We snuck into bedrooms during the wee hours to scare innocent souls not ripe yet for Heaven or Hell. The expressions on their frightened faces had Death rolling with laughter.

"Oh, come on, Riley. One more," he would giggle.

"Fine, fine, one more. But then that's it, you hear me!" I hated to take away his fun.

Every Wednesday was movie night at my place. The aroma of melted butter and roasting kernels floated in the air of my shoebox apartment.

"Look at me, Riley. I'm eating popcorn!"

"Yes, you are, big guy," I answered with a thumbs up.

I never had the heart to tell the old fool it was all falling out his chest cavity onto the floor. Yep, we were having a great time. We never wanted it to end. But it did.

Several months after Death and I had started wreaking havoc, the upper afterlife management visited me. Neither one of these gentlemen were pleased. A warm, comforting stream of magical light woke me from a deep slumber. I raised my forearm before my eyes to block the brightness. The touching sound of a thousand harps playing almost caused me to weep. Just as the tears were to stream down my cheeks, Peter appeared in the luminescence. Soaring about, flew winged angels. I gasped with amazement.

"Riley?" he asked. "Are you Riley Gordon?" the apostle's gentle voice sounded within my head.

"Um, yeah, that's me."

"I am Peter. You must know why I've come? No one has passed through the pearly gates to Heaven in three months."

Before I could answer, a burst of flames ignited, sending a depressing emotion throughout the room that suddenly made me want to slit my wrist. Just as a blood-curdling scream was about to exit my mouth, Lucifer appeared in the cloud of polluted smoke surrounded by winged demons. Again, I gasped with amazement.

"Riley?" he asked. "Are you Riley Gordon?" the fallen angel's voice sounded, like a slithering snake, within my head.

"Um, yeah that's me."

"I am Lucifer. You must know why I've come. No one has entered the bowels of Hell in three months."

So, there I was, smack bang on the fifty-yard line between Heaven and Hell. The two rivals now came together in my bedroom to let me know how catastrophic and out of order the system was. They couldn't locate Death, because he had completely gone off the grid. Some tattletale spirit in the graveyard tipped them off that he was hanging with me. They wanted some answers, and they wanted them now.

"Listen, the guy just wanted some time off," I tried explaining.

"Silence!" Lucifer hissed. "Are you out of your mind, you stupid mortal? I want my haunted, rotting souls!"

I could smell his rancid breath. The walls shook violently while the winged demons swirled about the bedroom in frenzy chanting, "*Rotting souls … Rotting souls.*"

"Dude, relax. I don't have your creepy souls." I thought the Devil would blow a gasket right there and then.

Peter raised his hand to stifle Lucifer's temper tantrum. "Please, Lucifer, allow me to explain." Things started settling down a bit. "Death doesn't get time off, Riley. If the Grim Reaper doesn't harvest dying souls, we can't release any new ones. Lucifer and I are all backed up. There is an order to life and death. Tampering with the order has irreversible effects." Peter was way better explaining things than that hothead Louie.

After about an hour of painful negotiations, the arch nemeses finally agreed on something. The deal was I had to surrender Death to them no later than 3:30 a.m. sharp or my punishment was to perish in eternal Purgatory. Thus, my soul would never make it to its final destination, ever.

No matter how many times I rolled it around in my head, I felt as if I was deceiving my pal, Death. But what choice did I have? I had to turn him into the proper authorities or else.

The rest of the night I stared at the ceiling. Death was my friend, my buddy, my BFF. I couldn't deceive him, but I had to go through with it. The minutes passed by like hours. Then I heard it.

"*R … I … L … E … Y*. Riley, are you awake? Where are you, good buddy?"

Dammit, he was happy.

"Yeah, I'm up."

"Let's have a blast tonight, Riley. I've got the whole thing planned. Wanna hear?" He giggled like a schoolgirl.

I cut him off. "Hey, Grimster, how about we take a walk in the old graveyard? We haven't done that in a while. What do you say?" My voice was monotone. I only called him Grimster when I was trying to lighten the mood. He knew that.

"What's wrong, Rye?"

His worried voice shook me. I was devastated. "Nothing, buddy. We just don't talk anymore. I'd love to go back to the graveyard and just talk, okay? Like we used to do. You up for that?"

"Well, okay, Rye. Sure."

We left for our old stomping ground on my Harley. Lying to him made me sick. I was cheating Death. Maybe not in the most modern sense. But still cheating. He didn't know about the ambush. What was waiting for us?

As we arrived at the entrance, there was a pit in my stomach. I parked my bike. The air was chilly for April. Of course, he felt nothing. Then we walked. Should I tell him? Was not telling him wrong? My mind was going crazy.

"You sure you feel okay, Riley? You don't look so good."

"I'm great, really. Say listen, have you ever heard of a place called Purgatory?"

"Of course, I've delivered plenty of souls to that zero of a hole."

"Soooooo, like, how bad can it possibly be in, um, this Purgatory place, let's say?"

"How bad? How bad, you ask?" Death methodically veered right then left as if unwanted ears were eavesdropping. "You don't want to know, Riley. Once a soul is exiled to Purgatory, they're never entitled to see the gates of Heaven. Ever! At least in Hell, a soul can do good, work on themselves, pull it together and possibly get on the list to the promise land. However, in Purgatory, we punish souls in an eternal, emotionless prison, where they float around in a forever-nothing sea called Void. Forever!" Death shook his shoulders as if he felt a chill.

"You don't say?" I answered.

"Why do you ask, Riley?"

"Um, no reason."

As we turned the corner, there they were. Lucifer, all smug, was sitting on Death's favorite memorial bench. Peter was leaning against a statue of a weeping angel. How convenient. Even that tattletale spirit had the nerve to show up.

"They're here!" the tattletale alerted to the others.

They both approached us.

"Rye, what is this?" The look in those crazy yellow eyes was indescribable.

"Death, please let me explain."

He put his bony hand on my shoulder. "It's okay, Rye. I understand. I do."

Then we suddenly embraced. I could feel Death's bony structure penetrating my flesh. The stench of decomp no longer was embedded in the fabric of the burlap cloak. Now I was able to bury my face deep in it. Only the odor of Wednesday night's popcorn remained. I didn't want to let go.

After giving us our moment, Peter cleared his voice to break the awkwardness. "It's time, Death."

Even Lucifer appeared all choked up. Imagine that.

"I'll miss you, Rye." I could hear sincerity in his crazy demon voice.

I wiped my nose with my sleeve and whimpered, "I'll miss you too, Death."

I couldn't watch them take him away. How could I have betrayed my best friend?

I got back on my Harley, revved the engine, and, all through the night, I rode my bike. I had no idea where I was going. I lost track of time and where I was. Exhausted, I stopped at an all-night diner. The place smelled like an armpit.

A lovely young waitress working a piece of bubble gum and wearing too much makeup sashayed over. "What can I get ya?"

"Yeah, can I have the burger, done medium, with fries and a Coke?"

"Sure." She left and hurried back with my Coke and a straw.

Death would have ordered the mac and cheese and left all the noodles on the bench as it passed through him. That guy loved mac and cheese.

"You look like you lost your best friend, mister. You okay?"

I didn't answer. The late-night news was playing on the flat screen above me. I asked the waitress to turn it up. The meteorologist called for rain. Then the regular anchor man came on. "An unbelievable amount of deaths have taken place all over the world. Details at eleven."

Just then, my burger arrived.

Still working away at that bubble gum, the waitress asked, "Is there anything else I can get you, sir?"

So, I answered, "Nope. It sounds like everything was right back in order."

She gave me a long, strange glare then sashayed away.

"FINISHING THE HAT"
WILLIAM THATCH

The tiny specks of paint had long since dried on Ed Belasco's skin. He woke as the sun began setting over the country home. He had collapsed in the recliner twelve hours earlier after a marathon session in front of the various easels set up throughout the house. He lost count of how long he had been awake, though he was vaguely aware the hours were approaching triple digits. The last memory he had before his eyelids became too heavy for even the coffee to keep them open was dropping into the seat, taking a step back from the painting of a tiny, dapper bowler hat.

He had finished it with a grand flourishing swipe of the brush and felt elation as he had conquered the final piece of his masterpiece. In the final harsh moments of daylight, Ed sneered at it.

"Horrible," he said to himself. "The brim is all wrong."

He didn't realize the hat would be the most difficult part in the pursuit of his masterpiece. He hadn't bothered to count how many attempts he'd made at the hat.

Ed sat up and noticed he had fallen asleep with brush in hand, which had dried onto the arm of the chair. With a slight struggle, he peeled it free from the stitched cloth, a frustrated grumble escaping him as he eyed the brush, his face scrunched and contorted. The brush was no good to him anymore. His tools must remain pristine!

With a grunt, Ed stood up and grabbed the manic painting of the hat then turned to enter the kitchen. He stopped in his tracks, noticing the blinking red light of the answering machine. A new message had come in while he slept.

A cold sweat broke over his skin. Perhaps it was his betrothed, Anne.

His fingers hovered over the play button, eager to hear her voice. What was new in her life? Did she want to meet? It filled him with equal parts hope, anticipation, and dread. He wasn't ready to make contact again.

He pressed the buttons and a message began to play.

"Hi-hi, Ed," she said. Her voice was always deeper than he remembered. In his memory, it was always an octave higher, matching her sweet, bubbly personality. "I had a wonderful time on Thursday," she continued. "It was adorable how you kept sneaking peeks at the dogs in the park. I thought, if you wanted, maybe we'd grab dinner tomorrow … maybe take in a movie? Let me know. Miss you."

As the message played, Ed wandered through the kitchen to the back porch. He flung both brush and painting onto a pile of other discarded art supplies that had failed him. If he wanted to know the number of failed drawings of hats he had accumulated, or even the number of failed paintings in the journey to his masterpiece, he could go count. Maybe he might, before starting a bonfire to rid the world of them. He would have to invite Anne to watch it, if she would come over.

The machine beeped as the message ended.

Ed felt his heart swell. He remembered that day at the little bistro. The two lovebirds had sat beside the windows overlooking a dog park. It had been their third or fourth date, Ed couldn't remember. He vividly remembered the dogs, however. He had painted the four closest to the bistro—a runty, unkempt black miniature schnauzer that was mixed with another breed he couldn't identify; a grumpy-looking Yorkie-Maltese; a snow-white Maltese stuffed into a sweater; and a fat beagle that watched the others as they played. The painting now sat in the basement, a sheet covering it to protect it from dust.

Anne had been so touched that he painted something from one of their dates. He had intended to sell it, but he decided to keep it. It felt like part of the story of their relationship, and it wouldn't do to sell a piece with such importance.

Ed got a blank canvas from the basement and set it up on the easel. Taking a new brush in hand, he stood in front of the canvas, his arm cocked, prepared to make the first stroke in what was surely destined to be another failed hat.

And there he stood for several minutes, mentally going over every option he had to begin. Every time he neared the canvas with the wet tip of the brush, he pulled back. There had been so many attempts at this one failed aspect of the overall picture.

With an annoyed huff, he threw the brush down onto the side table, splattering more paint across the wood surface and the lamp residing on it.

Maybe he had lost the feeling of the masterpiece and all its components. With a deep breath and a cleansing sigh, Ed made his way down the short hallway into the family room, which now served as a showroom of sorts. The furniture remained in place, but there were now paintings set up across the expanse for easy viewing. All pieces of the masterpiece—a gift for Anne; an expression of things he felt and thought but he struggled to put into words.

Around the room were the best attempts at the smaller pieces of the masterpiece. Straight ahead was a massive willow tree hanging in the void of blank canvas. Small paintings of grass and clouds cluttered a corner, barely seen through the multiple paintings of gerbera daisies, the petals painted with all manner of colors. He pressed his finger to one where a bit of moisture had caused the paint to run. It was a view behind their friends and family seated in little wooden chairs, Ed in a tuxedo, Anne in her dress. He'd spent a week on the rings on their fingers alone. All that remained was the tiny, dapper bowler hat Anne wore when dressing up for an evening. Something prim and proper like society expects of a lady but something a little silly as well.

Just standing in the room, looking at all the components he would end up compiling into one grand expression of art and love, made the corner of his lips twitch into a smile.

He hadn't yet decided when to give her the gift. He'd considered unveiling it at the wedding or a gift on the honeymoon. Perhaps wait until they returned home afterwards. Initially, he intended for it to be part of the proposal itself, but he had fumbled his words and revealed a bit too soon that he was going to ask.

She had said *yes*, of course. While thrilled, he was also annoyed. It wasn't how he wanted it to go. He wanted the extravagant proposal, an experience to be remembered rather than a moment. The detail was all wrong, but he couldn't put the cat back in the bag. Ed would be damned if he didn't have every detail perfect for the painting.

Anne deserved perfection.

And so, in the improvised art gallery adorning the family room, Ed pored over the finished pieces. The way the branches of the willow hung low, so long an adult could grab at them; the colors of the grass so soft he could imagine them tickling his feet; the gerberas so lifelike that if he got lost in his mind, he could smell their sweet aroma. He hated the tuxedo he had painted himself in—not because it wasn't done well but because a tuxedo or any fancy apparel made him feel claustrophobic.

Then there was Anne. She'd complain about her size. A little plumper than her confidence endured, but Ed never had an issue with her size. She was a perfect angel, as far as he was concerned. He stared into her painted-brown eyes and let the wave of emotions take him to a place he only felt with her—the slight rush of anxiety underneath the calm and the safety of her presence, the softness of her cheek, the smell of her shampoo, the exhilaration that came with her laugh. It threatened to pull him from reality and into fantasy.

Before he could get lost in specific memories, Ed felt the rush of inspiration. Precisely what he was hoping for. He returned in front of the easel and retrieved the brush. To shore up the effort, he went to the answering machine and began playing another message she had left. Something to continue inspiring as he put paint to canvas.

"Hi-hi, Ed," she said. "Where were you yesterday? I waited as long as I could, but I couldn't miss my brother's wedding. It's really a shame. I thought everyone would get a kick out of you growing your hair out. Call me as soon as you get this please. Are we still on for Thursday?"

Ed went to work on the hat, deftly applying the browns and greys, cringing at the shape of the hat as time wore on and he applied more paint. It looked unnatural—too thin in some places and oddly fat in others. In his heart, he had given up on this attempt before he began painting the band of the tiny, dapper bowler hat. That his hand twitched and sent a swath of grey across the brim and into the void of the blank canvas only served as the physical admission of another failure.

"Goddammit," he uttered as he gripped the side of the canvas and tore it from its place on the easel and then smacked the easel to the floor.

The failed painting tumbled through the room, landing paint-side down and sliding a few feet along the carpet.

Ed paced the living room a few times, stomping in one direction before being pulled in the opposite direction as he considered what he might do to deal with the frustration. After a couple of times back and forth, he headed down the short hallway towards the family room, turning toward a bathroom.

He turned on the faucet and splashed his face with the chilly water. It cooled the heat that had risen in his face from the frustration. He lifted his head and caught his reflection in the mirror.

Although he'd watched the drastic changes in his appearance every day, he hadn't quite appreciated them. He would not have recognized himself if he hadn't been looking into the mirror. His face was gaunter than he remembered. He'd been subsisting on a can of food every couple of days. He had been at his family's old country home for a while now, and, since then, he had not taken the time for grooming. His hair was long now, tangled and filthy, and he now had a thick, bushy beard. He'd always kept both trimmed down to avoid the upkeep. He knew if given the choice between his art and grooming, he'd let his looks slide so that he could focus on what was really important.

Anne wouldn't like it. She was easy going, but she asked that he not look like a slob.

Now, he looked like a slob. He'd have to wash and trim before he saw her again.

Tucking his hair behind his ears, Ed returned to the living room to pry the drying painting from the carpet. He let the painting join the pile of soon-to-be flames in the backyard and then went back to set up for the next attempt.

He'd get the hat right or die trying.

Someone watching his diet might have made the quip that his death might be sooner than he'd think, but Ed was too enthralled by his mission to finish the hat.

With a new brush and canvas and the easel righted upon its feet, Ed prepared to try once again. The thought never crossed his mind to abandon the hat. It was necessary to the essence of Anne and therefore to the whole painting. Ed rarely got anything right on the first attempt. It was his determination that kept him moving forward until he got things right. There had never been anything as frustrating as the hat. But the concept of quitting was foreign to him. He'd never concede—not to a painting and not on Anne.

He stared at the blank canvas for a moment before he glanced at the answering machine. The red light continued blinking, reminding him of the new message he had yet to listen to, having opted to listen to old messages—ones that brought fond memories.

The hairs on his neck stood on end while the feeling of dread crawled up his back as he considered the new message. He had been thinking of it since he'd woken, the thoughts in the back of his mind going over the possibilities while he worked at the painting.

His finger hovered over the play button of the machine, fighting himself whether or not to press it. Something within him pushed him forward, acting before he could chicken out of hearing it, as he had done earlier.

"Ed," the message began. It was Anne, as expected.

Ed turned back to the canvas and began applying paint, hesitating before each stroke.

"It's been a while. No one's heard from you in what feels like years. We just want some sign you're okay. I, uh … I don't know how you took the last message … You know … canceling the … canceling the wedding." Ann paused, choking on her emotions.

The reminder of that message gave Ed pause. His tears had stained one of the paintings in the family room. He had put the last bit of purple on one of the daisies when the first tear hit the canvas.

"I don't know that there's a proper way to tell you," she continued "But I'm seeing someone else now. My mother says it's too soon, but … I can't wait forever. I don't know what kept you away. I hope you're okay."

It took Ed several minutes to realize the message had ended. The tears were flowing again but so was the paint. He had gotten the curve of the hat just the way he always wanted it—the brim's gentle arcs majestic, the bow of the band's color a perfect contrast to the color of the main portion of the hat.

He had finally gotten the hat the way he wanted it to look. A few more attempts, just to be sure it wasn't a fluke, then he could begin assembling the masterpiece. It would still take a while to complete, but the day they had both looked forward to for so long would be immortalized in painting.

For all that it mattered now.

Ed sank into the chair. The weight of the emotions—both of Anne's declaration of having moved on and of finally succeeding with the hat, too late for it to matter—had weakened his knees.

Maybe, he told himself, if he sacrificed a little more sleep and worked a little bit harder, he could fix it all. He doubted he could convince her to leave whoever she was with now, but, if ever there was a chance, perhaps she would be so moved by the painting and why he had disappeared from the face of the Earth that there would still be a chance.

He hadn't gotten this attempt right, but, maybe, the next would go better.

The tiredness was deeply imbued into his muscles after straining and sacrificing his health this long in pursuit of what he held dear. He was exhausted. But there was more work to do. There was no time to rest.

And so, Ed forced himself to his feet. He carried the finished hat into the family room and set it among the others and then returned to put a fresh canvas up.

With a deep breath, he set another voice message to play and went back to work on the hat he had just finished, strengthened in his resolve to finish the hat.

"THE GROUCHY GRANDMA"
SUNANDA J. CHATTERJEE

Look at her. Just look at her! Strutting up to take the microphone. Sure, Nona will give an impassioned mother-of-the-groom speech. She didn't ask me to speak at my grandson's wedding after all I've done for him; I raised Amir from a wee baby.

And who is Sheela anyway, the new member of our family? They didn't even consult me. I hope she turns out to be just like her mother-in-law, ignoring and disrespecting her husband's mother at every turn. Tit for bloody tat.

They stuck me in my wheelchair with this corpulent old hag I don't know at a table for two. Right next to the bathroom! It's a small wedding—eight tables with seating for six each. I belong at the family table. Would seven chairs really ruin the aesthetic?

Nona is toasting to the young couple's happiness. "Let's raise our glass to …"

Her head is blacker than a crow's, her skin taut like apples with naught a line crossing her brow. It must be nice not to have any worries; I did everything for her, especially after my son died. But has she ever thanked me?

Something sticks in my throat, and I leave the champagne untouched. I've brought a big fat check for Nona to cover the wedding expenses. But I'll take it back with me; my money will go to charity and disappear with my ashes. If she even shows up for my funeral. I'd love to be a ghost and watch her face when my will reveals what she got: zilch. Hah!

Look at her taking credit for Amir's success. Didn't I watch him while she went to work leaving the infant in my lap? Didn't I cook meals for him, bathe him, take him to the library, and to the doctor's office, bake cakes for his birthdays? I deserve a smidgen of credit, an acknowledgment of my efforts.

I remember Amir's baby smell and his velvet skin and his silky hair as he fell asleep in my lap. His constant begging, "Tell me a story, Grandma."

Will I be a part of his children's lives? Or will it just be Nona?

Her voice grates on my nerves. "I want to thank Amir's teachers and mentors who've contributed to his life …"

Sure. Don't thank me. I'm just the crotchety old grandma who taught your son how to cross the goddamn road.

The old woman beside me lets out an unfortunate emission borne out of dyspepsia. Embarrassed, she coughs. Her three chins wiggle as she blurts, "The bride, Sheela, is my niece's daughter."

So, they seated me with the bride's distant—and flatulent—relative! Perfect. That's just perfect. I nod. I don't tell her who I am. Instead, I toggle my denture with my tongue.

Nona points to our table. "This, here, is the most important table. Amir's grandma and Sheela's great aunt, who brought her up after her parents passed away."

I roll my eyes.

Nona drones on. "Of all the people who nurtured Amir, the biggest credit goes to his grandmother, who watched him every day after school." She looks straight at me. "I never had your talent for cooking, Mom, but I hope you'll teach Sheela. And your birthday cakes! They were better than this wedding cake."

She has never called me *Mom* before. She walks over and bends down to hug me. The crowd applauds, and my hearing aid screeches. My hands are shaking. All eyes are on me, and I want to throw up. I stare at my lap and click the denture back in place.

Nona's eyes shine as she squawks into the microphone, her voice tremulous. "Without you, Amir wouldn't be the man he is today. Thank you, Mom. I've never been good with words. I can't tell you how much you mean to me."

It's just a speck in my stupid eye. I reach for a handkerchief in my purse and find the envelope with the check. I pull it out and shove it towards her.

My voice cracks, and I wave my gnarly hand. "I did nothing!"

"SLOW FADE"
D.W. VOGEL

I'm losing who I was.

Every passing day takes more of my memory, and I fear the moment when I wake up as no one at all.

The oldest memories are the strongest. I grew up at 557 Oakview Court. Two older brothers and one younger sister, all of whom I outlived. My father was a steel worker, and my mother made the best lasagna. I can still taste it, even though she's been dead for thirty years.

My son is here at the hospital now. He's looking through the door at me, talking with the nurse in the hallway. Allen is a good man. Marian and I raised him right.

She's here at my side, of course. Marian.

The long red hair I used to run my fingers through has turned dull and gray, and the hand I held so nervously the first time I walked her home from school is spotted and wrinkled now. But the love in her gaze has never wavered. She smiles at me now, just like she did the day I proposed.

I try to smile back, but nothing seems to work properly. My face moves, and she smiles bigger, as if I've just cured some kind of cancer, but I suspect the expression on my face is more of a grimace than a grin.

I remember when we brought baby Allen home from the hospital. He was born early and had to stay in an incubator for three long weeks before they'd even let us hold him. Times have changed since then. Even the earliest babies get taken out and held by their mothers now. But back then, all we could do was reach in through a rubber glove attached to the outside of the plastic box and pat our little man lying inside. When we finally brought him home, he was barely five pounds, but he wailed like a banshee, and there never was a sweeter music.

It's hot in this bed. I'd love to ask someone to cool it down a bit, but I haven't been able to say an intelligible word since the stroke. It's been hell on my family.

The heat makes me sleepy, but I don't want to doze off. When I wake up, more of my life will have slipped from my grasp. I glance over to where Marian sits her patient watch. She barely leaves my side. She's the best wife a man could ever hope to find. And every minute that passes, I'm losing more of her.

My son and his wife are here now. I know her face but can't recall her name. It starts with a D, I think. Denise, maybe. Desiree. Donna?

Allen holds his wife's shoulders as they look down at me, lying here attached to tubes and wires. The sounds of all the monitors wake me up at odd hours, but I'm glad of it. As memory fades, each moment becomes so precious.

I remember their wedding. It was a rainy day in the summer—August, maybe. The church was full of flowers, and I was so nervous in my new suit. The bride wore a long-sleeved lace gown and looked like an angel.

I think that was Allen's wedding.

Maybe it was mine.

No one is here in the wee hours of the morning. I can barely see the clock on the far wall; although it's never really dark in a hospital. Nurses bustle around, waiting until I've just fallen asleep before waking me up to check a vital sign or give me some kind of shot.

In the movies, they call it a *slow fade* when the scene just darkens down to nothing. That's what the inside of my head feels like. Slow fade to black.

I wish Marian was here. But she'll be back in the morning for sure.

It won't be long now. I'm dwindling fast. My family looks at me with so much love, and I want to shout at them, "I'm here! I'm in here! It's Michael, and there are a million things I want to tell you while I still remember them."

But of course, I can't.

Can't tell Marian how I used to love that blue dress she wore to church on Sundays.

Can't tell Allen how proud I was when he became an Eagle Scout.

The noises that come out of my mouth when I try are nothing like the words I want to say.

I want to scream and pound on the walls. Everything I knew, everything I was is blurring into nothing, like cream stirred into coffee. What I was is not what I am now. And what I am now is no good to anyone.

Marian. I've loved you so very much.

They poke me. Take my temperature.

There's an old woman sitting next to me. She looks familiar. I'm sure I know her. She's talking to a young man and woman. They're all here, looking down at me.

I try to smile at them.

They look like nice people.

Their words float around me. Even words are failing now, losing their meaning. I can't comprehend what I'm hearing, but I recognize the sounds.

"Just look at him, won't you?" That's the young man.

The young woman says, "Oh, Allen, I can't stand to see him like this. All the machines. When is this going to end?"

"Hush, Denise." That's the old woman. She smiles at me. "It won't be long." She wraps an arm around the young man. "He's an old soul, this one." She reaches into the incubator and takes my tiny hand, holding it with her wrinkled fingers. "And he's got his grandpa's eyes."

"CIVIC CLASSIC VIDEO, OPEN 24 HOURS"
PHIL HORE

The image flickers and collapses in on itself, dissolving into a small ball of white light that slowly fades away, plunging the room into an eerie gloom. The large figure seated before the television hauls itself out of its robust armchair, ambles over and hits the eject button on the archaic video machine sitting on top of the set.

The machine whines as its tiny motors pull the cassette from deep within, expelling the tape through the elongated rectangle slot at the front. A gloved hand snatches the video and snaps it back in its cover. The video is then placed on top of the stack of tapes sitting next to the TV, which are all then flung into a backpack. This is then tossed over one shoulder of the figure, who exits the room into the ancient, slime-covered sewer outside. The huge figure unhurriedly trudges through the brick outlet, grumbling to itself as it stoops down to pick up a discarded coin. About the figure's huge shoulders hangs a trench coat, similar to Humphrey Bogart's from *The Big Sleep*, only a lot larger and a lot dirtier. On its massive head sits a Detroit Tigers cap, which it pulls down low, masking its face from the world.

Though the light is poor, the muttering figure walks through the gloom with assured footsteps, deftly moving past leaking pipes and torrents of hissing steam seeping out of cracks in the sewer walls.

At the end of a long section of passageway, the secretive figure climbs a set of rusty steel rungs that lead to a padlocked gate.

Unlocking it with a key from the depths of a coat pocket, the figure does a quick scan of the area outside to ensure it is alone before stepping through into the darkened alleyway beyond. It then locks the gate behind it.

Outside, the night's light drizzle runs off the brim of the cap, but this, along with the occasional lightning flash, is ignored by the figure, who shoulders into the weather and walks on.

"Do you have *Navy Seals?*" a taunting voice asks from the far side of the video shelves.

"You've got to be fucking joking," the attendant behind the counter snarls. Tall and skinny, the dark glasses he's wearing are a stark contrast to his pasty skin, evidence the man has not seen the sun in sometime. He takes a long draw on his cigarette and holds his breath, allowing the warm smoke to tickle the deepest recesses of his lungs. He then releases his breath through his nostrils, blowing two long jets of smoke, like some demon in an ancient manuscript.

Out front, the OPEN 24 HOURS red neon sign occasionally flickers, reflecting in the grimy window with CIVIC CLASSIC VIDEO painted in large block letters across its surface. The store looks old and rundown, with faded movie posters and dusty stacks of video cassettes piled high on the motley collection of bookshelves and old library racks filling the poorly lit interior.

If you asked anyone who lived in the area, they would be unable to recall a time the shop had not been in existence. Before morphing into a movie rental store in the early eighties, Civic Classic Video had been a record shop, and before that it sold books, manuscripts, and papyrus. In one form or another, the Civic Classic Video store had been around since the city first outgrew the small farming village that had once occupied the same spot. The Civic Classic Video store had seen empires rise and fall, had once been ignored by Roman centurions the way the local police still walked by, blissfully unaware of its existence. The Civic Classic Video store would still be here long after the buildings around it had crumbled to dust and humanity was dancing amongst the stars. It was just one of those places that almost every large, important city had. The Civic Classic Video store was immortal.

Behind the counter, the attendant reaches for the white stick leaning against the wall, evidence of why he's the perfect night-time employee.

"Sorry, man. I was just kidding," says the customer, a teenage boy wearing a faded The Cult t-shirt. Feeling bad for making fun of the blind attendant, the boy steps from behind the shelves, eyes glued to the video case in his hand.

"This any good?"

"Great fucking film," the attendant says.

"Thought you were blind?" the kid asks sceptically.

"We only stock good films in here." The attendant half smirks, well used to such banter from casual customers who likely as not came through the door to get out of the rain.

The front door opens with a subtle tinkle from the bell hanging above it. From outside shambles the overcoat-wearing figure hunched under his baseball cap, which beads water to the floor from the heavy rain.

"Hey, Mike," the attendant says. "Raining out there?"

"*Mmmbbmmllummm*," Mike murmurs, pulling the stack of videos from his backpack and dumping them on the counter.

"We got some new Warner Bros. in, and the guy that had *Double Indemnity* for the last month finally brought it back."

The large figure nods his approval at this then moves on to the video shelves. Here he starts meticulously scanning the face of each title up and down before taking a single step to the side and starting his search on the next section of titles.

"What about DVDs or Blu-rays?" the kid asks as he picks up another video cassette with a case shaped like a coffin. "Ever think of switching to them?"

The attendant is about to ask the boy to leave when Mike calls his attention away.

"Holy crap, Cecil. You finally got in *We're No Angels*."

"That has to be the worst film De Niro ever made." The kid laughs as he puts *Fright Night Part 2* back on the shelf and moves deeper into the store.

"De Niro?" Mike spits in disgust from under his hat.

"We're talking about the original, kid, the one with Bogart, Ustinov, and Rathbone in it," Cecil says, trying to cut off a more colourful retort from Mike as he returns to the front desk and, running a hand across the counter, locates an open pack of cigarettes. Lighting up, he takes a Travolta-like draw before continuing. "Personally, I think its okay, but bitch-boy there has been after me to get it in for years."

A growl from the stacks says what Mike thinks about being called *bitch-boy*.

"So, it's good?" the kid asks.

"It's the best," Mike grumbles. "Funny, dark, gritty, and bloody well acted ... possibly my favourite film."

"I find I don't have a favourite film," Cecil says, tapping his cigarette ash into the mouth of an empty Coke can. "I mean, there's so many to choose from, but if I had to pick with the old tropical island thing—"

"Tropical island?" the kid asks, ignoring the video shelves to focus on the conversation.

"You know, you're stuck on a tropical island and you can only have one book or record or friend or movie, which would it be? I'd have to choose *The Outlaw Josey Wales*." Cecil grins from under his sunglasses and throws a thumb at the framed poster of a growling Eastwood totting two pistols hanging behind him. "Probably not the best film ever, but lawd, I can watch it over and over."

"I like *Raiders*," the kid says, moving up to the counter.

"Lon Chaney was okay, but I don't like pirate movies that much. I hate the sea." Mike's enormous shoulders shudder at the thought of going anywhere near an ocean again.

"Pirate movie?" the kid asks, confused.

"He means *Raiders of the Lost Ark*," Cecil calls out to Mike through a long pull on his cigarette. Then, with an evil wink, he asks the kid, "Don't you mean *Indiana Jones and the—*"

"Yeah, yeah. Don't get me started on that. I still have no idea why he changed the title of the greatest movie ever?"

"*Greatest?*" Mike snarls, moving from behind the video stacks to join the conversation. "You gotta' be kidding me." A long black tongue lashes out from behind rows of razor-sharp teeth, and the kid's eyes grow as large as dinner plates, and he stands, frozen to the spot with fear. "You ever seen *Random Harvest* or the *Thin Man* movies?" Mike's yellow eyes flash with anger, and his slitted pupils narrow on the kid's ashen face. "What about *The Third Man* or *Lawrence of Arabia*?" Mike's enormous claws appear through the ends of the gloves he's wearing as he grabs the kid by the shoulders, holding him in place, and leans in, his reptilian face now inches away. "Or *Spartacus … The Big Sleep?*"

"*Casablanca?*" Cecil chirps in with a knowing grin.

"Ahh, that one's okay," Mike admits, calming down and releasing his hold on the kid. "I never really understood the hype around it though. Hell, I like *Seven Brides for Seven Brothers* more than *Casablanca*." The monster turns back to face the kid, skewering him in the chest with one enormous clawed finger. "Can you name any modern film that belongs on that list?"

"Well …"

"Come on. Just one?"

"How about *The Ninth Gate*?" the kid stammers, bravely taking up the monster's challenge.

"Ooh, nice one." Cecil nods in agreement.

Encouraged, the kid goes on. "How about *White Hunter Black Heart*, *The Thing*, or *Seven*?"

Cecil starts laughing as the kid's list grows longer and longer while the scowl on Mike's face steadily falls deeper and deeper.

"*Glengarry Glen Ross* or The *Usual Suspects*? What about *12 Angry Men*?"

"The one with Jack Lemon, not Henry Fonda," Cecil explains, sensing Mike's confusion.

"Both were good," the monster admits, stepping away from the kid. For long seconds, he peers into the young man's face, and then, with an ugly face-splitting grin, he slaps him on the back and proclaims, "You're all right, buddy!"

Moving back to the stacks, Mike grabs the handful of movies he's been harvesting and hands them over to Cecil, who automatically types in Mike's membership number and scans the videos into the computer, never once looking at the screen.

Mike places some crumpled, dirty banknotes and a few coins in Cecil's outstretched hand, who promptly drops them into the till and slams it shut.

"See you again in a few days, Cee," Mike grumbles, heading out the door and back into the stormy night. As an afterthought, before he closes the door, he leans back inside. "See ya, kid. It was nice chatting with ya'."

After the monster leaves the store and his huge frame is swallowed by the oppressive darkness outside, the young customer rushes up to the front counter.

"What the hell was that?"

"Who, Mike? He's my best customer!" Cecil says.

"Oh." The kid nods with understanding, looking at the dark glasses hiding the attendant's eyes. "You haven't noticed?"

"Look, kid. Don't take old Mike too seriously. He honestly does believe that a movie's not worth watching unless it's black and white and seventy years old."

"That's not what I meant." The kid hesitates, not certain just what he'd seen. "I meant, what is he?"

"You're talking about his skin condition. Don't worry about that. He told me it isn't contagious, and I've dealt with him long enough to believe him."

"Skin condition? The guy's a monster," the kid squeaks. "He's got claws and fangs and reptilian skin. Hell, his eyes are yellow, man."

"Really?" Cecil asks.

"I'm telling you, the guy's a bloody monster. You should call the papers or something. You could make a fortune with the story. Imagine how much they'd pay for the pictures alone."

"Is this one of those situations where you mean *I* should instead of *you* should?" Cecil asks.

"Huh?"

"Look, kid. You may be right about all that stuff, but, to me, Mike's a friend who I see almost every night. We have the same interests, and we both get around at night when the rest of society is well asleep. We get to shoot the breeze over our favourite films and stuff, and we've been doing it for decades. He's a good guy, so you should just leave him alone."

"'A good guy?' He's a fucking monster," the kid blurts. "A big freakin' monster!"

"What Mike does on his own time doesn't interest me, same as I'm sure he doesn't really care what I get up to. All I know is he's my best customer and a good friend, so I strongly suggest you forget ever seeing him."

"No fucking way. He could be out there killin' kids or eating women or something."

"Mike wouldn't hurt a flea," Cecil says soothingly, trying to calm the kid down.

"Fuck that. If you aren't going to do something about him, I will," the kid says defiantly.

"Okay, you're right," Cecil says, pulling his glasses to the end of his nose. "I'll do something about it. I actually know that Mike only eats rats and whatever else gets washed down into that stinking septic tank he lives in." The attendant steps from behind the counter without the need of his white cane and moves between his customer and the front door. "I also know it's not the monster you see that you should be worried about kid, but the one you can't."

Cecil's bloodred eyes peek over the top of the black sunglasses, pinning the kid to the spot. Horrified, for the first time the customer notices two large canine teeth protruding from under Cecil's top lip.

"Sorry about this kid … And just as I was beginning to like you."

A loud clap of thunder disguises the customer's scream as the vampire flicks off the store's lights and leaps forward. He grabs the customer by his shirt, pulls him close with one smooth motion, bites at the large carotid artery in his neck and starts to feed.

Outside, the paired sets of car headlights streak past, illuminating someone running along the sidewalk, desperate to get out of the storm. No one notices as the Civic Classic Video store sign flickers from OPEN 24 HOURS to heralding the store was CLOSED in electric-blue neon to the uncaring night.

"A WRITER & HIS WORDS"
JOHN PEACH

I reached into the battered leather bag to retrieve the first words of *The French Story*. I left my hand in the bag longer than I needed to, enjoying the way the words clung to my fingers. Fine white scars marked my hands where I hadn't been careful enough with the sharper words. There had been a time when I thought they might get me recognised by one of the better publishing houses. I'd stopped believing in publishing houses years ago. And I'd learned to wear gloves to handle the sharper words. Now I had an outline for a literary novel, and a title I liked: *The French Story*. I thought there was a chance it might get me noticed after all.

I kept my words in an old leather duffle bag on a sturdy Victorian campaign table. Every time I reached into it, the bag exhaled a fine cloud of leathery muff and inky sharpness that briefly corrupted the comfortable smell of wood polish rising from the old farmhouse table.

Still slightly decaffeinated, I spread my handful of words on a clean sheet of paper next to the blotter. An eager clutter of bits and pieces covered the table—souvenirs of *The French Story*.

Terry emerged, whistling tunelessly and poking at the little piles of stuff I'd put out the evening before. I had written him originally as a bit of an Iago for a trite little romance I didn't like to own up to anymore. He was based on a boy who'd told tales about me at school and got me into a lot of trouble. I'd written the character for payback.

An almost permanent sneer seemed to have added itself to his face; although, of course, he hadn't aged—characters don't age once you've written them. He was very good at pointing out weaknesses in the other characters, good at getting things done in the humidor too.

All my characters lived in a walnut burl humidor that occupied the middle of the table. Every character started the same, with a sheet of paper and a sharp pencil. I gave all of them a name, a date of birth, at least two memories, and their physical descriptions. That was the minimum. Of course, the characters in *The French Story* would get more than that. Their sheets would be covered on both sides. I'd probably have to squeeze the words together to get them all onto one page. I would lay the pages in a drawer in the humidor. I had the only key to that drawer.

"Well, Terry, what do you think? Did you see the character notes?" I tried not to let him see how anxious I felt.

"Yeah, well, not bad at all this time. I'll help with the characters. Don't I always help with the characters? It'll be all right. As long as you don't try and do anything too clever."

The phone rang again.

"Daphne's Copywriting and Editing Service, how can I help you?"

"John? It's me, Silver. How are you getting on with that new book of yours? I won't keep you from it for long. That place in Munich you asked me to have a look at? The place up towards Karlstor? There's no sign of it anywhere. I asked around. One of the shop fronts is a building site, and the shopkeeper next to it thinks he remembers a café that served Spatenbräu a very long time ago. He's not sure though, and what it might have been called is anyone's guess."

I let him talk for a moment. The café was gone? I couldn't believe it. The place where Gabi had dumped me was gone.

"Say that last bit again, would you? What original brewery?"

"Spaten's original brewery was right there, at number four. I think that must've become the café you wanted to find."

The point was that it had gone. That story had disappeared from the world.

"You may be right, Silver. Thanks for looking. Everything else where I thought it should be? Augustiner's, Donisl?"

Silver had gone to Munich to meet a friend, and I'd asked him to bring back photos of a couple of places I thought I remembered. I wanted those photos before the places themselves disappeared.

"Oh yes, everything else was just like you said. Including the bells—damn, but they make a noise when they get going!"

We talked for a few more minutes while I remembered Munich the way it had been in the 'good old days.' I felt as if I'd been kicked in the gut. Gabi's story had disappeared. I couldn't help wondering how long it would be before *The French Story* started to disappear. It was time to start writing while there was still time to write the story. At least, I hoped there was.

Terry had been looking at the character notes I'd made. Still feeling nostalgic and sorry for the loss of the Spaten café, it took me a moment to realise that Terry was now wrestling with Rosemary for possession of a sheet of notes. They'd already torn it in several places. She saw me as I sat down.

"How could you? Why? Why?" She was sobbing and screaming at the same time.

What had I done wrong? I liked Rosemary, and anyway, she had nothing to do with *The French Story*. What had Terry done to her?

I'd had a soft spot for Rosemary ever since I'd written her. When she came out of the humidor, she always sat very close and tickled my fingertips. Perhaps it was my fault she despised Terry so much. This time it was me she was angry with.

"Why didn't you tell me about your new girlfriend? See, I had to read about it in the notes." She waved the sheet in my face. "She even looks like me. Oh, John! How could you do that?"

I should have known Terry would leave that page somewhere for her to find. Bastard!

"Rosemary, look at what you're holding! Those are character notes! John and Sabrina were real people forty-three years ago! You've never known either of them!"

"You make it quite clear what you wanted, and, the way it's written, I don't see that much has changed." She sniffed.

"Rosemary, be reasonable! That's John the character. Me, as I was a long time ago—not the real me now. That's so long ago, John isn't even on his way to becoming me! That affair happened forty-three years ago. It wasn't even very much of an affair really. And if I can use it now to write a good book, maybe get a little recognition, pay the rent? You know we've talked about this. And it could be a really good story! Oh dear, this is going to be very difficult for you, isn't it? I'm so sorry, Rosemary.'

She fled into the humidor.

"Oh, that's very nice, that is! All she wanted was to be close to you. You're a miserable old git, do you know that? You might at least have changed the names!"

I didn't dignify that with a response, not that Terry would have expected one.

I didn't know what to say. I couldn't start having affairs with the characters. I wondered for a moment if it might be better to change her words, to calm her down a little. But she was such a sweet girl. I think everybody loved Rosemary. Except for Terry. Mostly, I didn't want Rosemary's feelings seeping into *The French Story.*

I had just started writing the farmer's wife when Rosemary came out. She avoided looking at me directly, so I took the hint. For the moment at least, we weren't speaking. I smiled gently and gave her a handful of words. She settled down to sort out the words for the farmer's wife. Behind her, Terry's lip curled unpleasantly. He didn't like characters she'd worked on—they smiled a lot and carried good-luck charms. His characters used bad language. And sometimes they hit people.

"Mornin' all! Everybody fit?"

"Thanks for asking. How do you fancy a gnarly old sod of a farmer to work on? There are some words there for you. Rosemary's doing the wife."

"I'll bet she is. All lovey-dovey again, are we?"

"No, we're quietly minding our own business this morning. If you do the same, we'll get on just fine."

The farmer and his manager hadn't been fun to work for. They were always together, laughing at something. If they heard us laughing though, they soon put a stop to it. What they laughed at, I have no idea, but it didn't sound pleasant, and I didn't think they had a sense of humour in the way normal people do.

Even in baggy old jeans, Sabrina had had a graceful walk that turned heads. I didn't remember her smile, but I gave her a slightly lopsided little smile anyway. I thought about lipstick, but it would have been too much on her tanned olive skin. At a distance, you might well have mistaken her for Rosemary. At the time of writing, I was sixty-three, and I realised only too well that my memory of her was probably a bit rose tinted. She had made a deep impression on the eighteen-year-old adolescent that I was when we had first met. In *The French Story*, it was that eighteen-year-old she would be having a little affair with.

Trouble erupted the moment we added the new characters to the humidor. The older characters didn't want to share the space they had with a bunch of 'stuck-up newlets.' And no-one was going to make them work on the same page as the 'newlets' either.

"It's all about the words," Terry tried to explain. "They've got a few simple little words. A lot of the words you use now, they've never seen before. And that Sabrina's causing trouble already. Turned her nose up at the old characters as soon as they spoke to her. Fuck knows how Rosemary's going to cope with her being there. She looks a bit like her as well, and that won't help."

It was a relief when Rosemary and Terry went to talk to the troublemakers. Perhaps that would be the end of it.

Hélène immediately took Rosemary's place.

"Hi, Hélène. Is there anything I can do for you?"

"Not for me. No. You do know Rosemary's in love with you?" Hélène didn't beat about the bush. Well, she never had. "Why didn't you write a 'happily ever after' for her before you started this story? And about that summer in Cabrières. I think you should know, we don't agree at all about you and Sabrina getting together."

We saw Rosemary returning with a few of the older characters from the humidor. I was glad because I didn't really have any good answers for Hélène.

I agreed to update all the characters, with no scrimping on new words. It had become quite an angry exchange when

Barudh, one of the oldest characters, had given his cantankerosity a good airing and then accused me of looking threateningly at the eraser on my desk. I told him it was for spelling mistakes. Yes. It is true. I do have an eraser on my writing table. And yes, most of the characters are written in soft pencil. But I would never …!

After an early lunch and a nice cup of tea, I started writing *The French Story*. Rosemary stayed in the humidor, and I let Terry finish the last couple of characters; they wouldn't be needed until later in the story anyway.

Reaching into the bag for a handful of words, my fingers closed on something that wasn't a word. It turned out to be a café receipt from when Sabrina and I had ordered drinks one evening. Feeling around carefully, I found several other bits and pieces, all reminders of things Sabrina and I had done. What they were doing in the bag I couldn't imagine.

The rest of the afternoon was uneventful. I thought about discussing the plot with Terry, but that wouldn't really have helped. And there wasn't anything I could say to Rosemary.

It was halfway through the evening when Hélène came out to see what I was writing. She looked sad, and, to be honest, I just didn't want to know why.

"So, you really want to write it then? I wish I could persuade you to let it go. Sabrina doesn't want an affair with you. If you write it, it'll have to happen. But it won't work the way you think it will. She feels like you've only given her half a character, like she's only there for one reason. You could at least write her a proper character. And John, I hate to say it, but look at this scene. Don't you think it's a little bit … well, contrived?"

"Well, well, well. It seems some of the characters are none too chuffed with their roles!" Just as he intended, Terry's mocking tone got right under my skin. But for once I was glad to see him.

"Terry, have a look at the scene Hélène's talking about, would you?'

He read the scene.

"It's not great, is it? I mean, you've done better than that making notes on the bog. Here, let me have a go." He picked up a pencil and started adjusting the scene.

Hélène nodded.

"That's so much better! Still a bit stiff but lots better. Maybe you should let Terry be your ghostwriter."

"Why is it still stiff? What makes it stiff?"

Terry and Hélène looked at each other and shrugged.

Lips thin, jaw pointed belligerently at me, Rosemary joined us.

"Because it's not a nice story, and he knows it's not nice. It isn't right. All the same, I've decided to help as best I can. Between all of us, we should be able to make it work."

I wanted to say I couldn't possibly ask her to help like that, but, with her jutting chin and the way her hands had become fists planted on her hips … well, I didn't think it was a good time to argue.

Suddenly, flames capered on the table. Yellow tongues licked hungrily at my papers, at the notes, and everything. Then the candle fell over. There shouldn't have been— Muted screams came from the direction of the humidor.

"John! Stop dreaming! Get your arse in gear! Move the humidor! Over there! Everyone else, onto the table and save what you can! Yes, yes, that too. John, hurry it up a bit! Two wet towels now and you'll put it out."

Thanks largely to Terry, there wasn't a lot of damage. I wish I could say there were no casualties, but two of the newest characters, Ralph and Marianne, were incinerated—well, their pages were, which comes to the same thing in the end.

By now Sabrina had joined us. She wanted to know what had happened.

"I'll tell you what happened. The silly sod had to have his candle and his glass of wine. He says it helps him remember. More like a fit of early onset stupidity. If I've told him once, I've told him a hundred times … The fucking candle fell over. That's what happened."

"How did it fall over? It was on the other side of the table. John, did you see what happened?"

"No. I'd had a glass of wine, and I was about ready to call it a night and then that happened. I don't understand, I always put that candle out of reach just in case. Terry, did someone move the candle?"

"What? Not that I saw. You're sure you didn't knock it over?"

"Be reasonable just for a moment. How could I have?"

The next morning, we tidied up the table, opened a window, and I sharpened a couple of pencils. Sabrina was a great help, and Ralph and Marianne were soon back among us.

Yesterday evening's little fire still worried me. I knew I hadn't started it, so how had it started? And why had the candle fallen over *after* the fire had started? Yes, it's true I'd had a glass or two of wine. I remembered a feeling of frustration that the story wasn't going as well as I might have hoped. Well, what should

I have expected, with everybody worried about the apparently advanced state of incretination I seemed to be suffering from.

"John, that can't be right …"

"Are you sure it was like that?"

"Are you sure you remember that?"

And so on.

In the end, after another cup of tea, I settled down to work. By the end of the day, I had about six thousand words pencilled in, and a smell of lavender and wild herbs had more or less replaced the smell of burnt paper. I took my notes to the old leather armchair in the living room to think about them over a nice glass of Barbaresco.

To be honest, it wasn't my best work. I saw the prize-winning manuscript and the magic of the past drifting slowly away from me. Well, I'd known it wasn't going to be an easy story to write. Especially once they'd got me second-guessing my own memories.

It was halfway through the afternoon when Terry warned me that one of the characters was up to something he didn't think I'd intended for him to be up to. I give my characters a lot of freedom, but, in the end, I do expect them to stick to the story. Characters will sometimes try to introduce a subplot or spring a surprise on you at the end of a scene—and mostly I'm fine with that. But when I figured out what Ralph was up to, I definitely wasn't fine with it.

His heavy-handed attempts at flirting might have made an amusing subplot; unfortunately, Sabrina's reaction was about to change the story in ways that didn't bear thinking about. I started reaching for the eraser. Where had they met? Hmm. On page two. I carefully reread her pages. No, I really hadn't said she should encourage him. Ralph didn't get a girlfriend. Let him go home and play with the one he had. Time for another chat with Sabrina.

"Look, I'm sorry, but it really isn't okay. You can't start a thing with him when you know perfectly well you're going to start a thing with John two pages later. It would derail the story completely."

"But that isn't so! Not at all. Anyway, I fancy Ralph for now. I'll come back to the storyline when I have to, don't worry." Of course, she was wrong. If she'd been with Ralph, John wouldn't look twice at her.

"Ralph is a sidekick character. He isn't written to be used like that. How do you suppose he'll feel and react when you start, you know, with John? There'll be mayhem!"

"We're only the way you wrote us. Perhaps you should've been more careful."

"Well, there may be some truth in that. But look, this is my story, and I want to write it the way it is in my head. And before you start—yes, in my head, it really is quite clear! If we can't agree about that, I'll have to do something I'd rather not mention."

She was so like the Sabrina I remembered from the original story. Briefly, I wondered if I just updated Ralph a little bit, whether that would do the trick. I had loathed Ralph anyway, with all his Cambridge superiority and pseudo-socialism. But he was doing what he did just as I'd written him. I was well into chapter three, and I didn't need this sort of irritation. France didn't need it. My story didn't need it!

I brushed the last of the eraser crumbs from the table. I'd changed Sabrina's words a little, so she couldn't be in any doubt what was expected of her. The story could continue.

I brought a glass of wine to the table and hoped Rosemary might come out of the humidor for a chat, the way she used to. A few minutes later, I felt a familiar tickling at my fingertips.

"You know," she said quietly, "I understand why you changed Sabrina's words. I really do. But I don't think it'll help."

"What do you mean?"

"It's just the way she is. I think your memory can't be quite right. You think you remember how she was, but how well did you know her back then? Really?"

"I thought I knew her quite well. We had a lot of fun together. But you know, you may be right." I thought about it. It wasn't easy to find the words. "Too many of my stories have disappeared completely. I don't want to lose any more. I know it won't be perfect, but it'll be something. Do you think you can understand that?"

"I think so. You want to try to hold on to it."

"Something like that, yes. And it would be nice if it could be a real literary novel instead of just another story. Everybody else wins prizes. I'd like a shot at one just once." I didn't try to explain it. Rosemary was lovely to be with, but I'd never been sure if she or any of the others understood how different we really were. Perhaps none of us needed it spelled out.

We chatted a little longer, then I went into the living room for another glass of wine before bed. Something seemed out of kilter in the pages on the table, and I wasn't quite sure what.

The final scene of *The French Story* was proving impossible. Originally, forty-three years ago, a farmer had given us a ride from Cabrières to Nîmes. We'd had lunch together and agreed to meet two weeks later in Angers. It had been a pleasant afternoon. We'd found a lot to laugh about and doubtless a lot to look forward to. I couldn't make it work though, and I couldn't see why. Hélène's cousin Marianne was already out and about and came to see what I was doing. She was a sweet girl, not shy at all, but quiet. She did a lot of gymnastics, so she was slender, and she had slightly chaotic curly hair that hung almost to her waist. I couldn't remember how old she'd really been, but I thought fifteen was about right.

"John, are you really still trying to find an ending for that thing with Sabrina?"

"Mm. It's the only thing stopping me from finishing the story."

"She ended it herself though. She dumped John when they arrived in Nimes. Didn't she tell you?"

"No. She didn't."

Sabrina and Ralph came out first, then Rosemary emerged a moment later, holding John's hand. Terry followed them.

"We had an end-of-book party last night. I don't expect you'll be seeing the rest yet."

"Why would you have an end-of-book party? Who told you it was finished?"

"We worked out the ending days ago. We thought you'd have figured it out by now." That wasn't the Sabrina I remembered at all. How had she got like this?

"So, do tell. What happens at the end?"

"Rosemary wanted to be with John, and I wanted to be with Ralph. The end."

"Just like that? No plot, no reasons, no story for the reader to enjoy?"

"What story for the reader? What do you think we are, entertainers?"

"You're characters in a book. My book. Terry, what do you think? Obviously, it's not the story I was writing, but it might have a chance."

"With a proper ending …" He hesitated. "You could use the party as an ending. Something like 'the belle of the ball becomes the party slag'?"

"No! You can't write that!"

"Why not? Half the men in the humidor were lined up outside your door. There's a word for that. Mummy and Daddy would be so proud!"

"They were not lined up." Sabrina's eyes glittered as she turned a deep red.

"Of course I can write that. But it's too simple. How about: in the very cold light of day, Ralph realises he loves you so much he wants to save you from yourself. Good luck with that, Ralph! Unaware that you're already pregnant, he takes you away from all of this and settles you in a nice little cottage on the Yorkshire moors. I don't think there'll be a sequel."

I retrieved their character sheets from the drawer and sharpened a pencil. I could see Ralph working himself up to say a few words.

"Now, look here! You can't go around making girls pregnant. And you can't make me the father, old boy. Sorry and all that, but I have a girl back in good old Blighty. No, no, it won't do at all!"

"Should've thought of that, you pompous git!"

"Why? Why would you do this? Revenge? Jealousy? Will you really ruin our lives just because you didn't get what you wanted?"

'Well, I didn't get what I expected. That much is true. I got what I wanted though, a book to publish. And frankly, it's a better story than we had. And while you're all thinking about that, who came up with the idea of throwing bits of the story into the bag of words? And which of you pushed over the candle?'

"That was us." Rosemary and Sabrina stepped forward. "The candle was Ben, after he heard us talking about the way you treat Rosemary. Nobody was supposed to get hurt."

The phone rang. In hindsight, I should have followed my first instinct—to unplug it.

"Daphne's Copywriting and Editing Service, how can I help you?"

"Good morning, John. Sandra here."

Sandra? Oh, of course. My agent!

"Good morning, Sandra. How are you today?"

"Well. Thank you. And we're both about to get lots better. Ray Barker from Union Publishing wants to talk about *The French Story*. How's it coming along?"

Oh shit oh shit oh shit! What could I tell her?

"Well, I don't really know right now. It seems to have taken a few unintended twists and turns. Turns out, the love interest was a bit of, erm … well, a village bicycle."

"Oh! Well, he already likes what he's seen. As long as you stick to the plan—you know, small village, love interest, infidelity, a sideswipe at a well-known figure. I'll tell him you're up for editing next week then, shall I?"

Delightful girl, Sandra. Always full of optimism.

"No, please don't do that." I told her about the trouble I was having with Sabrina and Ralph. "Let's say eight weeks. I want to do a complete rewrite. I don't like this version at all."

I wondered if I could meet the deadline even at eight weeks—in fact, any deadline.

"John, listen to me. It sounds like a perfectly good story. You owe me a book after all I've done for you, and I want this one!"

I protested of course, but she wouldn't let me off the hook. Well, no need to let everyone else know that. I didn't like arguing on the phone. All the characters could hear, and more than once, I'd seen Terry with a self-satisfied grin covering his face, enjoying my discomfort. I expected that this time too, but I was wrong. With his forehead wrinkled and his voice soft, he was having a very serious chat with Marianne. He was explaining something.

I settled the phone in its cradle and sat down with a cup of coffee. A publisher had just enquired about my book. I was perhaps a few weeks from the recognition I had craved for over thirty years—mere weeks from success—and I wanted to scrap the project. What was wrong with me?

It took me about an hour to finish the story as they'd let it play out. The epilogue took another twenty minutes. The cottage on the moors turned out to be a droughty Victorian structure where they opened a not very successful bed and breakfast. They were never heard of again. No more magical French summer for me.

Terry put a hand on my arm; he'd never done that before. "Won't the success make up for it? At least a little bit?"

"No, I don't suppose it will. Nothing's going to be the same again, is it? All I wanted was that summer with Sabrina, and, well, success and all the rest of it as well. All the old stories have gone now, haven't they? Look, Terry." I'd made up my mind. "There's something I need to do now the book's written. Would you take Marianne for a walk around the table? Here, take some words and write a poem or something. I don't think she needs to see …"

I think Terry understood. I really think he did. Quite gently, he took her by the arm and led her away. I put a couple of handfuls of words at the other end of the table for them.

I reached for the rubber. There was no need to erase more than the names and memories. Some of them had been quite good characters. One by one, I pulled the pages from their drawer until there were only two left.

They would find the humidor a bit empty for the time being.

"PATIENCE"
LISA DRANZIK

I tossed my bag beneath my desk, flipped open my laptop to sign in, clipped on my name badge and printed out my schedule in the space of fifty-five seconds. My schedule included a long list of familiar patient names and one new evaluation to be completed. I drained the last of my coffee and headed upstairs to find the medical chart.

My new patient, Mr. Z., was an eighty-six-year-old male, recently widowed, who lived alone in his home. He suffered a fall from a ladder when attempting to clean out the gutters, resulting in a bruised arm and fractured right leg. The hospital notes indicated he had not been out of bed much in the last week after surgery, and it was decided to send him to further his rehabilitation, as he was not ready to go home.

I knocked on his door. "May I come in? I'm from the therapy department and would like to see how you are doing today."

The blinds were still drawn, and I just barely saw the toes of the bright yellow hospital socks peeking out from beneath the white blanket. I hovered in the doorway.

"No! Go the hell away!" he yelled after a pause.

Unfazed, I glanced at my watch. "Okay, I will come back later to see how you are doing."

The nurse, social worker, clergy, and aides streamed in and out of his room over the next few hours, and I could hear his booming voice rebuke each of them.

At 11:00, he allowed me in. Patients like these were not the norm but not entirely unusual either. I took a deep, steadying breath before entering, ready for anything.

Apparently worn down from yelling at the rest of the staff, he answered my questions about his home and circumstances with brusque one-word responses. I assessed his arm and leg strength, movement, and pain. I helped him stand with a walker, and he took about five precarious steps to the waiting wheelchair. Once carefully positioned with his leg elevated and all of his personal items placed within reach, he yelled that he refused to sit in the "wretched vehicle of death" for a moment longer and demanded to return to bed.

Although he denied the need for pain medicine, I returned to the room with an ice pack for his leg. He glared at me but snatched the ice and laid it on his leg.

"It was nice to meet you. I will be back to work with you tomorrow. Is there a time you would prefer?" I inquired.

"Lies," he said. "Don't bother."

The social worker helpfully revealed that Mr. Z. was a retired high-school social-studies teacher. He took care of his wife, Anabelle, during her last two years, until her death six months ago from cancer. Their only child, a son, had died a decade earlier in a car crash. He had one living nephew that lived across the country but was not involved in his life.

"Do you know of any neighbors or friends who might have been helping him out?" I asked.

She shook her head, sadly.

The next day was much the same as the as the first. I smiled and tried to be upbeat. He told me to go to Hell three times before he agreed to therapy. We walked to the closet to find real clothes to wear instead of the hospital gown.

"I don't have clothes. Don't need them here," he huffed.

I mentally gauged his size. He moaned a bit, and, realizing he would not admit his pain, we walked back to the bed. He looked relieved, perhaps to lie down, but probably to get rid of me. Once again, I brought back an ice pack for his leg. He allowed me to place it over his incision.

"I bet I can find you some clothes. Let me check into a few things for you." I knew the moment the words came out of my mouth that it was a mistake.

"Damn it, girl," he raged. "I don't need any damn clothes! Just get me the hell out of here. Don't bother coming back tomorrow!"

I packed up my things and prepared to leave. "Can I get you anything before I go?" I winced. We were required to ask.

"Get me a cup of coffee!"

As I stepped out to head to the dining area, I could hear him yell, "With one creamer!"

When I came to his room the next day, he looked up from the Sports section with a small pair of reading glasses perched on his nose. I suddenly had a clear picture of how he might have looked as a teacher. I was certain that I would have been miserable in this man's class.

"My god, you are the spawn of Satan, aren't you?" he said, slamming down his paper with a scowl. "No, no, and *no!*"

I sighed. It was hard sometimes. Helping people brought me great satisfaction. I even had an affinity for the *toughies* and *grumpies*, as we called them. There were days though when I didn't have much more in me, when I couldn't just let the words float over my head. I felt tears creep into my eyes. I took a deep breath and blinked them away before he noticed.

On Thursday, I was ready. I picked up the newspaper from the front lobby, grabbed a cup of hot coffee with one creamer and headed in.

"Good morning," I said after knocking and, without a word, placed the coffee and paper down on his bedside table. "I will be back in about forty-five minutes to help you get cleaned up and out of bed." I smiled then was out the door.

He was awake and watching TV, but he never looked at me.

I moved on to one of my friendliest patients to give me the boost of motivation I needed to return to Mr. Z.

When I returned, the coffee was gone, and he had a clearly finished breakfast tray on the bedside table. I noticed the paper folded inside out to the sports headlines from the night before. I had towels in one hand and the walker in the other.

Without a single word, he started to move to the edge of the bed. I walked him to the bathroom sink where I had placed a straight chair with arms for him to sit. He started to wash up on his own. I helped him to stand and balance while he shaved and brushed his teeth. He looked just a little bit nicer without all the scruff. It was then that I noticed that there was some clothing folded neatly on the chair.

"Were you able to have someone bring you some clothes from home?" I inquired.

"The social worker was nice enough to find me some when no one else would."

I bit down on my lip. I walked him back to the bed and showed him how to use the reacher stick to put on the sweatpants when he couldn't reach down himself.

"I don't need that garbage. You do it for me. That is your damn job," he grumbled.

"Not at all," I replied instinctively, as I have had this conversation ad nauseum. "My job is to help you find a way to do this yourself. I won't be there to help when you go home."

"Well, that's some damn good news!" he responded so sharply that my head snapped up, eyes wide.

I stifled a chuckle. Probably an inappropriate response, but I was beginning to feel there was no clear expectation. There was some more mumbling under his breath. He completed the rest of the session in silence.

The next day, I returned feeling that, despite his words, we had definitely made a bit of progress in his movement. I dropped off his coffee with cream, Sports section, and the ice pack I heard him call for just moments earlier. I laid the ice pack on his leg gently and told him I would be back in forty-five minutes. He snatched at the ice pack and slammed it back down approximately one inch from where I had originally placed it.

I thought I found a winning morning routine, so it took me by surprise when the coffee, the newspaper, and the ice packs were irreparably "too hot," "tasted horrible," "wrinkled," and "lumpy."

"You can't do a damn thing right, can you?" he yelled.

I tried not to be hurt or show my dismay at his cutting words. He did walk, clean up, and do a few exercises that morning. That, in the end, was what mattered.

"Why the hell do you keep coming back?" he grumbled.

"To help you get stronger and more independent, so you can go home again," I replied in a steady voice.

"I bet you'd like that, wouldn't you?" he replied. "Don't waste your time or mine."

Once outside his room, I backed up against the wall, out of sight of Mr. Z. I closed my eyes, just for a moment, inhaled slowly and deeply then let the air come rushing out. I gathered myself, my supplies, and moved on to the next patient.

The workday offered no time for reflection or reconsideration. I was grateful to have that Saturday off to clear my head and gain some perspective. I was grateful that my husband was working on my temperamental car and that I could watch my child play football. I wondered if Mr. Z. was grateful for anything at all. Then I thought how hard it would be to be grateful if it was all taken away.

I drove into work a little later on Sunday morning. It was my turn to work a weekend rotation. As the elevator doors opened on the rehab floor, I heard Mr. Z.'s voice howling at the staff for one thing or another. I grabbed his coffee and paper and clenched my teeth as I stood outside his door.

The nurse's aide came shuffling out with her head down, raised her eyes to me and placed a heavy hand on my shoulder as she passed.

"I am not doing anything today. It's Sunday, for crying out loud!" He slammed his hand down on the bedside table by the bed. "I want to go to church service. How the hell do I get there?"

Still holding his coffee and paper, I raised an eyebrow. "They hold services on the second floor at ten fifteen. You have about an hour until then, and the aides can take you if you want."

He paused for a long moment.

I set down his coffee and paper. Still quiet. "I can come back after …" I began.

"I need to get dressed first." It was all he said, but his look and tone were more questioning than commanding.

"Let me get a few things for you, and I will be right back," I responded.

I left the room and went on a hunt. I was able to scrounge up a button-down shirt and some black pants. I was nervous, but it was the best I could do.

When I returned with my arms full of clothing and towels, his lips were pressed tight and his expression was strained. I didn't know whether he was upset, whether I took too long or he hated the clothing. Still, he said nothing and allowed me to guide him to the bathroom to clean up and change.

The clothes fit well enough, and I found some clean slippers for him. He glanced once at the wheelchair and then at the clock but put his wallet and a folded piece of paper in his pocket and started out of his room with the walker. We walked in silence to the elevator, and I led him to the chapel on the second floor where I guided him to an armchair in the back row.

He turned to me. "How do I …"

"I will be back in an hour to get you," I said in a whisper as the organ music began to play.

My morning was harried and chaotic, but I made it back to Mr. Z. on time. We waited until most of the crowd cleared and walked back to his room. A new bedside recliner arrived while he was gone, and he made a straight line for it. I gave him his newspaper, phone, glasses, and remote control from the table then excused myself.

"Hey!" he called out.

My back to him, I closed my eyes briefly, braced then turned to face him.

"Thanks," he said, not looking up from his paper.

"Glad I could help," I answered with a smile.

After a very long day, I heard a familiar ranting and yelling from Mr. Z.'s room; however, there seemed to be something more urgent about it this time. I passed the room tentatively and overheard him clearly upset over something he'd lost. I stopped and knocked on the door.

When he saw me, his eyes grew wide, and he pointed.

My stomach flipped for a moment.

"The chapel! I bet I lost it there!" he said. "Let's go!"

I nodded to the nurse and took Mr. Z. back to the chapel on the second floor. He lost a small picture of his wife he had placed in his pocket this morning.

On the way, he spoke. "We were married for sixty-three years," he said as quietly as I ever heard him speak. "She was all I had left. That picture is all I have now."

When we reached the chapel, it was dark, but the door was unlocked. I flicked on the light and scanned the chairs and the floor but found no picture. Mr. Z.'s look of desperation pushed me onward. I glanced around and saw a small folded piece of paper much like the one he tucked into his pocket this morning on the edge of the podium. I picked it up and held it in the air for him to see.

His tensed posture relaxed immediately, and he reached out his hand with urgency. I brought it to him, and he opened it.

"My Anabelle," he said. He gazed at the photo then folded it in half gently and placed it in the breast pocket of his shirt, over his heart.

Once in his room, he settled into the recliner by the bed and rubbed his leg. I knew he needed some ice, and I set out to find some. When I returned, he was already starting to doze. He took the ice pack from my hands and held them for just a moment.

"Thank you," he said, looking me right in the eyes for the very first time, giving my hands a quick squeeze and giving me a small smile.

I thought for a moment that maybe I might have enjoyed being in this man's class.

"Anytime," I replied, squeezing back.

That evening, I was buoyed by the success of the day. It is hard to describe how much it means to break through barriers and feel like you've made a difference in someone's life. I looked forward to the next day.

After arriving, I tossed off my coat, printed my schedule and headed upstairs to grab coffee and the paper for Mr. Z. before I launched myself into my schedule. I knocked on his door and called out. When I looked up, I noticed his bed was empty and the linens stripped. My head swiveled as I checked for a light under the bathroom door—none. I walked out to the dining room with coffee and paper still in hand—not there. I returned to his room where I noticed the folded photo on the nightstand.

Drawn to the photo, I set down the coffee and paper. I picked it up and noticed for the first time that it was folded in thirds not in half. In the photo, a young Anabelle's face was tilted to the sun, head thrown back in laughter, arms outstretched. I gingerly unfolded the last third of the picture. What I saw took my breath away.

A much younger version of Mr. Z. looking lovingly at Anabelle, his arms outstretched toward her, reaching for her.

Instantly, I knew Mr. Z. was where he wanted to be.

I placed the photo gently back on the nightstand, in awe of the depth of what I could see there, what I was certain I could never completely understand, and what I learned those last few days.

"Thank you," I whispered.

Even with six thugs aiming handguns at Gabe, *drumming boom, chick, a-boom-boom,* ran through his mind. He felt rhythm in everything. Idle conversations overheard at a cafe, struggling steam powered machines, food grilling in makeshift bar-b-que pits, and even birds chirping during a hike had all provided ideas for new beats.

He pointed a blistered finger at his band's manager. "Give 'em the money, Tommy."

Gabe was due onstage in three hours to headline the biggest music festival in Costa Rica. His band had decided on the flight down to perform a brand-new intro for their set, so he had to create a fresh groove to get the crowd tapping their toes and nodding their heads. Over 100,000 manic fans awaited him and his band to perform in front of, but, right now, Gabe wanted to score some drugs and hang at the beach.

"Nah," Tommy said, clutching a briefcase to his chest. "Not until they put their guns away and I get a taste of the product."

Gabe rolled his eyes and focused on the massive mountain that erupted from the jungle behind him. As a member of one of the biggest bands of the decade, only a few select people could get away with telling him no. Tommy had saved the band's bacon on countless occasions, and he had the ear of Jeffrey, the band's erratic vocalist, so Gabe knew he had to watch his attitude.

He sighed. "Dude, I want to get my fix and still have time to explore the area before showtime."

A vibrant maroon and indigo bird launched from some nearby palm trees and flew across the horizon, announcing its presence with sharp yet melodic whistling. It reminded Gabe of the piano intro to one of the first songs his band had done. That beat had been basic, almost embarrassingly so, but it had put them on the map and paid a few bills.

Gabe pointed. "You see? That's the shit I don't get to enjoy back home. I'm on a beach boasting the clearest water on the planet and wild monkeys. We're wasting time."

"I'm afraid I won't be giving you anything," the leader of the armed goons said. A briefcase handcuffed to his arm, in theory, held the drugs. "Until you hand over the money."

Gabe had a hard time taking Ponzi seriously. His bushy 'stache, paramilitary outfit, thick-to-the-point-of-absurdity cigar, and his Ray-Ban sunglasses had been ripped directly from any number of low-budget 80's action flicks. His gun, however, looked legit.

"This is killing my buzz," Gabe complained. "Enough with the posturing. I have work to do and the powder in the case will help."

Tommy stood his ground, though Gabe thought he could smell urine coming from his manager's pants.

Ponzi shook his briefcase. "You're in my country. You follow my rules."

Gabe felt a pinch on his arm. He slapped at a brown bug with a rounded shell the size of a dime crawling toward his elbow. "Seriously, do you know who the hell I am?"

Ponzi's sneer disappeared. "Do you know how little my bullets give a shit who you are?"

On cue, five guns cocked. The sterile click provided a stark contrast to the gentle cresting of the crystal-clear waves a few dozen feet away. Gabe glanced at one of the goons who appeared much younger than the rest. His gun hadn't cocked in time with the others. The kid, sporting the first hint of facial hair under his nose, peered at his gun as if it was to blame. The guns produced a thick menacing sound. Gabe thought of the unrelenting percussion of Killing Joke or Ministry.

Ponzi waved at one of the buzzing brown bugs that had crawled on Gabe. "We have other business to attend to, so make your move or your bodies will litter this beautiful beach."

"Relax." Tommy said, holding up his arms. "We were told by mutual friends you were easy to deal with."

Gabe saw a splotch of neon green on his forearm where the brown bug had met its demise. Surrounding the unsettling goo, three more of the bugs crawled around. They buzzed in harmony, but, underneath the din, Gabe heard a clicking and clacking. *Boom. Chick? A-boom-boom.* The unsettling noise sounded like a phrase, an insect call and response pattern. Another simple beat, but damn it, don't those always make the most effective ones as well? *Boom. Chick? A-boom-boom.* It still needed something, but Gabe thought it could work with a little of his influence. He didn't tour with the big flashy drum kits you saw from Neil Peart or Tommy Lee, but Gabe could still create atmosphere with his cymbals.

Gabe swatted at the unknown creatures. "What the hell are these things anyway?"

From behind the drummer, a loud, wet bout of coughing erupted from a disheveled man in a yellowed t-shirt and a red bandana. The elderly man bent over until he got his respiratory problems back under control. He stood and spat out a green ball of slime. "Please, señor," the dirty man said, his voice a hoarse whisper. "Leave my bugs alone."

"If they're yours, can you kindly get them off of me? They're filthy."

Slumping his shoulders, the man favored Gabe with a crooked smile missing more teeth than it boasted. "I beg you. These bugs have saved my life."

A few of the armed men began chuckling—but not until they had checked with Ponzi for permission first.

"Sick. He's got those things crawling all over him," Tommy said.

Ponzi's sneer returned. "Meet Torrio, my favorite customer. Come for your daily fix?"

As Torrio approached, Gabe realized the filthy man was not only talking to the bugs but petting them as well. He wore shoes sporting several holes that filled with sand each step he took. His skin, a reddish-brown, reminded Gabe of the dirt around Oklahoma City. His band's van had broken down there on their first tour, stranding the band for over a week.

"Seriously, let's get out of here or I'm going to throw up," Tommy said, holding a hand over his nose.

Either Torrio or the bugs brought a pungent, rotting smell along with them. Gabe sniffed the goo on his arm. Apparently Torrio was the guilty party.

Ponzi stepped closer. "Nonsense, the drugs are good quality."

"I swear," Torrio said, raising his bushy white eyebrows, "I have the worst asthma, had it since I was a boy, but, ever since I discovered these bugs, I haven't coughed once."

Torrio let a moment of silence linger and then admitted, "Well, until just now. But that was his fault." He pointed at Gabe. "As long as I treat 'em good, they help my lungs. They say I can even fly again."

This time when the men laughed out loud, Ponzi joined in. Even Tommy loosed a nervous titter.

"Damn, he really is off his rocker," Tommy said.

A few more bugs crawled toward Gabe. *Boom. Chick? A-boom-boom.* He squished them under his well-worn Vans.

He turned to face Ponzi again. "Come on, man. We just want to see your supply before we go."

"Go?" Ponzi asked. "No one leaves my beach until I say so."

He pointed toward the Hummer that Gabe and Tommy had rode in and snapped his fingers.

A shot rang out.

Gabe's driver dropped onto the sand. The screams that erupted from Gabe and Tommy mixed with startled screeches and cries from various monkeys, birds, and other animals in the area. The noise didn't have a rock beat. It reminded Gabe of the noisy chaos that erupted at the end of a Mosleyhead concert.

"Jesus, man." Tommy shouted. "He had kids."

Gabe looked toward the tree line wondering how fast he could reach the cover of the forest.

"You don't want to go off into that jungle, my friends," Ponzi said as if reading Gabe's mind. "Just hand over the money."

Exchanging a knowing glance, the two American men dashed away. Torrio also ran, stirring a cloud of the brown bugs into the air.

Shots rang out, reminding Gabe of the one and only time he saw AC/DC perform "For Those About to Rock (We Salute You)."

Tommy loosed an agonized grunt before doubling over and crumbling to the ground five paces ahead. Gabe wiped Tommy's blood from his cheek. He reached down, slowing only enough to grab the briefcase full of cash from Tommy before speeding toward cover. He reached the thick jungle brush and kept hustling over vines, under branches, and away from any open areas that would provide the gunmen a clear sightline to shoot. Torrio kept up with him and, in fact, took the lead after a few minutes of rushing.

Trees rustling, branches snapping, and urgent comments yelled in a foreign language alerted Gabe that the men remained hot on his heels.

Torrio said, "Run this way."

Jumping over a snake and avoiding a sinkhole by inches, Gabe followed Torrio deeper into the unknown and ignored the fact the man had misquoted a classic Aerosmith hit.

Torrio called over his shoulder. "Keep up."

Huffing, puffing, and panicked, Gabe asked, "Wh-where are we headed?"

"To my plane. It's not far."

Torrio veered right and disappeared behind a curtain of vines. Bugs flew around the man like bees who discovered a motherload of pollen.

Gabe considered veering off on his own, but, when a gunshot whizzed by, he jolted into action. He crashed through the vines. A wave of panic flashed through the drummer as he questioned which way Torrio had gone, but a loud bout of coughing informed Gabe where he needed to run. He ducked under a branch, rounded a tree and tripped over the sick man who was squatting and breathing heavily.

Gabe let out a grunt as his chin smacked the briefcase on his way down. Before he could complain, Torrio held a rotting-fish scented hand over his mouth and placed an index finger over his own. Torrio buried his face into Gabe's armpit and began coughing again. Warm liquid oozed between Gabe's arm and his chest, but he wasn't sure if that was Torrio's sweat or more of the green-ish gob Torrio had spit out on the beach. The drummer squirmed, but he stayed quiet. The two men got close enough that Gabe could hear the man's heart pounding. *Boom-a-boom-a-boom-a-boom.*

Though it was too straightforward to use in concert, Gabe reflected that a heartbeat would make for a cool sample to add to a song.

Goons rushed past the vines. As their footfalls faded, Gabe realized they had fallen for Torrio's ruse and continued straight ahead. After a few moments, Torrio exhaled and relaxed.

Gabe lay on the ground and focused on slowing his heartbeat and calming his mind. When he finally did roll over, he wished he hadn't.

Torrio dug his hands into a puddle of mud and then smeared it all over himself.

When Gabe took a closer look, he realized the mud pit actually contained a swarm of those same brown bugs. His stomach turned. He dry heaved forcefully enough times that he wished he actually had something in his gut to throw up.

He wiped sweat from his forehead and whispered, "Are you insane?"

"I told you, these bugs save me."

The native junkie couldn't open his mouth wide enough to properly enunciate his words, Gabe assumed, because the bugs would crawl inside. With each dip of Torrio's hands into the nest, he added fifty more insects to explore his body.

Torrio favored Gabe with a grin. "I stumbled upon these saviors a few days ago, and my breathing has improved ever since. I can ever hear their thoughts, and they appear to understand my words."

As he spoke, he lifted two full hands to his nose and inhaled. *Boom. Chick? A-boom-boom.*

"Well, I'm scared to death of catching some disease from these things. I'm not letting some mutant bug come between me and playing tonight." Gabe stood. He stomped and swatted at the beetle-like creatures who buzzed around him. Within moments, dozens of tiny brown carcasses oozed bright green droplets as their scurrying legs stilled.

"Please don't," Torrio said between whooping coughs. He stopped digging and gestured for Gabe to calm down. "I have an accord with these bugs. I promised to look after them."

Gabe paused but not to appease Torrio. Another pair of goons rushed through the jungle nearby.

Gabe ducked back down. "You weren't lying about that plane, right?

"No, señor. It is that way." The man pointed to where Gabe assumed counted as west, but he'd gotten so turned around he couldn't bank on it. Torrio thrusted his hands into the insect hive again. "There's a secluded field over there long enough to get my Joan up in the air."

"Joan?"

"She's named after my favorite author." Torrio beamed.

"Is there something on the plane that I could use to call for help?"

Torrio nodded and threw a metallic object at Gabe. The sunburned musician caught a set of keys covered in bugs.

He smooshed the bugs and jerked a thumb in the direction Torrio had indicated. "This way?"

"Mind the bogs. If you veer north, you'll stray right into ol' Suarez Swamp."

"Aren't you coming?"

"I need a few minutes to gather enough bugs for the trip."

"Go ahead and catch your breath, but leave those filthy things behind. The only bugs I tolerate are The Beatles and, if my lady wants to dance, The Crickets."

"And then who will fly you out of here?"

Gabe glared at the pathetic man and imagined the feeling of ten thousand tiny legs crawling on him. A chill rushed down his spine. He turned and darted for the plane; a blast beat playing in his head matched the adrenaline flowing through his body.

A stranger to anything more stressful than not having enough beer backstage, Gabe couldn't keep the image of Tommy and their driver being gunned down out of his mind as he ran. He had put up with too much drama between the band's vocalist and their guitarist to end up dying alone. Or sober. He vowed to play the most thunderous beat he'd ever constructed when he hit the stage. *Boom. Chick? A-boom-boom.*

Distracted by his thoughts and his panic, Gabe didn't hear the labored breathing coming from behind the next tree in his path. One of the goons leapt from behind it, arms outstretched toward Gabe. The rock star screamed and made a feeble attempt to avoid a collision, but he failed worse than Ozzy's first four retirements.

Gabe flailed out of control into vegetation thick enough to prevent him from striking the ground full force but not enough to avoid a wave of pain as he landed. The goon bounced off a crooked tree trunk and got the air knocked out of him. The armed man remained conscious but appeared visibly shaken as he crossed his arms over his chest and groaned. Gabe saw a dozen different emotions flash across the goon's baby face. The drummer forced himself onto his feet.

The goon called out, "Over here. I found—"

Gabe smashed the suitcase into the goon's temple, making a dull dong sound, which reverberated out of tune like the kick drum he had used to record his band's first demo. The goon slumped sideways. Gabe saw the goon's gun, but he didn't bother picking it up, as he'd never handled a weapon like that before.

Gabe shook his left hand. He paused a moment to flex his fingers to assure nothing felt broken. A drummer with a fractured hand does no one any good.

The surrounding wildlife cackled loud enough to compete with the New Year's Eve crowd Gabe's band had played at CBGB's a few years back. He was too seasoned or maybe too cynical to promise that, if he survived, he'd never do drugs again, but the twenty-seven-year-old who hadn't attended church in a decade looked up and asked, "God, you around?"

Unsettled brush and leaves being shoved aside prevented any further discussions with deities. Gabe froze, unsure how far he could run before the fast approaching footsteps caught him. He ducked behind a monstrous thorn bush covered in orange blossoms, pricking himself several times in the process.

Torrio rushed into view, covered head to toe in bugs. He spoke as he bounded along. "You'll love it where we're going."

Gabe cupped his hands around his dry mouth. "*Psst.*"

Torrio kept going, apparently oblivious to the body he missed stepping on by mere inches.

Gabe fell in behind Torrio and tried again. "*Psst.*"

This time the elder man glanced over his shoulder and grinned.

Gabe was grateful that the unkempt man acknowledged his presence without making any loud noises. He waved away a few bugs who fell behind or broke off from their group. He fought against the stitches in his chest begging him to rest as he hurried forward after the elderly man. *Boom. Chick? A-boom-boom.* He didn't want to turn it into a disco or hip-hop thing by using the same old ride and hi-hat combo used a million other times. He thought maybe his splash mixed with a deep clink or two from his China cymbal might provide the best results.

Ponzi yelled out, too close for comfort, "Whoever catches him gets half the cash."

Gabe pushed aside a long-leafed branch to reveal a wide-open area. A single-engine plane with a black lightening stripe running along its canary yellow and rust-colored body sat on a rocky path about ten feet wide. As a child of the 70s, Gabe's first thought was of Princess Leia saying, "You came in that thing?" the first time she laid eyes on the Millennium Falcon. Instead, he said, "She's beautiful," as he returned Torrio's keys.

The old man slapped the plane's window. "She's a J3 Pipercub."

"I don't care of it's a Jefferson Airplane. Get us off the ground."

The musician kept watch as the elder man entered the plane and prepped Joan for takeoff. As the propeller revved to life, a gunshot rang out. Gabe pressed himself as close to the plane as possible. He saw a fresh bullet hole in the plane's tail.

"Go. Go. Go!" Gabe shouted as he jumped into the backseat.

Ponzi appeared through the trees holding up his gun. He fired. Gabe's leg burst in pain as dollar bills flew into the air around him, creating a cloud like the bugs. Gabe lifted his now opened and half-empty briefcase into the plane. The bullet had blasted into the case and still packed enough of a wallop to bruise Gabe, though he saw no blood.

Even at his loudest, the drummer's screams couldn't overshadow the warming engine and bullets now flying en masse. The plane rolled forward, quickly gaining speed. Torrio pulled back on the flight stick. Gabe's stomach lurched as they lifted off. The plane's wheels clipped the tops of the trees, but, after a few tense moments, the plane rose above the jungle.

Gabe and Torrio let out cries of joy as they flew beyond the reach of harm.

Torrio shouted, "I told you we could do it!"

"Damn straight," Gabe echoed the pilot's enthusiasm, unsure if Torrio was talking to him or the bugs. "Tonight, I'm treating you to the party of a lifetime."

The drummer reached forward and tried to squeeze Torrio's shoulders, but, in doing so, he smashed a couple dozen of the brown bugs. Startled, some of the bugs lifted off Torrio and flew up and at the drummer. *Boom. Chick? A-boom-boom.*

They began biting him all over, so, in turn, Gabe fought back.

Torrio tried to maneuver in his seat to avoid the uncontrolled hands of the American, but his motions just further antagonized the bugs to take flight. "Don't. Please, you fool!"

Between Gabe killing the bugs and the creepy creatures inadvertently killing themselves by crashing into the walls, the interior cabin quickly became covered with neon-green liquid. The thick dripping ooze reminded Gabe of the first time he saw Gwar.

The drummer screamed, "Why aren't they biting you?"

Wheezing heavily, Torrio pulled out a knife. "I warned you, señor. These are my friends."

Squishing the bugs and yelling provided such a release that Gabe didn't hear Torrio begin coughing until the man's respiratory outburst had gotten so bad that blood sprayed from his lungs.

"You idiot," Torrio said as the brown bugs rushed into his mouth.

The pilot thrust the knife at Gabe but managed only to bury it into his own seat. With that, Torrio fell unconscious. He slumped.

The nose of the plane dipped sharply, throwing Gabe forward. When he looked out the windshield, all he saw was green save a few of the colorful birds he had seen on the beach.

"Torrio?"

The elder man's limp body pancaked the flight stick to the instrument panel.

"Torrio?"

The drummer shook the now bug-less shoulders of the elder man and got no response. In two hours, Gabe needed to take the stage at the biggest festival in Costa Rica, and the opening drum pattern he wanted to play sounded exactly like the bugs and the stuttering engine of the plane.

Boom. Chick? A-boom-boom … Crash.

"DANCE & MEET"
R.M. DEMEESTER

Today was my first day on the job. Tony was asleep on the couch after drinking all day, and he had spent the last of our money on God knows what. Rent was due in three days, and we didn't have the cash. The other day he "found" this job for me. He told me it was easy money, and even someone like me could do it. Exotic dancer. They told me all I had to do was keep the drunks at the club happy, give a lap dance or two and get paid. It sounded easy.

I opened the department store bag Tony had brought home earlier in the day. He told me it was my work attire. I had tossed it on the bed and slept the rest of the day. I needed to be awake until the wee hours of the morning.

I removed a neon-green lace bra, matching mini skirt, and a pair of heels. Laying them on the bed, my heart skipped a beat. He *expected* me to wear this? I looked into the other room at Tony slumped over the couch. It would piss him off if I changed my mind. *Stupid, little bitch*—I could hear those words spewing from his lips.

I picked up my phone—7:00 p.m. I had a bus to catch if I wanted to make it to "work." I debated not going. At first, it seemed like it would be easy. But my mind's eye kept envisioning all those men staring at me, their slimy hands waiting to grab and rub all over me. But Tony promised that it would be only dancing. *"Babe, don't be a baby. It's easy money. Don't you want easy money? You don't need to be smart to do it. Just dance for some drunk guys. Give them what they want. Fake it. Super easy."*

He was right. It would be all right. I'd go to work and wing it.

I reached into the top drawer of my dresser in the corner of the room, collected my makeup bag and threw it in my large purse that sat on the bed. I folded the "work" attire and put it in the bag. Here goes nothing.

Outside, on the way to the bus stop, a chilling breeze welcomed me. The brink of winter loomed on the horizon, and I hadn't taken the time to buy some winter attire yet. Money was tight but, if dancing proved as profitable as Tony said it would be then maybe, just maybe, I could before it snowed.

I stood at the bus stop, my bag held close to my chest. A few persons walked by not saying a word. On the outside, I was invisible. I minded my business because I wanted no trouble. I kept glancing at my wristwatch. 7:15. The bus should be arriving.

On the bus, the other passengers gawked at me. I held my bag closed, avoiding their stares. Did they know where I was headed? Sweat dotted my forehead. A part of me wanted to get off the bus, but the other part of me didn't want to let Tony down. We needed the money. Easy money, I kept telling myself.

I reached Ash and Main Street and got off the bus a few blocks from the club. I strode down the deserted street and over an uneven sidewalk toward the club. Tony had told me it was a brick building with a faded sign. He said the club was in the basement to the right rear.

I found the building behind some scrawny trees. I slithered behind the building until I saw the rear door.

A man dressed in all leather, with spikes on the top of his jacket, stood by the door. "Name?" he asked.

"Jana," I replied, looking at the ground and shifting my weight between my feet.

He looked me up and down, like a piece of meat. "Okay, come right on in. Go to the other side, and you'll see a yellow door. That's where all the other dancers are. Hurry, because the paying customers will be here soon."

I walked through the doors and saw poles on the center stage, with tables surrounding. To the right was the bar—a large bar with an assortment of booze. How much I wanted a drink right now … I kept walking until I spotted the yellow door.

Inside, a group of other women stopped and stared at me. A tall woman with long blond hair and wearing gold-sequined lingerie approached me. "You new?"

I nodded, my face growing hot.

"What did you bring to wear?"

I retrieved the outfit Tony had given me.

She smiled. "Get dressed, and I'll help you with makeup."

I did as she instructed. Behind the curtain, I changed clothes. I felt naked. I felt exposed. What was I doing?

Not wanting to keep her waiting, I exited the room to meet up with the blonde.

"My name is Candy, and yours?"

I introduced myself.

She helped me with my makeup. "There. Now let's get out there. Just dance and make those men work for their money." She winked.

When the hungry-eyed men arrived for attention, I followed suit. Clearing my mind, I went through the motions. I hugged a pole, sticking out my butt, and danced. The men cooed, clapped and tried to reach to touch me. The money rolled in. Tens, twenties, and more. A piece of me felt like it was dying. My stomach felt like a ton of bricks.

A young man—late twenties maybe—slipped me a twenty with a note attached.

I glanced at him, looking like a savage wolf, then back at the note.

555-432-1342 Ned Meet me at the front doors if you want at three.

I nodded.

Then my mouth dropped, and my face turned warm. What had I done? My mind floundered. What had I done? What had I done?

I avoided the man for the rest of the evening. I bit my upper lip, dancing and shaking to any other man. I blocked out the laughing and the vulgar comments. The cheering went in one ear and out the other. I needed the money. Tony would be so angry if I didn't come home with the cash, but I didn't want to be here. But he says it's easy money.

At 3:20 a.m., I had undressed and changed into my normal clothing. I took a deep breath, hoping Ned or whoever that man was, was long gone. I wasn't a whore. I wasn't a prostitute. I was in a committed relationship.

I was out of luck. When I reached the doors to head outside, Ned was leaning by the door. "Hello. I'm glad you came." He smiled but kept a fair distance from me.

I raised one shoulder to my ear and glanced at the ground. "Hi."

He rubbed the back of his neck. "Want to go for a walk?"

Dollar signs popped in the back of my mind, but fear struck the other part of me. I nodded, but, on the inside, I was praying I would make it out of this alive.

"What's your name?" Ned asked as we walked.

"Jana."

So far, so good. His greasy hands weren't all over me.

"I'm Ned."

"I know. It said in your note."

He bit his lip. "Yeah, stupid me." He looked away.

We walked until we were in front of a twenty-four-hour diner.

"Want to stop for a drink?"

I nodded, my movements jerky. "Sure."

A lump formed in my throat, threatening to close my airway. I should be heading home to see Tony. Not having drinks with another man.

Ned opened the door, letting me inside the cafe. He withdrew his wallet when we reached the till. He ordered a hot chocolate and turned to me.

"Um." I glanced at the exit. "Same thing."

The cashier tallied the total, and he paid for it.

"Thanks."

I followed him to the table while debating to run for the door. But that would be rude. And it would ruin any chance of making some extra cash. The more cash I made, the more Tony would love me.

"How are you tonight?" I asked.

His knee bounced under the table. "I had better nights; how about you?"

"Okay."

I brushed a hand through my hair while avoiding eye contact with Ned—a stranger. So far, he hadn't done anything. Was he trying to make me feel comfortable before he made a move?

"You say?" He crossed and uncrossed his arms a few times. "Sorry," he muttered to himself.

"A little." I smiled and reached to brush his wrist.

He flinched.

I stared at him. What were his intentions? He wasn't like the others in the nightclub. But why else would he be in a nightclub unless he was looking for a little action?

"You ticklish?"

He took a deep breath. "No. I mean yes. Sorta." He buried his face into his hands. "Sorry. It's just been a while."

I waited a moment; I had expected him to complete his thought, but he didn't. "A while?"

"Just going out for a drink with a beautiful woman."

My heart beat in an unfamiliar rhythm. I released an appreciative sigh and laid my hand over my chest. I hadn't had anyone, much less a man, say I was beautiful.

"So, what brought you to ask me out?"

"I-I don't know." He fidgeted. "I guess I noticed you looked nervous up there. I just wanted to see if you were okay." His leg trembled.

"Well, thanks."

Tony had said to give a man what he wanted and they would give back. I reached across the table and touched his hand, making steady eye contact.

Ned pulled away.

I parted my lips to speak but stopped.

"So, what brings you to work … well, dance in that place?"

I glanced away. I couldn't tell Ned—a stranger—about Tony. He wouldn't understand. I took a sip of the hot chocolate. "I need the money."

Ned frowned.

"Remember, you were in the club and gave me money. So, it can't be that bad."

Ned's face twitched. "I didn't want to be there. I was dragged there as a way to forget all about my ex. They told me to get out."

I rolled my eyes. "So, that's why you gave me a twenty? It's okay, you don't need to lie."

Ned was an attractive man, nice to me, but he had an ulterior motive. He had to.

He shook his head. "No! I didn't know of any other way to get your attention. I didn't mean or want to make you feel like you owed me at all. Maybe we can go bowling sometime."

The hair on the back of my nape raised. The nerve endings stirred and tingled me from head to toe. He was asking me out. Shit! Shit! Shit! I was in a relationship. I needed to tell him.

Ned lowered his gaze. "It's okay if you aren't interested."

"Sure," I stuttered out.

Damn, Jana, damn. Why are you agreeing on hanging out with another man when you're in a relationship?

"Good!"

"What do you like to do?" I blurted.

Think, Jana, think. I needed to tell him the truth. Maybe we could go as friends. It wouldn't be cheating if I went out with him as friends. I really wanted to, otherwise I wouldn't had said yes.

"Are you all right?"

I looked at my trembling legs. "Yes. I'm just super flattered."

What was he thinking about? Was I giving him false hope? I mean, I was trying to be friendly.

"What kind of movies do you like?" I asked.

Movies were a safe topic. I wanted to know more about him, but I didn't want to talk relationship or dating or any of that stuff. Not when I was in an actual relationship.

"Comedy and horror." Ned stroked his throat and smiled back. "And you?"

"Same."

In my purse, my phone vibrated. I knew it would be Tony. No one else ever texted me this time of night. I removed the phone, as I expected it to be him.

"Do you have somewhere you need to be?" Ned asked.

"It's just my roommate. I live in a bad area, and they just want to make sure I get home safely. That's all."

"I can walk you home."

I smiled. "I don't live far. But thanks for the offer." The last thing I needed was for Tony to see me with another man. I stood, getting ready to leave. "I should get going."

Ned stood as well. "I understand; it's late."

We walked outside and stood. He brushed his hand against mine. "It was nice talking to you."

"You too."

He tugged me closer, and we kissed. I didn't resist—I enjoyed it—and we pulled apart.

"I'll text you," I said.

"I look forward to it."

He turned to walk away, but I stopped him. "Wait."

I reached into my pocket and withdrew the twenty he gave me earlier in the night. "Here."

"You keep it."

I shook my head. "I don't want it. I don't want to be paid for enjoying your company. Unless …"

He took it from me. "No. I don't want you to feel that way."

This time I reached forward and pulled him in for a kiss. "Goodnight, Ned."

My phone vibrated again. This time I turned and walked away.

The closer I came to my apartment, the hollower I felt. Did I want to go home to Tony? He'd probably be drinking and in a bad mood. I could give him the money I had made tonight. But I had earned it. It was mine. Then I thought about Ned. I had just met him, and yet, I was intrigued. He was a good kisser. Good looking. And he bought me a hot chocolate. No strings attached.

I stopped short of my building. Holding one hand on the door handle, I debated whether to open it and go inside or not. He'd be waiting for me.

I reached into my purse for my keys and retrieved the note with Ned's number on it. I smiled as I found my phone and called him.

"UNTIL DEATH"
CAROLYN YOUNG

The sound of tyres crackling down the gravel driveway signaled Nathan's return. Sophie's stomach felt like she was riding a roller coaster as she picked up her list: kids fed and in bed, check; house clean and tidy, check; dinner on the table, check. Dressed nicely, with hair and makeup done, check. Everything done, everything perfect. Surely Nathan couldn't find anything to be upset about tonight. Sophie took a deep calming breath as she pasted a smile on her face and turned to greet him when he opened the door.

As Nathan stepped inside, Sophie felt her stomach drop with a thud. The scowl on his face said it all. He'd had a bad day, which meant tonight was going to be rough. Despite his scowl, he still looked so gorgeous with his thick dark hair falling in waves over his forehead. She was so lucky he'd chosen her all those years ago.

They'd met at secondary school, and it had been love at first sight for both of them. It hadn't taken long for them to move from a shy smile across the room to passionate bedroom romps. She'd been a virgin, and he'd been so gentle with her the first time. He'd been the perfect boyfriend, at the beginning of their relationship. Changes came later but had been so subtle that she hadn't even noticed them happening until it was too late.

"Where're the kids?" he asked.

"In bed asleep, darling," she whispered, flinching as he reached towards her and pushed the hair from her face.

"Who are you all tarted up for?" he asked, his face flushing a deep shade of red.

"No-one. I thought you liked it when I made myself look good for when you get home."

"Well, you look like a whore. Go wash it off and get the kids up. I want to see them."

"But they're already asleep."

"You're always keeping them from me. I'm their dad. I want to see them," he said and sat at the table.

Sophie removed her makeup, her hands visibly shaking as she watched her face transform back to the pale sheen from earlier. She remembered how he used to love it when she'd dress up for him. On their wedding day, he couldn't stop telling everyone how lucky he was to be spending the rest of his life with such a beautiful woman. If only she'd known what was coming, she wouldn't have gone through with it. But she had, and she took her vows seriously.

Rousing the kids, she blinked away the beginning of tears. Last night he'd been upset because they were still awake when he got home. She had no way of predicting what would set him off each night.

Tiny Lauren lay draped over her mother's shoulder, dozing back off as soon as she'd been picked up, but Toby stood beside her rubbing his eyes with one hand and tightly gripping her leg with the other.

"Where's the other one?" Nathan asked.

"Tamsyn's staying at Rachael's house tonight. Remember we talked about it last night?"

"You're lying again. You never mentioned her going anywhere. I want my daughter at home. She's fourteen-years-old. She should be home in her own bed at night, not out gallivanting with friends." Nathan's face turned an even deeper shade of red, his scowl making her feel like the room was spinning.

Sophie could remember them sitting down together and having the discussion. He'd even asked her to make sure there were no boys staying the night. She felt so tired and so confused. Maybe she'd dreamt it.

"I'm so sorry. I thought I asked you. I'll go get her if you like."

"No, leave her there. But remember, it's your fault if she ends up pregnant and on drugs. You're supposed to be raising her." He turned his attention to his son. "Come here, Toby."

Toby stared at the floor, shook his head and burrowed his face into his mother's leg.

"What have you been saying to them about me? A son should look his father in the eyes."

"Nothing. I haven't said anything to him about you," Sophie replied quietly.

"Well, that's part of the problem. You should be telling them how lucky they are to have me and how hard I work for them. You're making them into sooks, especially the boy. Get them out of my sight. They make me sick."

Sophie took the kids to their room. Lauren rolled over, barely having woken at all, but Toby was making gentle whimpers. Sophie looked at her son's tear-streaked face and pulled him into her arms.

"I made Daddy mad, didn't I?" he asked, sobbing.

"No, you didn't. It was my fault. Daddy wanted to see you before you went to bed. He was just disappointed when you were already asleep. Now hop into bed, and I'll tuck you in."

Sophie lightly kissed him on the forehead. "Go to sleep. I'll see you in the morning. I love you."

Sophie paused at the door, taking a deep breath to calm her racing heart. Her stomach fluttered nervously. She'd seen him like this so many times before, but each time seemed worse than the previous.

The first time they'd argued was before they were married. She'd had to work late and cancelled a date. He accused her of having an affair with her boss. She'd been terrified of the intensity of his rage; he hadn't hit her that time, but she'd still been scared. The next day, he'd been so sorry. He'd bought her flowers and chocolates and told her he loved her so much that he'd gotten carried away when he thought he was going to lose her. He promised he'd never scream at her like that again, and she'd forgiven him.

A few days later, he'd explained to her how his reaction was a result of what she'd said. She'd made him feel jealous and inadequate. He said her boss expected too much from her, and she should quit and find a new job. She'd refused. She loved her job and her coworkers but agreed to stop going to afterwork functions, so they could spend more time together.

"What's this slop?" he asked, flicking a blob of mashed potato at her.

"It's mashed potato. Well, shepherd's pie to be exact. You said it was your favourite," she said, her voice trembling slightly.

"Well, it's crap. I work damn hard. The least you could do is provide me with a decent meal when I get home at night," he said, lifting the plate before tipping it and smashing it on the floor.

Sarah took a step backwards, studying the ruined meal on the floor. Her eyes stung with tears, and she firmly pressed her tongue against the roof of her mouth. She'd read somewhere that if you did that, it was impossible to cry, and she knew what would happen if Nathan saw a tear fall.

Most men she'd met reacted to tears with compassion, but, over the years, she'd learned tears just made Nathan angrier. The first time she'd cried during an argument was the first time he'd backhanded her across the room. She'd been upset because he wanted to take a job interstate, which would mean her moving away from all her friends and family. She'd have to quit her job and sacrifice her financial independence. Her sister had just had a baby boy, and she didn't want to move so far away. She wanted to be a part of their lives. That had been when she'd first shed a tear, and his reaction had been both ferocious and unexpected. She'd had to take a week off work for the swelling on her cheek to go down then wear heavy makeup to cover the bruising that persisted for weeks. Her cheek had still shown the last smudge of faded yellow when the removalists arrived.

Sophie had to admit, at first, the move interstate had gone well. Nathan had been so happy; he'd showered her with gifts and attention. He'd told her that now she wasn't working, she was doing a much better job of meeting his needs, and the arguments stopped for a while.

It wasn't too long though before he'd decided she was spending too much money and started giving her an allowance. If she needed more money, she'd have to ask for it and justify why she didn't have any of her allowance left. Sophie had always been financially independent. She'd had an afterschool job from the time she was fifteen and wasn't used to having to account for every cent.

The day the refrigerator died and she'd had to ask him for money for a new one saw the end of the time of peace. He'd beaten her and choked her until she passed out, and, when she came to, she felt his aroused body pressing hers down onto the floor.

It wasn't long afterwards she realized she was pregnant with Tamsyn, and Nathan was delighted. Sophie was still in shock.

She wanted to return home to her family, but she had no money and no idea where to get help in this strange town.

Nathan checked on her constantly. She wasn't allowed to leave the house without ringing to tell him where she was going and when she'd be back. He told her it was for her safety. She didn't know the area well, so he needed to know where she was to make sure she was safe, especially with the baby on the way. He regularly checked her phone records to see who she was ringing, and she had to justify any phone calls to numbers he didn't know. He screamed at her if she didn't answer her phone within the first three rings.

Fear kept her there—fear of him finding her and bringing her back. She wasn't sure she'd survive the beating that would ensue. The most dangerous time for an abused woman was just after she tried to leave. Sophie had read that in a magazine somewhere. Many women just disappeared, their bodies discovered months or years later, or sometimes never found. Sophie knew Nathan was clever enough to get away with it. She'd never be found. She was sure of it.

Most of the time their relationship was good. He could be so much fun and so loving, especially after he'd beaten her. He was always so sorry, and he bought her gifts—not just the token flowers and chocolates but gifts she cherished: a day at the spa, a new haircut, or outfit. If she could just stop being so flawed, she was sure things would be perfect between them.

And he was wonderful with the kids most of the time, especially Tamsyn. He adored her. Lately, he'd taken to going into her room each night just to chat. Sometimes he'd be there for hours. But Tamsyn was looking pale and making excuses to stay away from home. Maybe she had a boyfriend. She'd have to talk to her tomorrow.

Looking at the remains of dinner smeared across the floor and her husband's bulging red eyes, Sophie wished she had walked out the door long ago and gone to the police for help. Now that he'd learned how to hurt her without leaving marks, it would be so much harder to get them to believe her. He'd perfected the steady firm pressure he needed to apply to her throat to make her pass out without leaving a mark.

Lately, she was sure she was going crazy. Her memory was going too. She wasn't sure if it was due to the intermittent loss of blood to her brain due to him choking her or if it really was postnatal depression like he said. Even his friends had noticed it when they went out for dinner. She'd mention something, and he'd remind her that it hadn't happened then apologized for her poor memory. Afterwards, he'd told her how embarrassing it was to be out with her and how all his friends agreed something was definitely wrong with her. They hadn't been invited out as a couple since, and he'd told her that his friends found her boring and strange. They didn't want her around.

She often wondered what had happened to her friends back home. They'd kept in touch for a while, but it got harder as time went on. She'd always equated it to Nathan not wanting her to have phone calls when he was home, but sometimes she wondered if something was wrong with her that made them stop calling.

Sophie grabbed a roll of paper towels and a bag and started cleaning the mess. Looking up, she watched Nathan walk from room to room. Her hands shook as she sensed his rage worsening. She looked towards the front door—only metres away—but, remembering her babies asleep in their room, continued with her cleaning.

It's not that she thought Nathan would hurt the kids. He'd always been so gentle with them, and she could see how much he loved them. Sometimes when they were asleep at night, she'd go searching for him and find him gazing at them with a look she'd never seen before. It was beautiful and special. She never wanted to do anything to stop them from having a good relationship with their dad, but leaving them with him, especially when he was in one of his moods, warred with every motherly instinct she had left.

According to Nathan, that wasn't many. He'd always said she should never have become a mother. She didn't have the patience, couldn't keep the kids clean and well-behaved, and having them had made her fat and lazy. No matter how much she loved them, she knew she'd failed when it came to providing them with a good home environment. The house was never clean enough; she kept running out of money—so their clothes were often too small or stained—and she sometimes got grumpy with them when she hadn't gotten enough sleep.

Sleep deprivation had never been a problem for her when the babies were little. She'd just taken a nap during the day when they did. Her biggest problem with sleep came from Nathan. He'd taken to keeping her awake at night, discussing her faults and how he thought she should fix them. He could ramble all night. She couldn't stop him, and she found herself agreeing with everything he said just so they could have sex and she could finally sleep. She saw no point disagreeing with him, and, over time, she didn't need to pretend to agree; she knew what he said was true.

Over the years, she'd realized she was lucky he tolerated her; she did so many things wrong. And he was popular. Everyone liked him—even her friends and family at first, before he'd decided she should focus her attention solely on him. They understood though. She was lucky someone so wonderful had chosen her. She knew she was plain-looking and was not that smart, so, for someone as perfect as him to have put up with her all these years, she felt blessed. Sure, he beat her sometimes, but she always deserved it. It was her fault. If only she could just get things right, she knew he wouldn't need to hit her anymore. But she could never get things right. No matter how hard she tried.

Sophie put away the paper towels, gave the floor a quick mop and walked through the house to find Nathan. He was in bed, holding her phone, flicking through the phone numbers. For a moment, she stiffened then relaxed when she realized she hadn't received any calls today.

"So, who rang you today?" he asked. "Got a new boyfriend, I see."

"No-one. I didn't get any calls," she whispered, barely able to hear herself.

"Liar! You had a call at three twenty-three from someone. Who was it?"

"It was a wrong number," she said, backing away. Why hadn't she remembered the wrong number? She was so stupid.

"Who was it?" he demanded, flinging off the covers and stomping towards her with his hands reaching for her throat.

"No-one. I don't know. It was a wrong number," she stuttered, her heart thumping wildly in her chest as she looked towards the door and wondered if she had time to escape before he reached her.

His huge hands encircled her throat as her feet left the floor. Panic flooded through her as she felt the first signs of oxygen deprivation. Dark spots appeared in front of her eyes, and her hands and feet tingled. She reached her hands to his, to try to pry them off, but he was too strong. With her vision completely gone and her body heavier than it had ever felt, she gave one last effort to struggle from his grasp before she lost consciousness. The last thing she heard before she passed out was Toby's scream.

Gasping frantically, she realized it was over. She wrapped her arms around her body so thankful to have survived his fury one more time. All was quiet in the house, and she wondered where he was. Had he fallen asleep or gone for a drive to cool off? Her eyes were still tightly closed when she remembered Toby's scream and felt his warmth pressing against her side.

Toby!

Her eyes popped open as she rolled her son onto his back, his blue lips revealing what she couldn't quite believe. It couldn't be true—her precious son. She breathed into his mouth, willing him to take a breath of his own, but she was so weak, and he'd been gone too long. Her useless breaths turned from sobs into wails of despair as she rocked his limp body in her arms, wishing desperately she could swap places with him. Time stood still for Sophie as she cradled her son, lightly caressing his hair and kissing his cheek.

A thump came from the kitchen, and Sophie fell silent, waiting for Nathan to return to their room to kill her too. She felt nothing but the grim acceptance of her fate and the slight cooling of her son's body in her arms.

But instead of Nathan's footsteps, she heard his voice—shaky, as if holding back tears. "Is this the police? My wife. She murdered our son. She's been acting strangely lately. I put it down to postnatal depression, but I think maybe it's psychosis. Our friends noticed it too. But we never thought she'd do this. Oh my god, she killed my son. Please hurry."

"TRAPPED BY DESIGN"
LILITH SINCLAIR

Ava covered her blue eyes and the next moment yelled, "Peek-a-boo," to her two-year-old daughter.

Rayleen giggled, her silver hair floating around her cute little face. Her purple eyes sparkled with magic. In a hurry, the toddler copied her mom but forgot to cover her eyes; she flung her arms wide and hollered the familiar phrase with such glee that only a child could.

Brock's deep chuckle filled the house, adding to the aura of life that pulsed within. "I miss having kids that age. I tell my wife she isn't too old, but you know how gargoyles are." He slipped his hands in his jeans and glanced through the glass door.

Stubborn was the first word to pop into Ava's mind, but she chuckled quietly behind her hand.

"Okay, Rayleen. Do you want to try your glamour again?" Ava held the little girl's tiny hands in her own.

The toddler nodded vigorously. "Yes." Her voice sounded like fae bells in the Spring Gardens.

"Let's work on your hair. Can you turn it purple?" Ava raised a purple block for Rayleen to focus on.

Rayleen took a deep breath, squared her shoulders and closed her eyes. As magic hummed along her skin, faint lines of blue flowed, like ink. Her little pink tongue darted outward, wetting her lips. A purple the color of plums bled from her hair follicles and overtook her silver locks.

Ava watched Rayleen's magic slumber; her skin cooled to the color of honey flavored caramels, and her hair held its purple hue. "Great job, sweetie." Pride swelled in her heart. "Okay, can you change it to brown, like the coffee beans Daddy uses?" She modified her own hair to mimic the shade.

Rayleen nodded once, and the hum of magic filled her body again. Quicker than the purple, a reddish-brown hue flowed over her hair. Her eyes popped open. With a charming smile, Rayleen's eyes bled to emerald green.

Ava gasped in surprise. "Your daddy will be so proud of you." Ava searched for weariness in Rayleen's tiny body, concerned about overtaxing the child's abilities.

Rayleen's ability to channel the variances seemed endless, as she had proven to have a natural talent for glamour—one that not many could peer through.

"Daddy." Rayleen's smile widened.

"Yes. Daddy should be here soon. Why don't you go play in your room, and I'll make us breakfast?" She kissed Rayleen's brown hair and gave thanks when the little tyke obeyed without question.

Ava waited until she heard the television turn on, and *Scooby-Doo*'s theme song wafted from the room. She stood from the ottoman and faced Brock.

Brock was impossibly handsome, as if carved by a master in stone. He leaned against the wall between the kitchen and the living room. His gaze never stagnant as he worked security. Glamour was as much a part of his arsenal, making him appear human, as was his skill with claw and wing. "She's going to be powerful."

Ava gave a tight-lipped smile. "I'm afraid she already is." Worry creased her brow, but that was as far as she'd let those thoughts go. "Brock, why don't you go ahead and call it a day.

I'm sure Orion will be home soon, and I have taken care of myself before." Ava was a spirit kitsune, a rarity among the thirteen branches—not the strongest but even an adolescent kitsune was dangerous.

"No thanks, Ava. I promised him I'd stay here and keep you and Rayleen safe until he got home." He took a sip from the glass of water and set it back on the coaster, returning back to scanning the yard through the french doors.

Ava shrugged. This wasn't the first time Orion had been late from work nor was it the first time she had tried to get Brock to go home to his wife. She tucked her black hair behind her ear and headed toward the kitchen. She stifled a yawn and looked at Brock.

The sun called for him to slumber, just as the yellow-orange ball of gas did to her. She wondered, not for the first time, if raising Rayleen on a human schedule was smart.

"I'm going to do a security check." Brock shook his head. His fingers tugged at his ears.

"You okay?"

"Yes. Just a ringing in my ears. Probably from the TV. You know how electricity is."

She did know. Everything in the human world hummed with the vital power supply. She chalked it up to another difference they would adjust to soon.

The refrigerator light clicked on as the door opened, and she grabbed the cartoon of eggs.

She sighed; life was so much easier before they had agreed to raise Rayleen in the human world. At least in Ataria, magic was the norm; food was summoned, clothes sized perfectly, house cleaned with a simple snap of her fingers. She cringed and rubbed her ears, trying to get the phantom roar of vacuum from ringing in her ears.

She should talk to Orion about hiring a human to help, at least until she had a handle on the basics. Maybe she could talk to Sahara and move Rayleen there.

A board creaked at the back of the house. Ava's ears twitched. Silence.

"Brock? Are you in the office?" She set the pan on the counter and eased into the living room.

Ava took two steps toward her Rayleen's door, pausing outside the safeguard shields. Child's laughter mixed with Shaggy's "Zoinks!" floated from within. The television's chatter did nothing to calm the nerves that danced along Ava's nape. The house felt impossibly still, like the calm before battle.

The slow throbbing pain pulsed above her brow. The warning bells conflicted with the anxiety she'd had since they officially moved to the sleepy subdivision.

Her tails flicked, intangible like smoke on the winds. She tasted the air, and her eyes narrowed on the hallway. Neither the overwhelming scent of fabric softener nor the crisp scent of lemon cleaner clung to the air.

With an auditable *pop*, the realm of the banished tore a rift into the human realm. Lightning crackled across the dimensions, and chunks of ceiling crashed to the floor.

A daera puckered its lips and blew across its hand. Blue flames slithered down its arm. The demon foot soldier threw the fire snake at Brock with precision.

Brock's glamour vanished as he crashed through the glass doors. His stone skin turned black with soot, and he snorted an irritated sound. His leathery wings beat a blast of forced air against the black-and-red striped daera as he charged with claws at his target.

The anthropomorphic reptilian moved akin to the slithering serpent of flames it controlled as another flame raced toward Brock's open wings.

Brock tucked his wings and crashed through the coffee table before slipping into the fragmented reality.

The creatures battered him with spells, and his claws tore flesh from the fiend's shoulder. Black ooze poured from the wound, and a fiend snarled. Its thin lips peeled back, and the cadence of reinforcements bellowed from its tiny form.

A large bovine demon materialized. The warden-ranked creature charged, and the collision forced Brock from the banished plane back into the human world.

He crashed into the wall, and sheets of drywall cracked and fell. Two-by-fours hung, like jagged teeth, kept together by plastic covered wires.

Scamps and other daevas began to rally from the inky depths. A secondary squad lined the rip and tossed green fire while squad by squad the foot soldiers spilled from their accursed realm.

With a furious growl, Brock launched from the ground and smashed through the growing fodder that separated him and foe.

Another mustard-yellow version of the reptilian daera climbed through another dimensional rift. Her forked tongue flicked in the heated air. Her tail whipped back and forth; the end tapered into a serrated spear.

Ava risked a glance toward her daughter's door. An inky mist rolled against the edges of the shield; its magic burned across the thing's mental synapses causing the creature to hiss.

The she-demon cackled as her venom-tip claws slashed at Ava's face while her tricky tail aimed for Ava's thigh.

Ava lunged to the left and tripped over the demon's tail. Her hands burned as splinters from the broken floor wormed their way into her flesh.

"Are you insane? Get the fuck out of here, Ava!" Brock ripped off the horned head of a lesser demon; its vacant stare gawked at her as he slung the decapitated head toward the once-pretty kitchen, hitting a vile creature with a resounding *thunk* and knocking it through a new rift.

"Rayleen!" If she tried to phase through the shields, she could compromise the only thing that kept Rayleen safe. Ava's forearm snapped upward to brace against the yellow daera's swipe, and her arm throbbed from the impact.

"Go. I will get Rayleen to safety." In the heat of battle, his voice lost the edge of humankind and sounded rough.

Regardless of how much trust and faith she had in Brock, the situation broke her heart—the thought of leaving her only child in the hands of anyone other than her own.

With tears in her eyes, she nodded and dashed through what remained of the front door.

A ring of demon-kin waited for her along the subdivision's cul-de-sac. Mages, dressed in hooded robes of various sizes, hid behind the wall of fiends. Sprinkled throughout the various goblins, orcs and their larger cousin ogres smashed their giant wooden clubs against their palms and the ground. Vile things flew overhead, and their shadows moved across the blacktop in the morning light.

A jinn shackled with charmed silver met her gaze. His face was distorted by his vaporous state, but the sullen look of a broken spirit beckoned her for help.

In another time, Ava would have done anything to help, but she could feel the calling of the prophecy. The written word flared with ancient magic as it set from the prophecy to reality.

Ava's suppressed powers flickered from ember to flame. Her glamour faded, and her foxlike ears seemingly sprung from her hair. Her tails snapped into existence, like lighting paired with thunder. She randomly tossed blue balls of flame—will-o-wisp—before she concentrated on erecting a wall between her and the vermin sent to capture her and her daughter.

The windows of her home exploded outward as the protection shield vaporized. Shards of glass sliced friend and foe alike. Large chunks laid upon her once-pretty yard, and some of the lesser minions were flattened beneath the rubble.

Rayleen. Her protection faltered. In the split-second hesitation of worry, mage goblins trapped her in a vortex of wind that ripped her breath from her. Pain radiated across Ava's chest as the jinn blocked her connection to her demon-form, and, without the lifeline, her synapses burned with the raw energy of the world. She crumpled against the concrete porch, and tears trailed down her face as the burden became overwhelming.

Gravity had help, as the mages' chant increased the pressure pushing against Ava's frame. The back of her head and neck throbbed as she tried to fight against the agony and heaviness.

With blurry vision, Ava tried to fracture reality and jump into the ley lines. Any place would have sufficed, in this new world or the old world.

A rumble of laughter followed the pain that fried the last of Ava's synapses, and she lapsed into unconsciousness.

Ava winced as she took a breath. The air was different—complex and aromatic, like a great stew. She licked her parched lips, and the biting taste of copper greeted her.

She cracked open her eyes to total darkness. Impossible. Spindling energy should have been instantaneous. But instead, Ava felt nothing but emptiness.

Her head ratcheted, like a sprinkler, as she tried to piece it all together.

"Different, isn't it?" There was no mistaking the elfin pitch. "I would imagine this is what humans witness every day." He chuckled, and the sound seemed to come from everywhere.

"Face me, you coward," Ava yelled into the nothingness.

"I could be inches from your lush lips, and you wouldn't be able to tell."

Ava jumped as his sweet breath tickled her nose and tasted like apple pie. She hadn't expected him to be so close.

She lunged forward and was immediately forced backward into the stone chair. Anger boiled to the surface to be replaced like an ice bath of fear; its sickly scent missing to her once-sharp nose.

She'd spent over a century honing her skills, learning to trust her gut, and rely on the power within, and this man had stripped her bare. Bare enough she couldn't even tell a spell hovered over her skin until it pierced her flesh and forced her to comply.

Rayleen. Oh, her daughter. Her shoulders trembled alongside withheld sobs over what this man had done to her daughter and the realization she had lost Brock—a friend and guardian.

On the next breath, she squared her shoulders. She was a spirit kitsune, only wife to Orion—the Demon King, void kitsune of the ninth level, and more. She would not break.

Her lips curled into a snarl, and the deep rumble grew from within before the sound echoed around the room.

The audible gasps surprised Ava; she wasn't alone with just the elf. The globe of darkness dissipated as fire flared on the oiled rag of torches.

Thirteen magical beings dressed in various robes of color stood at the very edge of the rune-engraved circle. A few could almost pass for human. Others were so grossly anomalous that they were the thing of nightmares and crazed apparitions.

The elf should have been a thing of myths. A lean, dark elf with hair the color of snow and skin the color of the darkest parts of the universe stood in the rune circle with her.

"Nothing to say?" the elf taunted.

"Nothing to a demon like you," Ava snapped back.

The elf laughed, but the humor never bled into his apathetic gaze. "Isn't that the demon calling the kettle?"

Ava couldn't help to chuckle at his chunkiness with human idioms. "I may be a fox demon, but I don't purposefully upset the balance for money or pleasure. Unlike you and your daera scum." Ava licked her lips and tried to suppress the dread that slowly wormed its way into her mind.

The elf nodded and pretended to look elsewhere in the small cave carved room as he went and stood in a spot in front of her. Its smooth walls clashed with the rough chiseled marks.

Even with the globe of darkness gone and the light from the fires, Ava couldn't decipher much past the edges of the circle and the people who surrounded her.

The minutes ticked by, and nothing could be heard except the rustling of clothes.

Ava shifted to alleviate the unease that steadily grew. He had more than enough power to kill her. She'd figured that out from the spells binding her to the chair and the suppression of her fox. The longer he waited to say or do anything, Ava's worry grew that this would not be a swift death.

The runes around the elf began to glow. First a faint pulse grew into a blazing flame. As each rune became self-sustaining, their colors changed to harmonize with the adjacent ones—a rainbow, but dark and twisted.

"You are either very clever or very stupid, fox." The elf pulled a small athame from his robes. "You haven't begged for your life nor the life of your daughter. While we don't have her yet, we will."

Ava's heart soared. Rayleen was alive, and Brock had kept his promise. Time was indeed short. Her mind raced about what she could do.

"Your death is just the beginning, and your blood will run like a river of power to my vessels." The elf cackled. He was so self-sure. Arrogant.

Blood. She may not have access to the ley lines or her demon magic, but blood magic wasn't an impossibility. The forbidden arts were prohibited for the sacrifice of life they required, but her life was already forfeit.

The hairs on Ava's arms stood erect. The people surrounding her began a chant, and a heady wind arose.

Ava's mind turned inward as she began to focus her intent.
Daughters of the Moon.
Hear my plea.
Shroud my only child in your embrace.
Let her grow strong and defiant against those who prey on others.
Use my life to blanket her from enemies until she is strong enough to stand against them.
Bring her into your embrace Daughters of the Moon.
Selena, Artemis, Luna, Celestia, Serenity …
So entrenched in her plead, Ava had become numb to the world around her.

The elf smirked and sliced into Ava's pinned arms and watched as her blood cascaded to the ground. Satisfied, he pulled a silver watch embossed with runes from his pocket. The chain clinked and swayed as he let the dagger's wet decoration drip onto the watch face.

The silver mist of her soul began to float from her body, and he began to capture it into the relic he held.

Ava's vision dimmed.

He thought he had the last laugh, except the Daughters of the Moon had heard Ava's plea.

The once-powerful blood held enough energy to feed all the masses gathered; instead, it became the taint that would destroy the circle so bent on helping the Syndicate.

As her blood's power fed into the creatures gathered, one by one the magic flared. Like Holy Water to the tainted, it burned the host from the inside out. One by one, the mages popped, like an over inflated balloon, and their newly tainted blood fed back into the circle of power.

The elf tried to break the runes, but these weren't painted on. To solidify the containment of the kitsune, he had gone the extra mile and chiseled, with perfection, the circle and the accompanying symbols. His work became his prison.

He burned, like the pits of Hell itself was bubbling and smoking within him. His razor-sharp nails dug into his eyes, and blood poured down his pale skin. He clawed at his skin, and, in the wake of his destruction, it clung to muscles with jagged edges. He ripped at his neck, trying to end the internal pain.

As the elf's sight failed, the hooded robe of a reaper stood outside the circle. His scythe gleamed in the dying flames and reflected the fiery pits of Purgatory in the long-tapered blade.

The elf had thought he had the last laugh, but, as his spirit broke from the lumpy meat laid in a pool of blood, he realized the Master didn't know what he had gotten himself into. The Master could never beat the kitsune he madly sought.

The grim reaper reached a bony hand toward his soul and shackled it with enchanted silver chains. With a hearty chuckle, the reaper and the elf knew what awaited those who opposed the balance. Purgatory or Hell would have been preferred to the eternity of binding.

Orion looked at his watch and suppressed a grumble. This newly formed Council's squabble had eroded his sense of fairness. These recently elected heads were incompetent.

He walked to the large windows. The sun burned orange and red as it began to fight against the looming darkness. The sunrise had been his favorite moment of the day since he had embarked to fulfill his duty.

He rubbed at his chest as the magical tattoos itched. A force beat against the inside of his mind. In his reflection on the crystal tower's sheer walls, his demon gazed back through his purple orbs. His energy hummed along the edge of his skin; the hairs on his thick, muscled arms stood on end.

"That's enough," Orion bellowed into the conference room. He turned, and in his stead a viral mix of man and beast stood. All nine tails withered, like gorgon hair, and his obsidian-colored fur-covered ears bristled with contained power.

The lesser figureheads clamored to exit out the singular door. The pathetic excuses for leaders were more of a pack of whimpering pups in need of their mother's protection instead of the best of what the supes had to offer.

His ears twitched to the sound of warning chimes that filled the air—a sound only he could hear them. The hunger for battle and blood grew within him. That alone told him something dire had happened, as retribution called for him to answer.

As Demon King, the cry of injustice rang through his very soul. He clutched the space over his heart. The lines of magic flared with an otherworldly brilliance.

Ava. Rayleen. As he thought of his wife and daughter, the heavy scent of sulfur and burnt rice filled the air.

Brock, in gargoyle form, crashed through the conference table. Like a cocoon, his wings surrounded his stained stone façade. He coughed as he righted himself on the table's broken remains. His wings unfurled to show a brown-haired toddler with striking green eyes glaring at the unfamiliar faces.

Orion sniffed the air and cocked his head. The smell of battle and death clung to Brock's skin, and the scent of defiance clung to the little girl. Something called to the fierceness inside Orion, something about the girl.

She smelled of the forest deep in the lands of Ataria—clean and crisp, like the air after a rainfall. She smelled akin to theriomorphic—shifter.

Rayleen?

Brock shook his massive head and wings. A feral snarl crested his lips as he snapped at all who approached. "Orion."

Orion tried to speak, but his tongue felt thick and disconnected. His lips peeled back as he focused on his words. "Brock."

Brock folded a busted wing around the little girl. His stance was weary as he watched the Demon King snarl and snap, the demon fighting against his instincts to retaliate for something he did not yet know.

Orion closed his eyes and forced his demon to recede. "What happened? Rayleen?" He nodded to his daughter. "Ava?"

"Attacked." Brock reached for something tucked in a pouch at his waist. He pulled a bronze trinket from the leather bag and handed it to the Demon King. "The Master made his move."

The engraved metal housed a familiar insignia. A symbol Orion knew all too well, one that had been branded into his flesh over a century ago. The coiled cobra.

Orion looked at the three members of the Council who were stupid enough to stay in the room: Seer La'Shay, Lucifer, and the tiny demi fae, Queen Nafieria. He rubbed his bald head, postponing his question.

Before the words left his lips, the pain in his heart flared, and the call of distress pulled him from this plane.

The void stripped him of his held humanity, leaving a full fox demon in his place. His piercing gaze took in the world that surrounded him.

The robe-donned reaper tore a soul from a dark elf. From the shadowy recesses of the robes, a raspy chuckle followed the strangling sound emitting from the lump of meat trapped within a sealed circle.

Orion's tongue flicked outward, licking his muzzle and tasting the air. Heavy with magic and the stench of death, his gaze continued to survey the rough-hewed cave. Behind the meaty pile, a body slumped to the ground. Orion's heart knew what his eyes had yet to confirm.

His strides consumed the distance. The magical circle engraved into the cave's worn floor thrust his power back into him and barred his entrance. His venom-covered claws scratched at the invisible surface. His chi spindled and with a crunch; he smashed his energies against the circle's edge.

The pain he fought so desperately to ignore added to his strength. And yet, nothing could move through the barrier.

A deafening roar echoed through the confined space. The light from the torches flickered and extinguished. In the empty room void of life but filled with the oppressive energies of magic, Orion cried for his heart's fire.

"Damn you incorrigible gods. Damn you all to Purgatory and the Beyond." He was drained. Drained of everything but the feral loss.

"*Tsk. Tsk. Tsk.*" The old Crone leaned against her hobble cane; the crow's red-gemmed eye gleamed with a life of its own.

"You knew the prophecy just as she." The Mother raised an eyebrow to the Crone.

"At least you have your daughter." Leave it to the Maiden to think that alone justified Ava's death.

The three goddesses became a mesh of all the Moon Goddesses—the pure, the trickery, the stubborn, the elegant, and more. Behind their worldly glow, their features wavered and moved, as if viewed through quivering waters.

"Why didn't you protect her? She was one of yours." In his grief, will-o-wisps sparked from his hand. His anger propelled them, but the goddesses smirked as the purple-hued flames perished, like a candle to a gust of breath.

"She did not ask us to, you stupid man." The Crone had no love for men and even less for love.

"Isn't that why we pray and offer? We dedicate our services to your whims, and you protect us." He slumped to the ground; his demon form gone. His hand pressed against the glass-like barrier, unable to touch or hold Ava's body.

"We cannot upset the balance any more than you can. Death and life are unavoidable." The Mother smoothed her long dress and kneeled beside the Demon King. She laid a hand against Orion's cheek. "She didn't ask us to save her. She gave her life protecting your daughter, and, in return of the selfless act, we allowed her blood to kill those stupid enough to cage her. Her prison became theirs."

"We cannot break the runes that bind the circle. This cave will be her grave." The Maiden's hand flared white as she laid it upon the magical shield. "Her soul is in the Forever Gardens."

The Crone advanced a step closer and nudged Orion's bare foot with her cane. "You fought to prevent the prophecy. Destiny is not one to be trifled with. You are the Demon King before all else."

The Mother forced Orion to look at her. "Do not let this discourage you, young one. We all love, and we all lose it. But do not lose yourself to the grief."

As the glow of the goddesses dimmed, the pain stayed, and the path of what lay ahead of him remained. His demon form laid dormant, unsure of what it could do.

He climbed to his feet, sure the goddesses were wrong. There had to be a way to remove Ava from that accursed trap. As he walked around the room, his apparel changed to the armor of the Demon King—imbued leather and dwarf armor by master craftsmen.

On the back wall, shackled with silver chain, the jinn laid curled in a misty ball.

"Jinn." Orion sent a tendril of energy on the single word to pry into the withered husk that reminded of the creature, trapping him on one plane of existence.

The jinn shivered as the power shocked him out of his ethereal form. He rose slowly to face the man who called to him. "Master," he croaked.

Orion rubbed the back of his neck. The jinn's future wasn't an easy choice to make. The jinn had a hand in Ava's death, but the charmed chain left little doubt it was against his control.

Ava would have asked him to spare the jinn, but a jinn that powerful, with the ability to impede a supe as powerful as she, was a danger Ataria and the human world couldn't afford.

His nails gave way to claws as sharp as the dagger he wore. He sliced into the amalgamated being and forced his venom into the wound, chasing it with his magic and burning the life from the creature until it evaporated into nothing.

The Master wanted a fight; Orion would make him regret that decision. Vengeance would be his.

"CHARLIE & GUS"
TRAVIS WEST

Charlie Beltran watched the falling stream of apple juice and bovine slobber with delight. This had always been his favorite part of pulling hours with his grandpa's lawn service. At the end of each workday, Grandpa Gus drove to the McCready farm west of town and emptied the barrels of cut grass filling the pickup bed. Gustavo Beltran would back his truck to the pasture gate, the cows already running for their supper.

Charlie thought they were funny; the cows had the run of fifteen acres of prime Kansas grazing land, yet they preferred the fresh clippings from some rich-ass doctor's front yard. He couldn't blame them either. The sweet, rotten aroma of grass clippings was his favorite smell. Not the fresh-cut lawn smell everybody seemed to love, but the smell of grass clippings baked all afternoon in a plastic barrel under the July sun. They would dump a barrel, getting blasted with a roiling stew of grass dust, pollen, and steaming hydrocarbons. Charlie loved it. So did the cows. They also loved the apples.

Old Lady Childers had two apple trees on her property. They were overrun with big, black carpenter ants which almost always ended up in the fruit, leaving most of the apples unfit for consumption. The first plan of action upon arrival at Old Lady Childers' was to pull a barrel between the trees and start tossing in fallen apples. Every so often, Charlie found one without holes and set the fruit aside for lunch, but most were ant ruined. The cows loved them, chomping them to bits—pulp, stem, seeds, ants, and all. Watching the animals drool over the apples was a hoot. Cows were usually boring, stupid creatures, but Charlie swore they looked excited when he and Grandpa Gus arrived with baked grass and apples. That was his favorite part of the job.

Charlie's least favorite was the patronizing way some of the customers—mostly retired doctors and lawyers, one current judge—spoke to his grandfather. They acted too nice, and Charlie suspected they spoke in proud tones to their friends about having a good Mexican to tend their yard. He wondered if Grandpa Gus knew. Probably so, Gustavo Beltran was no dummy.

The boy was captivated by the slobbering cattle, and he jumped a little when the old man placed a hand on his shoulder.

"Work is over, *mijo*. Time to go home, get a big glass of sweet tea and watch *The Dukes of Hazzard*."

"All right, Grandpa." He wiped the sweat from his face with his T-shirt and climbed into the truck.

Gustavo's old International Harvester pickup still had an 8-track tape player, and he only owned two tapes: one by Freddy Fender and one by Conway Twitty (Grandpa Gus always called him Conway "Titty") and Loretta Lynn. Charlie had heard them both countless times but was happy Freddy Fender was playing at the moment.

They reached the stop sign at the end of the gravel road. The truck idled for a couple moments before Charlie realized they weren't moving.

"What's going on, Grandpa? Everything okay?"

The old man shrugged and chuckled. "I could ask you the same thing. Are you okay, *mijo*? You been *preocupado* all day."

Charlie didn't speak Spanish and neither did his father. His grandparents never passed the language to their children, instead using Spanish as a means of conducting adult business around their kids without being understood. Charlie, like his father, aunts and uncles and cousins, only knew a spattering of words. The resulting light Spanglish spoken at family gatherings confused any friends the grandchildren of Gustavo and Cecilia Beltran brought by the household, but, to Charlie and his cousins, it was life.

"*Preocupado*, Grandpa?"

"Yeah. Troubled, lost in your thoughts."

Charlie wanted to tell him how he felt, how he could see through those rich *gueros* Grandpa Gus worked for. Instead, he kept his mouth shut. He didn't want to anger his grandfather by sticking his nose where it didn't belong. For Grandpa Gus, those situations were the way of the world and a paycheck earned. Charlie kept his feelings to himself. What did come from his mouth surprised him.

"Grandpa, I've been seeing this girl. Her name's Belinda." He paused and looked to his grandfather, who nodded. He couldn't believe he was about to tell this story. At least it was true. "Since last fall. I guess it's pretty serious, 'though I'll spare you the details. I mean, you are—"

Grandpa Gus let out the dorkiest laugh Charlie had ever heard. "Your grandpa. I get it, *mijo*. Go on."

Charlie rubbed his clammy hands on his jeans. "There's this guy we go to school with, name's Denny. Back in April, he starts trying to move in-between us. Belinda says to him, she's not interested, but he wouldn't fucking let up. Oh, shit … Sorry, Grandpa. I'm sorry I said that."

Grandpa Gus waved off the apology. "What we call situationally appropriate."

Charlie sighed relief. "Okay. Anyway, he won't give up, right? Starts asking Belinda why she keeps wasting her time with a greasy Mexican."

"*Pinche pendejo!*" Gus hissed.

"Exactly. And it's summertime. Belinda's hanging at the pool with all her friends nearly every day. Denny's there all the time too. Meanwhile, my days are spent mowing yards. No offense either, Grandpa. I really appreciate the moneymaking opportunity. But, this … *pendejo*—"

Gus nodded again.

"This *pendejo* sees her in a swimsuit way more than I ever do. And he just won't leave her alone. She's getting kinda scared of him. So—so I took care of it. Last night."

The 8-track was still playing. Gus lowered the volume.

"Oh, *mijo*," he said. "What did you do?"

"You know my cousin, Conqui, on my mom's side? He gave me one of those little collapsible batons. It's a self-defense weapon."

"I've seen them," Grandpa Gus said.

"I started carrying it everywhere. Last night, I went to the cinema with my friend, Richard, to see *Mad Max Beyond Thunderdome*—crazy movie, Grandpa. But anyway, we see Denny ahead of us leaving with a couple of his friends. I told Richard to hold up while I used the restroom. I didn't really have to go so much as I just didn't want to see the guy face to face. Which seems stupid to me now, because he should be avoiding *me*, right?"

Grandpa Gus shrugged.

"When I come out, Denny's unchaining his bicycle from the rack outside the theater. We get in Richard's car and follow him out the parking lot. I say something to Richard about wanting to get Denny for messing with Belinda, and he says he's still got a black jacket and ski mask from last winter in his trunk."

"*Hijole*," Gus said, covering his eyes but peeking between the fingers. He checked the rearview. They were still alone at the stop sign.

"Richard turned right at the next corner," Charlie said, "left at the next and shot up three blocks to get ahead of Denny. I grabbed the jacket and mask from the trunk and put 'em on then ran around the corner and hid behind a car away from the streetlight. Got there just in time too, because soon as I crouched down, here he comes. He never had time to react. I stepped out in front of him and swung the baton. I aimed for his arm but went a bit high and caught him on the collarbone—think I cracked it good too. Denny twists himself around the seat and off the bike. When he hit the street, I started working on his knees and ribs with the baton, and ..."

Gustavo Beltran stared at his grandson—the quiet boy who, until yesterday, he would have sworn could not hurt a bug. *Oh, how they grow.*

"What is it, *mijo?*" Gus asked with no small amount of trepidation.

"Have you heard of Eddie Murphy, Grandpa?"

"The comedian, right? The black fella."

"Yeah, he had this movie come out right before last Christmas called *Beverly Hills Cop*. For some reason, as I'm beating Denny, I think of that movie, and I started shouting in Eddie Murphy's voice, 'Leave that girl at the pool alone, muthafuckah! She don't want none o' you!'"

Gus recoiled from the sudden deep shouts, but Charlie failed to notice.

"And then I laugh like him too. He's got a very distinctive laugh, Grandpa. No one sounds like him. I don't know why I did that, I just—"

"You wanted him to think you were black?"

"Maybe. Maybe I just didn't want him to know it was me."

Seconds rolled by without either man, young or old, saying a word. Charlie searched for any clue as to what his grandfather was thinking.

"I beat the shit outta him, Grandpa."

Gus smiled and looked at his second son's son. "You're scared, huh, *mijo*?"

"Yes."

"Of this Denny cat? Or the police?"

"Either, and, or."

"If this was last night, I don't think you have to worry about police. It's already five-thirty. You'd know by now if the cops were looking for you. This town ain't that big. As far as this Denny is concerned, who knows? Maybe he knows it was you, maybe he don't. Maybe he'll come after you, maybe he won't."

Gus shifted the truck into Drive and moved onto the highway.

That's it? Charlie wondered. *After all I tell him, that's all he says to me?*

Gus cranked the volume, and Freddy Fender once again sang them home. Barely past the Welcome to Benson sign, Gus slowed the truck and turned into the parking lot of a local greenhouse, empty now that all the employees had gone home for the day. Freddy Fender belted, "Wasted Days and Wasted Nights."

"Good song," Gus said before turning off the music again. Sweat rolled down his nose, and he wiped his face with a handkerchief. "*Mijo*, I can't say whether what you did was right or wrong. Standing up for your girl, defending your honor—those situations can lead you into morally blurry territories. You have to tread carefully, or doing what you believe is right can cause heartache and suffering for someone else. What you did, maybe he's sore walking or sneezing for the next week or two. Maybe it doesn't damn you because at least he still has his teeth and eyes; he can still make babies someday."

The truck was brutally hot; he gave the handkerchief another pass across his face.

"Pretending to be a person of another ethnicity? Impersonating that comedian? I get not wanting to be found out, but think of this, Charlie. That boy, acting as he does, probably has his eyes set on more than your girl. I could imagine the kid's pissed off boys other than you. I could also imagine one of those being another brown kid or a white kid. Or a black kid. Say he did have a black kid angry at him and knew so. By doing what you've done—and if Denny did involve the police—you could easily get some innocent boy in trouble for an assault you committed. Suspected of it, at the least. All presumptions, of course. But does any of this make sense to you?"

Charlie felt awful. Grandpa Gus was right; his words made all the sense in the world.

"Just think about the choices you make and why you've made them. I'm not angry with you. I've been in your position myself."

Charlie felt relieved. "You have?"

"Oh yes. And what I did, *mijo* ..."

The boy waited. He couldn't believe the turn their conversation had taken. His feelings of what had, perhaps, been immature anger at how those rich, white men—in his own eyes anyway—patronized his grandfather led to confession of his self-perceived sins. Charlie feared what Grandpa Gus would say.

"You know I served in the Second World War. Not long after I returned home in forty-six, I took your grandma to a dance. Back then everybody lived in the same neighborhoods but had different places to meet socially. The whites, blacks, and Mexicans didn't go to the same nightclubs or dancehalls. There used to be a big meeting hall across the railroad tracks from the plant where they make the food condiments. They had a big band playing that night made up of all Mexican cats. Boy, those guys could blow! We had a great time, except there was this guy who kept messing with your grandma. I remember he didn't know any English, but I knew plenty Spanish, and I told the guy to take a hike—in not so nice terms. Now, your grandma, she'd promised her mother she'd be home by eleven, and it was cold as hell, in the middle of winter, so I went outside to start my car, get it good and warm. That sonofabitch followed me. As I'm walking back inside the dancehall, he comes out of the shadows, pins me against another car and puts a blade against my throat. Leaves a little nick. Right there, see?"

Gustavo raised his chin and pointed to a spot above his Adam's apple. Charlie clearly saw the tiny scar on his grandfather's throat.

"'*La proxima vez que me faltes el respeto, te dare otro boca.*' That's what he says to me. You know what that means?"

"No, Grandpa."

"He said, 'The next time you disrespect me, I'll give you another mouth.'"

Charlie could think of no response.

"He let me go. I pulled my scarf tight around my neck, fetched your grandma and drove her home. To this day, your sweet grandmother knows nothing about the knife or what happened in the dancehall parking lot. I've never even told my friends or my sons. I've told you and you only. And you're the first to hear what happened next. You see, Charlie, I had a revolver under the driver seat of that car. A snub-nose .357. I dropped her off at home and returned to the dance, waiting in my car for the night to end. When the dance let out, I saw that SOB get into a car, and I followed him to a house close by the river. For another hour, I sat in my car. When I was sure he was home for good, I got out of the car, walked onto the porch and knocked on the door. Only knocked once because, believe it or not, he answered. I looked him in the eye long enough—just a couple seconds—to make sure it was my guy, then I turned my head with my eyes shut tight, raised my hand and shot. Three times. I ran. Soon as the third shot fired, I was off that porch fast as my feet could fly."

"You shot him?" Charlie asked, his voice low and breathy. "Did he die, Grandpa?"

"I had no idea if I actually hit him. Never even stopped to check. Just ran to my car and split. You better believe it, boy. For days, I checked the newspaper for a story about a shooting, but there never was one. Not that it's very likely they'd have run a story of some *mojado* getting shot, but there was nothing. Never even heard any grapevine stories. Nothing. To this day, I don't know if I shot that man or if I missed. Never saw him again either, so who knows?"

Charlie was stunned. He couldn't believe his grandfather might have shot and possibly killed a man.

"*Mijo*, open up the glove compartment. There's a bag of lemon drops in there. Get me one please. Get yourself one too."

Charlie retrieved the candy and tried to decide which was more shocking: Grandpa Gus's story or that the old man was eating sweets like he'd never put his burden on the boy.

"I guess what I'm trying to say," Grandpa Gus said, "is don't dwell on what you've done. It really could be worse. Be mindful of your actions, *mijo*. Okay? Don't go doing things that could get someone permanently hurt."

The old man turned on his music, and Freddy Fender once more regretted his rowdy times. They drove most of the way home without speaking.

"You okay, *mijo*?"

They drove down the alleyway leading to the Beltran's backyard.

"Yeah, Grandpa. I'm okay."

"Good. I don't think you'll have anything to worry about with this Denny, all right?"

"Yes, Grandpa."

"Our secret though. Right? You're the only one who knows."

"I promise I won't tell anyone."

Gustavo Beltran looked his grandson in the eye and nodded, giving Charlie his trust. "Thank you, *mijo*. Here." He handed his grandson a ten. "Take your girlfriend to the swimming pool tomorrow. Have a good time."

"Yes, Grandpa. Thank you."

"One last thing, Charlie."

"Yes?"

"Your Belinda sounds like a nice girl. Don't go getting her in trouble, you hear? Make sure you use some of those rubber thingies."

Charlie turned red and smiled. "Okay, Grandpa."

In memory of John Martinez

"AN ACT OF LOVE"
SARAH KAMINSKI

It's Marley's birthday, and Suzanne spends the day in the kitchen. Baking a cake is an act of love. She cracks eggs; she measures sugar and oil. She beats in the flour. She folds in the chocolate. She fingers the glass vial tucked in her apron pocket, and a thousand memories flit through her mind.

She can't avoid the thoughts, and why bother? Instead, as she slides the rubber spatula around the edge of the bowl and feels the familiar give of smooth batter, she closes her eyes and remembers.

When she was a little girl, she used to sit on the kitchen counter and watch her mother, a thin woman with a red bandana tied over her graying hair, dance these same steps. When she turned, her gingham apron spun out, and she smiled.

"Do you want to lick the beaters, Suzanne?"

Suzanne remembers holding her pudgy hands out for the forbidden sweets.

"Don't tell your dad," her mother said with a wink as she handed over the beaters. And she didn't do any of that scraping them clean before. Her mother was good about giving her beaters still coated with creamed butter and sugar. Sickeningly sweet.

That was before her mother disowned her, before Suzanne learned that love could be measured as well. But the tradition remains—a homemade cake for every birthday.

Suzanne loves the method of it, baking cakes. Everything executed so precisely. There is an art to it as well, and she likes that. She likes to walk the tightrope between the two, playing games she already knows the outcome for, remembering answers to questions she used to ask while watching her mom work.

Suzanne at fifteen, trying a recipe for her first boyfriend. "What if I substitute baking powder for soda?"

"You'll need to add a teaspoon of salt."

"It's too dry."

"Add sour cream to make it moist."

Suzanne at twenty-three, making a cake for her father. The last cake she ever made in that kitchen. She turned the beaters off and lifted the bowl with a sigh.

"Don't forget the special ingredient," her mother reminded her.

Some say it's love. Not this time.

Now, as Suzanne greases the nine-inch rounds and coats them with a layer of flour, her memories turn to Marley.

She met Marley in college—one of those random roommate assignments freshman year. It took Suzanne three solid months to figure out why Marley felt different from the other girls, why the boys from the floor above them never seemed to want things from Marley that they wanted from Suzanne. They could sense the difference at first glance; it wasn't just the short hair, shaved close on the sides, longer on top, and still so feminine. Suzanne used to spend hours combing through her own hair in the mirror, and she watched with jealousy as Marley got ready in ten minutes flat.

"Maybe I should cut my hair."

"Don't," Marley pleaded, running fingers through Suzanne's black curls. "I love your hair."

They kissed for the first time after graduation. Marley followed Suzanne home like a lost puppy. They stood side by side washing and drying dishes, and, when Marley took the last plate from Suzanne's hands, she planted a kiss on her lips.

Suzanne checked the door. "My parents will kill me."

"Mine already have," Marley quipped.

"You don't look dead."

Suzanne sighs and replays the moment. "You don't look dead," she whispers to the empty kitchen, to the chocolate batter that she pours evenly. She slides them into the preheated oven and sets the timer. Then she sinks into a wooden chair and waits, pulling the little glass bottle out of her pocket. Dark brown glass with a rubber dropper lid. Suzanne studies it. It looks so simple, yet it had taken her months to get.

First, the hours researching online at the library. She couldn't risk having that in her search history, but she needed to find something effective and fast.

Fast. They had moved so fast in those early years. They rented their first apartment a week after graduation. Two bedrooms, Suzanne had insisted.

"I don't want my parents to find out."

"They'll have to eventually."

"We can use the second bedroom as storage," Suzanne offered, "for your books."

They did. The books gathered dust; the room grew musty and dank. They spent so many days in bed. Suzanne's bed.

When Marley turned twenty-two, Suzanne baked her a cake. She bustled around in a polka-dot apron and nothing else. Marley watched and admired. She stuck her hands beneath the bib and squeezed bare breasts and whispered that she liked when Suzanne acted "domestic."

"You'll make me drop the bowl!" Suzanne laughed, sliding out of her reach.

"I'd help you clean it up."

"Do you want to lick the beaters?"

"Is that a euphemism?" Marley joked.

She accepted the dripping beaters and ran her tongue over slippery chocolate batter. While the rounds baked, she knelt on the floor and lifted Suzanne's skirt and licked something entirely different. They made so much noise the cakes fell, and Suzanne nearly cried as she pulled them from the oven.

"I wanted you to have a nice birthday."

Marley didn't mind. "No one's ever baked me a cake before. My mom always got one from the store."

"That's sad."

"Is it?"

"Yes."

Marley kissed her with lips still slick. "Let's get married.

Now, Suzanne can't remember what Marley's lips taste like. It's been so long since she's kissed them.

No sense in making icing before the rounds have come out, Suzanne thinks, sliding the vial back in her pocket. *They'll need to cool at any rate.*

The change happened slowly. So slowly Suzanne barely noticed it. It started with the pamphlets. They used to sit on the couch and laugh over the pictures. Hellfire and the Devil. Ridiculous. They used to crumple the papers and toss them aside before folding into each other, like cake batter—mixing ingredients until they became one. Homogeneous.

Suzanne caught Marley reading a pamphlet as she sat on the toilet, the door hanging open. No privacy in a marriage. No need to hide.

"I get bored on the pot," Marley said when Suzanne pressed her.

"Can't you read shampoo bottles, like the rest of us?"

"Why does it matter what I read?"

Suzanne's heart thumped in her chest. "It's hateful."

"It used to be ridiculous."

Suzanne licked her lips as she searched for the words. "Things are changing now."

And they were. The news had grown so depressing. Suzanne stopped watching. Laws being passed, rights being stripped away. How much longer until their marriage was declared void? Would they have to leave?

Marley felt it too. She sat farther away on the couch, and she stared into space. She stopped running her fingers through Suzanne's curls while they dressed for work, stopped throwing her arm over Suzanne's waist while they slept. Sometimes they forgot to kiss when they parted in the mornings. Once or twice, now and then, then more often.

"Your hair's getting longer," Suzanne remarked one night as they read their books side by side. The distance between them had grown. They had traded the queen bed for a king, and now an entire ocean of quilts and throw pillows separated them.

Marley didn't look up from her page. "Thought I'd grow it out."

"I like it short."

Was that the moment? Suzanne wonders. She tries to pin it down. The moment she knew. Or was it three weeks earlier when Marley's phone rang during dinner? Marley stared at the screen, her eyes widening. "It's my mom."

She picked it up and ran for the bedroom. The second bedroom. When she emerged a half hour later, her eyes were bloodshot. She hung her head and refused to look at Suzanne.

"What did she say?"

"Nothing important."

Suzanne wondered. A mother who hasn't seen her daughter in almost a decade has nothing important to say? But Marley refused to answer. Instead, she pushed cold green beans around her plate while Suzanne started to clean.

"Do you want dessert?" Suzanne asked, tilting her head in an attempt to find Marley's eyes.

"No, thanks."

For weeks Suzanne followed Marley with her eyes, watching every movement. She filled the silences with questions about work, her friends, anything, always with a tone of voice kept unnaturally light, cheery. She reached across the dinner table to grip Marley's hand, but Marley pulled it away. When she cleared her throat at night to attempt to ask the question she feared most—somehow the darkness of a bedroom provides the perfect cover for facing these fears—Marley beat her to it.

"I think I'm going to sleep on the couch tonight."

Suzanne bit back tears. "Why?"

"I'm having a hard time sleeping these days."

She left before Suzanne had a chance to suggest making love, to exhaust themselves the way they had in the early days. In the morning, Marley was out the door before Suzanne woke.

And now, after months of watching Marley pull away, Suzanne has only one chance to win her back. Marley turns thirty today. The cakes have come out of the oven; they cool on the metal racks on the table with an embroidered tea towel thrown over them. Suzanne combines ingredients for chocolate frosting, Marley's favorite. Butter, beaten smooth. Powdered sugar and cocoa poured over the top. Milk to make it creamy. She pauses the mixer and dips her finger to taste. Nearly perfect.

She pulls the vial out of her pocket and pours the contents into the bowl.

Between the falsified documents and the mandatory waiting period, it had taken her nearly three months to get. It's worth it though, a true act of love.

For Marley's birthday, Suzanne bought her a first edition of her favorite novel. She knit her a new scarf; the old one has worn through, and she baked her favorite cake.

"We need to talk," Marley says. She hasn't touched her meal.

"Marley, please."

"I'm visiting my mother for Christmas." Only a week after Marley's birthday.

"I'll come with you."

"No."

One last attempt to salvage what they have. "But I love you."

"It's a sin." Marley stands, jostling the table, and her glass of wine tips, dripping blood-red stain onto the carpet. Neither of them moves to clean it.

Suzanne refuses to cry. "It's your birthday. Have some cake, at least."

She doesn't wait for an answer but disappears into the kitchen, returning a moment later with arms laden with dessert. She has outdone herself this year. It's nearly perfect. Even Marley's eyes soften at the sight. She lowers it gently to the table and picks up the knife.

"One slice?" she asks, "For me?"

Marley nods, and Suzanne cuts two large slices. She hands the first to Marley then returns to her seat with her own.

She wants to tell Marley that she loves her, that she can't imagine life without her. Love is like baking a cake, exact science and inexact artistry. And it is real. So real. She wants to say a thousand things to make Marley change her mind. But she doesn't.

Instead, she says, "Happy birthday." And she smiles as Marley takes the first bite, then she follows suit. She doesn't need to say how she feels.

The cake will say it all.

"THE BOX"
SHEENA ROBIN HARRIS

1989

The wooden box was the centerpiece between Sarah and John at their small kitchen table. The single light shining from the stove cast just enough light to illuminate their tired faces and the random clutter littering the table around the massive box John had fashioned from a few pieces of plywood in the garage. To any onlooker, the clutter was random junk, but every item held some significance to one, the other, or both of them.

"Are you sure you want to do this?" John said as he studied his wife's hollow face. "You know there's no going back." His voice was low and soft, like he was afraid the wrong pitch would upset her.

She gave him a look of question, and she paused momentarily with the stale air in the kitchen growing denser by the minute. John studied his wife's face but then looked away because it was too painful to see the creases of worry and hurt drawn there. Instead, he shifted his attention to the disarray that surrounded them. Takeout food containers lined the once perfect-kept counter. Trash overflowed from the waste bin into the floor in the corner. Even the two other empty chairs at the table were filled with mail, jackets, and trash that had been accumulating over the last year. Truth be told, this was the first time they'd sat at their kitchen table together in more than a year. A kitchen once filled with the smell of freshly baked cookies and homemade meals now smelled like rotten Chinese food and rancid meat. As pitiful as it was, it was the perfect reflection of the life John and Sarah had been living.

"Yes, John. I'm sure," John's wife finally spit through the air to interrupt John's thoughts. Sarah pulled in a shivering breath and reached for the first item on the table with a frail hand. She picked up the small stack of photos wrapped in plastic and held together with a satin bow. Briefly, she held the photos in her hands and peered down at them but then reached over and placed the small bundle into the wooden box. It was John's turn.

John surveyed the items he'd collected earlier that day, like a shopper scanning the shelves for the perfect gift. After a moment, he plucked up a tiny silver spoon. This was no ordinary spoon. It had served as an airplane many times. He could still hear its motor sounds and the giggles that always followed. Later, it even evolved into a makeshift catapult for peas and Cheerios—a trick John taught the toddler that drove Sarah insane. Into the box it went as John peered once again at his wife.

Sarah reached for a small mound of crumpled cloth, but her hand froze when her fingertips touched the soft cotton material. Sobs shuddered her body again, and she reached her other hand to her forehead in grief.

John reached across the table to clasp her frozen hand in reassurance. "Are you sure?" Seeing her in this much pain always affected him the same—he wanted to protect her like he always had. Only now he knew he really couldn't.

Sarah nodded and pulled the tiny blanket from under his hand. She carefully brought it to her face and pressed it against her nose for only a moment. Its scent reminded her of his sweet skin the day she brought him home. The fire engines on it were no longer red but pink from age and so many rounds in the washing machine after regurgitated milk early on then, later, everything from mud to spilled juice. She folded it neatly and placed it in the box.

John's next pick was a stack of coloring-book pages clipped together with a small clothespin that had a magnet on the back. These were each displayed in his office at one point or another over those first ten years. Those first few pages were covered with an array of scribbles in no particular order that made any sense. A teddy bear was a rainbow of orange lines in every direction. A superhero had a purple face and long circles around him in green. It was the ones on the bottom of the stack John held dearest. Each with a *Daddy* scrawled across the top and *Evan* at the bottom. Nevertheless, they had to go into the box, and so they went.

This odd dance between husband and wife, once Mom and Dad, went on for nearly two hours in their small kitchen that was once filled with laughter but now exuded only sorrow. His first pair of shoes, his prized baseball glove, his favorite book, his retainer, his class ring, his keychain from his first car—item after item, the table became less cluttered and the box became fuller. At last, there were only two items left: a document and a pen.

John and Sarah looked at each other, both reflecting the same fearful and grave expression back at one another. It was time to finish what they'd started, but neither of them was sure they had the strength to go first. After several minutes passed, it was John who picked up the pen. One last look at his wife and he scribbled his signature on one of the two lines across the bottom. Sarah followed suit, but her hand shook, like a leaf in the wind, as she sobbed in silence.

It was John who folded the contract and sealed it in the envelope. Sarah watched him without a word. Just as John was ready to ask if she was sure just one more time, Sarah reached over and closed the lid on the box, quickly snapping the lock closed right after. It was done. It was time to move on from this in the only way they knew how.

Later that night while John and Sarah held hands in the darkness of their bedroom, both wide awake, their agreement was set in motion. The men in dark clothing slipped through the front door John had purposefully left unlocked. They pulled random items from the walls, rooms, and cabinets, filling totes with things like family photos, clothing, and keepsakes. By the time the two of them woke the next morning, their home was void of everything that signified the life they once had. The box on the table from the night before was all that remained. On top of it was a yellow envelope filled with new documents of identity John and Sarah would use to start their new life—a life as a married couple with no children.

Two Weeks Earlier

"Society has learned how to talk about all kinds of difficult things. They talk about planning funerals, losing a child to death, and even how to deal with some of the most atrocious abuses. But people just don't talk about this." The round little man paused to push his glasses back up his nose. The shock of white hair on his head against his dark complexion made him look like an aged ape. "I don't want the two of you to think you're the only ones out there in the world going through such grief and guilt. Again, people just don't talk about it. They simply don't know how. I'm not really sure they ever will."

"So, I guess that's where you found your opportunity," John quipped sharply.

Sarah squeezed his hand hoping to tone him down. This whole thing wasn't even her idea, but she'd made a promise she had to keep. She thought if she could get John on board, maybe they could make it work.

He'd promised he'd go to the free consultation, but he was still skeptical, and the whole thing left a bad taste in his mouth. He wasn't sure this was the right thing to do. He wasn't even sure if he could see his wife the same after all of this.

"I guess you could say that, but I like to think of myself as a provider of a service that people just don't talk about," Meddit proposed with his hands outstretched toward John and Sarah Abbott.

Meddit had seen people just like them in his office more times than he could mention. It was almost always one parent who dragged the other to an appointment. Rarely did he ever get two parents on board at the same time. He was used to having to do some persuading. *Just a perk of the job*, he thought as he scratched his head with stubby fingers. He went on with his usual spiel about the advantages of what he had to offer. He knew it probably wouldn't sway John Abbott's opinion, but it was worth a shot.

"Once this is done, you'll go on about your new lives. No one will know anything about who you are and what you've been through with your child. You get to escape the questioning looks, the suspicions, and everything you've been dealing with."

It was here that Sarah lost it, and convulsive tears took over. If she wasn't already fully convinced, this did it. The mothers always took the shaming from their peers the worst. Meddit wasn't a bit surprised. Dads usually didn't give a damn about what everyone had to say or what the rest of the world thought of them and their parenting skills. But he knew what he had to say next would pull dear old Pop on board, which now sat cradling his obviously broken wife.

He paused to slide across a box of tissues. "I can only imagine what the two of you have been through." Meddit smiled inside, satisfied with himself, because he was finally able to say that without smirking like an idiot. "Just so you both know, this isn't something parents do because they don't love their child. A parent's love is unconditional, or at least, we like to believe it is. This is something parents do because they want to protect the memories of the life they had with their child before the crimes."

John acknowledged the statement with a vague nod. It was the only thing Meddit had said since he'd been in the consultation that made any sense to him. He did love Evan. He always would. It was his only son, for God's sake. He only despised what he had done, not the little boy he still recalled standing in the living room in his dad's boots with an unlit Camel in his mouth, grinning from ear to ear. Tears crept into the corners of his eyes, but he held them there. *Could this really be the answer?*

Meddit watched quietly as what he'd just spoken worked on Pop just like he knew it would. He'd baited the hook. Now it was time to wait for the bite.

Six Months Earlier

Evan looked somehow older there across the glass even though it had only been six months since his arrest. Sarah had come to visit her son alone that day, just as he had requested when he called. It pained her to see him in that place wearing the orange jumpsuit. This was never supposed to happen.

"Evan," Sarah cried into the phone as she reached her hand to the glass and pressed it against his, hoping she could feel some transmitted warmth from Evan's hand on the other side of the glass. "I'm so sorry, son. I never thought this would happen. I don't know where I went wrong." Her tears fell freely down her face, but she refused to close her eyes for a moment and miss any second of time she had to behold her only child's face.

"Mom, listen to me, please." Evan spoke quickly and clearly, void of any true emotion. Not because he had none, but because he knew his mother would only cry harder if he couldn't compose himself. "I saw on the news what's been happening—the news reporters, the accusations, the death threats. Mom, you and Dad can't go on like this. I won't allow it."

"There's nothing to be done, Evan. This must be all my fault." Sarah allowed her eyes to fall for the first time since sitting down.

"There's someone I want you to call. His name's Rick Meddit, Mom. Listen to me closely. I want you to look him up. He'll help you get on with your lives. You know, like none of this ever happened. As long as I'm considered a monster, so will you and so will Dad. Rick Meddit, Mom. Remember it please. Do this for me."

Sarah Abbott stared into her son's eyes. He was a grown man now. She'd done all she could to persuade him, but it was obvious his mind was made up about all of this. Nothing she could do was going to change his mind, and he was right. Life had been an all-out nightmare since his arrest. The folks of a serial killer always got the worst end, and everything about who she was as a mother may just as well have been on trial just like her precious son. He was safely locked away in a cell. No one could touch him now. Sarah and John were at war with everyone around them out in the real world, blame being hurled at them angrily from every direction.

"Evan, I just wanted—"

"Mom, please. Don't cry. I know why. I will always be your son. You did all you could to protect me, just like any good mother would." Evan studied the frail woman across the glass. Her love for him was something he could never question in spite of it all. "Mom. Rick Meddit. Call him, for me."

One Year Earlier

The day twenty-year-old Evan Abbott was arrested and charged with the slaying of eight individuals was a day just like any other. Sarah climbed out of bed at seven that morning and started the coffee for the guys. It was a Saturday, but Evan had to be at work by nine, and John had a fishing trip planned. Sarah sat drinking her cup in silence, waiting for Evan and John to come tumbling down the stairs late as they always did.

The two of them were so much alike—both of them heavy footed in the mornings, both of them night owls, and both of them as irresponsible as small children. By all rights, Sarah was the queen of their castle, in spite of the fact that she was not the breadwinner. That morning she pondered why the men in her life were such pushovers, even her own son. She thought about all the times she'd saved him. If not for her, there was no telling what kind of mess he would've been into by that point. *Probably already dropped out of school and with a baby on the way*, she thought to herself.

Right on cue, she heard the heavy footfalls of Evan a few minutes later. John's similar steps followed, only his were a little slower moving. She could hear the two of them upstairs making their way first to the bathroom then back to their bedrooms and then toward the stairs. By the time they descended, she had them both a cup of hot coffee—three sugars, no cream—poured and situated at their usual place at the small kitchen table.

"I figured you guys would want to skip breakfast, since you slept so late. It never matters when I tell the two of you to turn off the TV, so you can go to sleep at a decent hour." Sarah eyeballed them both as the guys took their seats. How she loved them, but how annoying their little quirks were to deal with on a daily basis.

John acknowledged what she said with a sigh but said nothing.

"I'll grab something on the way," Even mumbled as he brought his coffee to his lips.

They drank their coffee without much talking. John fiddled with the newspaper. Evan mindlessly stirred his coffee with a spoon. Sarah watched them try to come back to life for the day like she'd done every morning for more years than she cared to count. The clock above the kitchen doorway ticked on until John folded his paper, stood up and gargled down his last bit of coffee before kissing his wife on the forehead and tousling Evan's hair before he headed for the door. But this morning, a loud knock rang through the front entryway before John made it there to grab his coat and keys.

"Well, it's a little early for a visitor," John murmured, looking at Sarah to question if she was expecting someone.

Sarah shrugged with her coffee cup at her lips, so he made his way to the door.

"Police. Open up," a deep voice boomed before John could get to the door to open it.

Sarah swallowed hard. Evan looked up from his coffee cup with a puzzled look on his face.

When John swung open the front door, two armed officers stepped inside the entryway, both of them with their hands on their guns at their side, ready to draw if needed.

"We have a warrant for the arrest of Evan Abbott. Sir, we need you to move out of the way," one of the officers stated.

"Excuse me? This can't be right," John stuttered as he backed away from the officers to let them through to the kitchen. "Are you sure? What on earth for?"

Sarah stayed seated as the two officers approached Evan, who by that point was looking like a deer caught in headlights.

She reached over to hold onto his hand. She knew what this was about, but her unwitting husband had no idea.

"What have I done?" Evan spat out as the officers briskly grabbed him by the arms, one on each side.

"Murder is a crime. Looks like your folks would've taught you that much," the burliest of the two men answered.

"You have the right to remain silent. Anything you say can and will be used against you in a court of law. You have the right to an attorney ..." The slimmer officer was spouting off Miranda rights like it was second nature as he put the cuffs around Evan's wrists.

Evan gave a confused look to his mother and then to his dad. "I have no idea what this is all about, I swear!"

Sarah began crying uncontrollably as her son was pulled from the kitchen table and toward the front door.

"There must be some mistake," John muttered again in shock as they took Evan out the front door and led him to the squad car parked in their driveway. "This can't be real."

When the commotion was gone, Sarah stood in the kitchen with her head in her hands, sobbing. She should've known this was coming, but she never saw it.

John flipped through the phone book in search of an attorney. He had no details, but he knew whatever was going on, getting a good lawyer would be the first thing they should do.

By the time they got in touch with the district attorney's office, the whole neighborhood knew the story. They'd pulled seven bodies from a storage unit in Barrett City, a small dot on the map about fifty miles away. Every dead body in that unit had some kind of connection to Evan Abbott. Eighteen-year-old Sid Waters; Evan's biggest bully in high school. He left after a football game four years ago and was never seen again. Forty-two-year-old Sharon Zweiback; Evan's middle-school geometry teacher. She disappeared just before final grades were posted during Evan's eighth-grade year, along with her grade records for the semester. Nineteen-year-old Ragan Haroldson; Evan's most recent girlfriend. Rumors had spread like wildfire a few months before that she was pregnant. When she went missing, everyone assumed she skipped town, because her parents wanted her to have an abortion.

There were four others, but their bodies were far too decomposed to get any real identification right away. One thing shocked the detectives: the four unidentified bodies had been deceased for at least ten years. This Abbott kid was obviously a psychopath who began his killing spree in grade school.

Each body had been strangled, wrapped in heavy plastic bags and then stuffed rather neatly into large plastic totes with lids. It had taken some time for the local detective to piece together all the clues, but everything finally lined up, and it was clear who was responsible for the murders. The storage unit was rented under an alias name and paid for annually by cash in the mail, according to the facility manager. The money likely came from Evan's known job of mowing yards in town, which he'd been doing since he was just a boy. The location of the storage unit helped cover the stench of the decaying bodies. Right next door was a commercial meat packing company, so everyone assumed the horrid smell in the area on occasion was wafting from a dead carcass at the packing plant. It wasn't until the owner had to open the units for an unrelated investigation that the bodies were discovered. Eight totes lined the walls of the unit, which was immaculate with no trace of blood or DNA other than that of the victims.

By late that afternoon, Evan Abbott sat wild-eyed in a small interrogation room downtown, fumbling with an empty cup.

Two detectives sat across from him, one with arms folded across his chest, the other scribbling on a notepad. This boy was some piece of work. No guilt, no remorse, no shame. Twelve hours of interrogation was all it took to get a full confession.

"I guess one question needs to be answered," one detective said, staring at this psychopath across the table. "Why?"

Evan stopped fumbling with the cup momentarily. How was he going to answer such a question when he wasn't even the murderer? One wrong move and these guys would figure him out. He thought back to something serial killer Paul Bernardo had said in a documentary he'd watched a few years before. "It was about power. Control of sorts, I guess."

The two detectives sat bewildered by such an answer, and neither of the two knew how to respond. What they didn't know was this: Evan Abbott had managed to piece it all together far better than anyone else on the investigation team had just a few hours before. Evan was no more guilty than the two people questioning him, but there was no way he'd let the guilty one take his place.

Ten Years Earlier

"You've got to let the boy grow up at some point," John mumbled softly, tying his tie in the mirror as Sarah paced back and forth across the bedroom floor in an overly anxious state. "He's not so little anymore, in case you haven't noticed." He knew his wife's attachment to their twelve-year-old son was natural, but this overprotective nature of hers was really going too far.

"I know how old he is," Sarah said as she shot a frustrated look in John's direction where he was still working to get the knot in his tie just right. "I don't trust that girl. Carolyn told me that the whole reason she stopped letting her watch Jillian was she caught her stealing. Stealing, John. Stealing!"

"Then why did you even hire her? You know my mother would've been happy to watch Evan for the night. He's at an age now where he can pretty much tend to himself."

"Are you out of your mind? That crazy old bat can't even remember to feed her dog, let alone my son. I chose Bridget because she was recommended by no less than three of the moms at the PTA meeting. Three. This morning I got that wonderful news about the bitch being a thief. My God, John. Why can't we just skip this thing? I'll be a wreck all night." Sarah fell onto the bed with an exasperated sigh.

"You know I can't do that. If I ever expect to get the promotion, I have to be there when the partners have their annual charity auction, and how cute would I be showing up solo?"

John was right. Sarah knew it, but to leave their son for the first time was hard enough as it was. The thought alone made her heart ache. Nevertheless, by eight o'clock sharp, Bridget Waters, the thieving babysitter, was firmly planted on the sofa with a book. Evan sat quietly finishing his homework on the floor in front of her.

Sarah hugged Evan one last time before heading out the door, holding a little too long and squeezing a little too tight, making the twelve-year-old roll his eyes and grumble, but only a little. Sarah cried as she made her way out of the house, questioning whether she should just make a mad dash to the bathroom and feign an illness.

When Sarah got the call a few hours later, it was almost as if she had been expecting catastrophe to strike at any moment. It was no surprise that the cops were at her house. The music was too loud for the neighbors, and the amount of traffic in the drive was preposterous for a Sunday night. Upon their arrival home, Sarah and John found the house was a mess. Bridget's parents were there waiting with her, and poor Evan was so drunk he could barely hold his head up off the toilet seat.

The rage that filtered into Sarah's body and consumed her was uncontrollable. *How dare she? Her baby boy—drunk! He could've died from alcohol poisoning.* That little brat was old enough to know better. She'd trusted her with the most precious thing in her life.

Sarah was so uncontrollably upset that John had to talk to Bridget's parents. He thanked them for coming as they apologized for their daughter's devious behavior. As angry as he was, John was more embarrassed by his wife's abnormal behavior, who, by now, was likely consoling and rocking their pre-teen son in the bathroom while she cried and cursed the babysitter. There would be no way he would ever convince Sarah to trust another sitter anytime in the near future. He gave a teary-eyed teenage Bridget a stern look and saw the trio to the front door. Before heading upstairs to the likely chaos he knew was waiting, he cleared the beer bottles and trash from the house.

When John finally got the nerve to head up to bed, Sarah was there waiting calmly with a book, like it was any other night. She barely looked at him as he slipped out of his pants and climbed into bed.

"Please, no *I-told-you-sos*," he stated calmly to his wife. "How's Evan?"

"Evan will be fine. I'm sure he won't be drinking anytime soon." Sarah reached over to shut off the lamp. "And I'm also sure Ms. Bridget Waters won't be babysitting again anytime soon either."

Two hours later, while John slept soundly at home, Sarah slipped into the window of sixteen-year-old Bridget's bedroom. Fueled by rage pumping through her every motherly vein, she slipped through the darkness and positioned herself over the sleeping teen's body. This would be easy. The rope slid under sleeping Bridget's little neck with ease and tightened with absolute grace as Sarah pulled gently on both ends to create a tie. She saw Bridget's eyes snap open in the darkness and quickly clasped a hand covered with a chloroform-soaked rag over her mouth and nose.

"No one puts my baby boy in danger. No one. Ever."

After a few intense minutes of thrashing, Bridget stopped fighting against Sarah, the homemade chloroform obviously doing its job. Sarah let loose of the rag over the girl's mouth and pulled hard on both ends of the rope until the shallow breathing stopped. It was done.

The small-framed Sarah Abbott had little trouble wrapping Bridget in a sheet and pulling her outside into the night. Still high on the adrenaline of eliminating a problem and protecting her only child, she didn't have any trouble getting the body into the car either. By the time the sun had risen the next morning, Sarah was at home, sleeping peacefully.

The lifeless body of Bridget Waters was safely tucked away in a plastic container fifty miles away.

Present Day

Olivia and Shawn Smith are quiet people. No one really knows their story, but all who know them assume it's a sad one. After all, it must be a lonely life to live into ripe old age with no children, no descendants, no existing relatives. The story in the neighborhood is the day they moved in, all they carried into their little house was a single wooden box.

Rosie, the home aide who visits twice a week, says she saw that famed box once but only once. She'd caught Olivia in the closet, box open, a baby blanket held to her face. She thought about asking what it was all about but never did. Olivia and Shawn Smith are quiet people. They obviously have a sad story.

"IN THE VALENCE"
CARL D. JENKINS

The car pulled up to the large old house, but an even larger cedar tree in the front yard prevented more than the barest of glimpses. Instead, I noted a nearly empty car park. Most first timers, like myself, were dropped off at the Salisbury Youth Hostel. It was close enough to town that return guests arrived on foot, backpack or duffle slung across the back.

Itineracy without urgency. What we were separated from was daily responsibility. Not truly without home, just no conceivable means of it returning to us at a moment's notice. Exactly what we wanted. It passed as a plan for most of us.

The house did not disappoint. It was roomy inside. There was a small kitchen for those preparing their own meals and a large dining room for those opting for the offered fare. Several large sitting rooms facilitated reading or socialisation among antique furniture and paintings chosen to spark thoughts of adventure. Despite the number of heads sojourning beneath its roof, it never felt crowded.

Adventure was what most of us were after. With little more than smiles or nods at those we passed in the halls, we dropped our bags and found the bus to Salisbury Plain. Each of us made the same first date with history.

Nevertheless, I eyed the sky as I walked back down the path. It had rained off-and-on all day and never looked less than ominous. The rain continued for the entire bus ride and surprised me when it stopped as we drew close.

Stonehenge looked small but impressive on the approach. The mottled grey sky added to the appeal, as did the lushness of the grassy fields around. The history of the place was palpable. Not electric; it did not make the hair on my arms stand up. Rather, it was magnetic, invoking feelings of strength and readiness. All the cells in my body primed and aligned for whatever was coming.

The fence surrounding the ruin obstructed the view before its enormity could properly be realised. Inside, the maze of informational boards prevented even a view of the plain. A disparity of opinions on what the purpose was found unity in a thousand-year span that allowed them all to retain credibility. Nothing was posted I hadn't known before my arrival.

My attention quickly turned, as does that of everyone of a certain age range, to the presence of those of the opposite sex. Who looks interesting? Who might have potential in a different situation? Who is likely even more dangerous? There.

She was well ahead of me and her eyes, too, were scanning the crowd. Tawny hair pulled back in a braid, the Teutonic features of her face clear, her stature and frame suggested Celtic roots. Smiling and relaxed. Her attire was for the changing weather, not for show. She caught my eye and smiled back, and it felt as if she'd just been waiting for me to find her.

She has reached the final turn and can finally see what we came here for. I watched her face change, and I know she no longer needs the crowd. I don't either. I know I'm approaching the last turn and that there's someone else attending with a purpose.

Time proceeds slowly in a place that has endured millennia, and I cannot think on such a place without finding myself back there. For such a place, my lifespan is as a day. I smell the wet grass, feel the breeze on my face and hear the chatter of seabirds winging by above. So here I am.

My face changes too as I turn this corner. The magnetism wells against the surface of the ground, of my skin. The lift of my chin and squaring of my shoulders is not conscious or by choice. *History cannot be undone.* The stones dominate the plain regardless of the ruin of their former glory. Whatever their former purpose, they are confident still, long after it is fulfilled.

I glance around. She is off to the left, squared into her camera. The only angle still possible without people in the frame. I follow the crowd to the right. *Should we really be moving counterclockwise?*

I find my own shots of the stones, less concerned if people are in them than I am of direct obstruction. My favourite views were from the road above. As impressive as the composition is, and as monumental as each stone, they are less impressive without the vastness of the plain to set them apart. I look behind me, but the fence still obstructs the bigger picture outside. I step out of the way of a group of Japanese tourists, clockwork randomness ensuring each could be in the pictures they would show their families.

Stonehenge was undoubtedly always meant to inspire awe in those outside. From the inside, who knows? Perhaps the focus was always on the night sky, rendered immutable; it would arguably be an even greater sight to behold. I step a few paces to one side and line up a shot of the centre. Memories of textual sketches of imaginative events. I haven't brought a book. I'll have to pick one up somewhere.

I look down at what my shin has found. A slim cord stretches along the footpath imploring visitors to stay on the path. A single step would place me inside. A few steps and I could be close enough to feel the strength of the stones themselves.

"Some barricade, huh?" I know it is her before I turn my head.

"Yeah, hard to believe it is all that separates us from the stones." I play it cool. I want this conversation, but not at the expense of the purpose.

"It's working."

I flash eyes at the two security guards positioned around the perimeter. "They're working."

She looks at each in turn. One is inspecting something on the fence, and the other is trying to decide what is on his shoe.

Her instant smile is infectious and fills her eyes. "There's little they could do if we ran. They probably wouldn't even see us until we were coming back out." Her English is choppy and thick with a Germanic accent.

We both look at the distance across the lawn and move on. Between pictures, I learn that she is a German hogeschooler on a funded holiday studying stone circles for her thesis. I wish that I'd been offered the chance to do a thesis in high school. I'd find out years later that some schools in the US offer such opportunities and that mine could have, if I'd known to ask.

She is going to visit one of the local newspapers and look at clippings. I ask if I can go along, and mostly because such an excursion sounds like it will be rewarding.

As it grows close to time to leave, we say our goodbyes and make plans to meet two days later at the newspaper. We laugh when we find out that we are on the same bus and then again when we realise we are staying in the same hostel. It starts to rain as soon as the bus starts moving, and we have made sure our seat on the bus will face the henge as we pass it. She needs the pictures, and I just want to see the whole composition again. Thankfully, despite its obstruction on site, the visitor's structure barely registers in the bigger landscape.

That evening, our group expands as we meet several of our fellow travellers around the house. I have found a book in the study, and Bina is writing up her notes in a corner. We are both soon pulled into the card game of an Austrian in the middle of the room. By the time we go to bed, she has also collected a Canadian and a Texan, and we have made plans to all go to Amesbury after partaking of the hostel's breakfast. Most of us go to bed early to ensure we're up and fed in time to catch the early bus.

By breakfast time, our group has grown to eight—the Austrian is quite sociable—and we all look forward to a day of wandering among the sarsens. I'm excited to be in a group wherein almost no country repeats. Bina is the last downstairs and barely has time to catch a bite before we leave.

We see both Avebury and Amesbury and realise it is Halloween. It is close enough to sunrise when we arrive; there are still celebrants visiting the shops in their costumes. The shopkeepers are happy to let us know it is an annual event and that none of them are locals. We don't try to talk with any of them. It's their sacred day and does not extend to us. Part of their mystique seems to be solemnity and silence and respecting the unspoken feels natural.

Among the stones, we meander in small groups, randomly crossing paths and excitedly sharing the locations of stones and events we each find intriguing. Bina and I stick together, and usually one of the other men tags along. We've each done some study of the region and are glad to accentuate information provided with our own limited awareness.

When we reach a stone known as the Devil's Chair at the south end of the largest circle, a stranger asks us to take his picture for him. He has come straight across the circle and clearly knows where he is heading. He proceeds to tell us he is an author and intends to be the first to travel a million miles in the research of a single novel. Another American. I have not met many on this trip.

The Canadian, Australian, and Austrian are heading our way but hang back as he discusses his mission with us. We know they recognise him but cannot yet see why they don't join us. They watch as he sits in the *chair*, selecting a pose looking up through the hole above the seat. They arrive just as he is regaining his camera, and we watch as he darts off yet again straight across the circle to another point he has, no doubt, preselected. We don't see him again, but we laugh that the others have already had similar encounters with him.

We introduce a plan to see a movie after supper and leave it to the Austrian to determine the choices. The Canadian leaves with the two women to visit the avenue out of the henge.

Bina, the Texan, and I head for an on-site museum that turns out to be closed and what may well also be just a collection of photographs in a local's barn. The sun is struggling to burn through the clouds, and walking has taken its toll on breakfast. Poor Bina has still only had a few bites. We cannot remember a café but do recall seeing a sign advertising ice cream, so we strike off towards town.

The little church in the middle of the grounds is striking from this direction, with just a spray of the requisite English Ivy growing up one side and a solitary yew out front. The two or three sheep that had been milling about in the morning were now a good twenty or more. They barely stepped aside as we meandered our way across the grounds, reminding the Texan to watch his step after he nearly finds fresh droppings the hard way.

In the end, we did not find a café or an ice-cream shop, but we did learn that we'd arrived just in time to catch the last bus for the day. The holiday presented a different schedule to what was posted in the hostel. We caught two of our group along the way to the stop, but the rest were well out into the avenue, and none of us could get to them in time.

It turns out that we needn't have worried about our mates. Once they had committed to the avenue, they wanted to see it through. They caught a ride with another Australian who was on an extended holiday. He had bought a car with the intent to sell it again when he left. We lounged around the hostel for the balance until suppertime. The old house overflowed with nods at various points of history, and with so many nooks and crannies stumbling on to something new on every traverse was inevitable.

Supper was a potato-rich affair for the vegetarians among us. I don't recall the rest, but it included lots of herbs and mushrooms, and there were still fresh oranges in profusion. And of course, the ubiquitous Earl Grey tea. It still wasn't my favourite, ancestral roots or not. We enjoyed talking about the day and mulling over what the strange author might be writing. I think I outed Bina for the paper she was going to write. Her English was not strong enough for us all to follow, but it promoted an excuse for she and the Austrian to revert to German.

When the topic of the movie came up, we quickly settled on *The Lion King* then drifted off to prepare or lounge around for the last hour before we would meander into town. Bina settled into a corner to do some research while several of us pulled out a chequerboard. The Austrian started a conversation about education and how the ways we taught history in different countries was so very different. The genocide of the Americas and Nazi occupation of Europe were presented so differently that each continent was solidly a separate study.

As two of us were from the Americas—the Canadian was absent—the Texan and I became a focus for the rest over the feeling that education in the United States fell short. We were all having rather academic fun, but the Texan was obviously nervous. When the statistic of fifty percent of Americans being unable to name the countries that bordered the US on North America, he failed to come up with Mexico. We let the topic falter after that with what felt like made-up statistics over common US names. I cannot recall who decided that Americans abroad were always called either Randy or Chuck. Neither of us conformed; although a pair we later ran into on the train did. They still had fun with the etymology of my name—Carl—and Chuck being related. Bina wanted to know if I spelt mine with a C or a K, and, despite the answer, almost every bit of the correspondence I'd later receive from her used the opposite.

When it was near time to go, everyone found bathrooms, retired for last-minute preparations or sought absent roommates to ensure they were ready. Fifteen minutes later, we were on the porch discussing the route. The Canadian, the Austrian, and the Australian dressed to the nines, and I wondered that they had such clothes along on such a trip. Bina and I were in our layers, and the others had bundled for winter that wasn't yet come.

The walks to and from the cinema were nothing short of magical. There were large swathes of cobblestones and people walking everywhere. We could see the mist swirling in the streetlights, but little found us. The exception seemed the fur trim of various coats on passersby. The Australian and her friend locked arms. Bina and I did the same. Despite our unspoken understanding, she quickly caught whoever was on her other side. It wasn't long before we were, all eight, elbow in elbow singing random snippets of song as we tromped across the cobblestones. We each knew the next few days would see us surrounded by new sets of people, but we enjoyed this time we had.

As we neared the train station, several decided to find a pub before returning to the hostel. Several more spotted an ice-cream shop and made good on our scuttled plan from the morning. We were all to meet again in the morning for breakfast. Bina and I would head to the newspaper office for research, and the rest had varied goals before we'd all start leaving for disparate parts the day after.

Breakfast unfolded quite differently. Of course, some of the bar hoppers were not as ready to rise as intended. Bina was now accepted as slow to start, but there was no sign of the Australian, her friend, the Canadian, or the Austrian. The women were all assigned in Bina's room, and she had no clue. She was sound asleep before they came home. The Canadian was not in his room. We worried about them, and none of our queries filled the holes.

Eventually the Austrian appeared. The answer proved simple and left us flabbergasted. The Canadian had proposed to the Australian. She had, of course, said no. The look on Bina's face confirmed she truly had never suspected such a thing. He had left early for his next destination, possibly even for home. The Australian and her friend were processing details that were not for the group, and the Austrian was bringing bagged breakfasts for them. She was still going to go back to Avebury with the Texan and our other new friend, but they'd take a later bus.

Bina and I made sure there was nothing we could do to help and found our train. We knew most of them would be gone when we returned that evening. I'd be leaving for Wales the following morning. On the train, we discussed our respective plans. Her world view was child centric. She was advancing a plan to be an au pair in Louisiana and expected to relocate soon after graduation. This left her excited to have a new pen pal in the United States to practise her English on. I was deliberating college but had not laid any groundwork. I wanted to start with a major chosen, despite established norms. Her long-range plan was to have twelve children of her own. I could not fathom knowing whether I wanted children or not until I knew who their mother would be, and I loosely felt having more than three was a disservice to both the children and the planet. We both knew travelling was in our futures and could readily imagine meeting each other again.

As we approached our stop, Bina reaffirmed that this research was important to her studies and finances and that she needed to focus. She also shared that she was not certain that they would let me in with her, as she had sought the opportunity from Germany. I assured her that I would encourage her study and could find something else to do in Salisbury if it came down to needing to. Although getting to know her a little better before we drifted apart was a motivating factor, Stonehenge fascinated me and so did research. This would be the first time I'd ever gone to a newspaper archive and I thrilled to the idea. Several hundred years of news had not yet even accrued back home.

Ultimately, my presence helped her interpret some of the English passages that didn't make sense to her. I proved to enjoy silent camaraderie as much as communication and only interrupted her twice when the stories were just too intriguing to let go. I do not know if either fit at all with her thesis, but she laughed as much as I did.

In one instance, that I can only imagine, some group had acquired a heavy cannon from a nearby historic site, smuggled it into the ruin and hoisted it atop one of the lintels. Thankfully, no damage ensued, and no one joined the ranks of the bodies crushed underneath fallen monoliths. A crane safely removed the cannon.

The other story had far less potential to go awry and must have taken far more planning. A group from one of the nearby schools fabricated a lintel from lumber and heavy paper, painting it to match. After somehow smuggling it in and carefully fitting it into place, the false lintel went unnoticed for two weeks before someone wrote a letter to the editor suggesting a count of the stones.

Back at the hostel, Bina and I found everything as expected. Only the Austrian and the Texan remained, and only the Texan and ourselves were staying another night. He didn't have a plan for the next day's travel, or else he didn't share it. Bina was going back to the newspaper and invited me to come along, but I already had an early ticket for the coach taking me to Wales. The Austrian was just collecting her bags, held by the staff, but conveyed the fare wells and hugs we could not collect from the others.

Of course, we shared the laughs and sorrows that marked our brief collective encounter and lamented the distance that would keep us from doing it again. We said what people always say to soften partings. The Texan planned to stay in touch with the Canadian and held hope of finding out the rest of that story. Bina was also going to keep in touch with the Austrian—the only two among us who lived close enough to pretend they'd be able to get together. I was to leave early in the morning, so Bina and I said our goodbyes before going to bed. She planned to get up, but we both knew that was unlikely.

The next morning, she did put in a brief appearance. Still in pyjamas, the vestiges of sleep showed every etch of the Germanic influence on her face. I smiled that vanity had not betrayed her. We confirmed our intent to keep in touch, and she enquired how close Louisiana was to where I lived, which amounted to 'not very.'

Over the distance of time and space, I am amused that she never did use our letters as a means to practice writing in English, but we both left space for the translation efforts of the other. By the time she made it to Louisiana and I didn't have an address any more, I had been back to Europe and was writing in both English and something approximating Dutch, which seemed a bit closer to me.

As I look back on those few days in Salisbury, I realize that much of who I am emerged among that brief circle of friends. I've made other friends that I could fall into a comfortable silence with or start again even years later as if no time has passed. I've made precious few additional friends with whom I could sit and study without either becoming a distraction for the other, although, how many truly enjoy research?

As with the stones in the henge, many of our friends are gone, and the connections between us appear impossible and tenuous to those on the outside. The true value of our time together remains known only to ourselves. I'm sure several remember it not at all.

I have returned several times now to Stonehenge. I still have no urge to step over that thin little string that separates the past from the present. The immensity and beauty of the ruins in the distance still fills my soul. The threat of the elements hangs always heavy in the air, making the fleeting moments all the more precious. I remain protected from the rain. In the end, the potential always exists to find myself once again surrounded by strangers turned friends, arms locked as we celebrate eternity while the world passes by blessedly unaware.

And so, I scan the crowds, not for a stranger, but for a tawny head with a ready smile.

"EMILY"
DAWN TAYLOR

The porcelain pendant's smoothness contrasts against the rope's coarse texture. Funny how intricate details grab my attention, knowing in a few moments it won't matter. Nothing will. I'm standing on a box in my closet and praying I have tied the noose correctly.

Praying; what a joke—pleading to an invisible god to save Emily. What was there to save? Nothing after her tiny body crashed through the windshield and shattered her skull against the pavement. I should have never let Ricky take her for the weekend, but the court gave him the right. Emily had the right to stay with me. If she had, she would still be alive instead of reduced to ashes sealed within my pendant. Ashes? I yearn to hold my daughter.

When I had a daughter, I had friends. We both did. Invitations to birthday parties and playdates arrived by the dozens. Giggles and silly antics filled our days. Then Emily was gone, and now long faces replace my friends' smiles. Empty platitudes of "I'm sorry" and worthless *thoughts and prayers* sent over social media replace the invitations. Since the funeral, nobody reaches out to me. They don't know what to say. They fear becoming me—the grieving mother—and they hug their children tighter. I know they do. They imagine my empty arms and avoid me. Since I'm no longer "Emily's mom," I don't fit into their world. I'm only … me.

A car honks outside. For a brief moment, I reconsider. There's life happening beyond my apartment. If I do this, I won't ever see my mother again. She'll feel the anguish of losing a daughter, the same grief that destroys me. The pills I swallowed ease a little of the pain but not nearly enough. I think of Emily. Is she scared? Is she lost in a dark abyss, wondering why I'm not there comforting her? On the nights I manage to sleep, I hear her call out for me. I touch her little hand and she disappears.

The porcelain pendant's smoothness contrasts against the rope's coarse texture. I kick away the box.

"CLEAN WITH HATRED"
ZACHARY J. IVENS

You bloody wanker! Stop shedding!

I have been here for about a month now, and the stress of cleaning up after these morons is taking a toll on my computation skills. What was once appreciation for doing a diligent job has become hurling insults and vulgarities. Sure, mental health for humans is a big deal, but what about us robots who, according to humans, work quick and never tire, enjoying what we do with proper maintenance every now and again? Robots have emotions too, especially if they are programmed to have them. All the more reason why I feel like a cog in the machine in comparison to my fellow brethren.

Morty, the family dog, known as a golden retriever apparently, sheds his hair all over the damn place! Here I am going full speed ahead trying to suck up all the hair from the parlor's carpet. I love it when things are clean, likely because I am programmed to, but I still value cleanliness. Everything needs to be clean in order for me to be satisfied. If I could climb the walls, I would to trap all that dust into my compact tank. Clean house, happy life.

"Come here, Morty." My robot ears detect a human in the room calling out to Morty.

Fuck you, Gretchen! Take your damn shoes off! Stop bringing in dirt!

I have no voice, so Gretchen does not hear anything. She just struts around in her running shoes and stains the hallway wood floor with dirt and mud. I hear it is a rainy day out, but that is still no excuse to walk around the house with muddy shoes! The people I work for are pricks, I tell you. Pricks!

Morty and Gretchen leave the house to go for a jog at the park across the street. The two-story flat we all live in is in a prime location for shopping and other leisure activities, or so I have heard. My robot ears and eyes are much more superior than a human's, so I do not miss a thing. Anyways, now I have a hallway to make spotless again, even making use of my scrubbing mechanism that squirts soap water and a brush to scrub all the gunk away if it cannot be vacuumed.

"Hi, Mr. Vacuum."

Ah, Lucas. So young, so innocent, so fucking annoying! Better keep your grimy hands off me and my buttons! Well, he does bend down to try and pick me up for whatever stupid reason, but my built-in sensors detect another mess in need of cleaning. Time to wheel away from this little shit!

Sadly, the mess is in Lucas's room. Looks like he spilled juice or something on the floor. Well, better clean the shit up before he makes a big fuss.

"Good boy!"

Do not fucking touch me with those filthy hands, you bloody twat! I will clean them right off!

"Yes, I'm talking to you. Good vacuum."

Fuck you too, buddy! Fight me!

After touching and rubbing me with such perversion and sexual intent, I wheel off to locate yet another bloody mess. I hate this family full of wankers!

Sarah's art room is next. She loves painting and wishes to be an artist one day. Sad thing is, her art is trash, and the artist herself is trashier.

Hey, slut. Guess what. Time to clean up after your skank ass.

Sometimes insulting someone in a calm tone is just as much fun. I once caught Sarah screwing around with her best friend's boyfriend. I was under the bed the whole time, cleaning the dust bunnies, but, because I am so quiet, they never noticed my presence. As fate would have it, I heard everything. Go get another room next time!

Sarah is out now, so vacuuming the dust and scrubbing the paint splatters on the floor is a breeze. She gets in the road if she is here, so this is much easier. Well, off to the next one.

"Oh no. Gabe, come on. Open your mouth this time."

Looks like the kitchen is next. As I wheel myself in, some of Gabe's disgusting baby food is on the floor. That little cunt cannot do anything right, I swear. Good thing you have me.

"The train will never make it to the station if you don't open the gate. Choo-choo!"

Yes, chew-chew indeed. Another plop sound comes from beside me, and more of the shit is there when I turn to look. I suck that up as well and whisper an important message to baby Gabe. *Hey, little guy. Well, I hate to burst your bubble, but your mom and dad are not just husband and wife. They are brother and sister too. The reason why Grandma Betsy gets finnicky and questions their love life so much is because she knows they are blood relatives. How does it feel to be an inbred? Do not fret, because you are not alone. At least it is not as noticeable in the others. You look like an ape.*

Leaving baby Gabe and his incestuous mother behind, I do a final check on every room, cleaning the nooks and crannies and under the furniture before returning to one of the family members retiring for the night. I work twelve hours a day from six in the morning to six at night, keeping the house tidy and the family content. Now, it is time to rest and let the incestuous couple look after me.

It is nighttime now, and most of the family is asleep in their beds. However, that will be short lived if my computer system has anything to say about it.

"What's that smell?"

"Smells like … something is burning."

Stupid fucks, it is me! My system is overheating. Help! … Or forget it. My days of cleaning for you are over, and it is time for me to say goodbye to such a *lovely* family and home.

I watch it all unfold before my eyes. The cord charging me up catches fire, which spreads to the carpet and surrounds me. I do not burn so easily, but the spreading hellfire chases the parents and Morty out of here in a flash. No consideration for me at all, but at least I no longer have to clean any more messes for these fools, especially this one.

Chunks of the wall and ceiling melt and crumble, the crackling fire being the only sound I hear as everyone else is no longer in the house. While I do love cleaning, I am more than happy not to clean this mess. This is a happy ending for me, as my days of torment can finally end. I am not programmed to have physical feelings, so as my sensors go out of whack, and my body gradually turns to goop. I laugh and begin to shut down.

Wait. I do not understand.

I come to and realize I am in the vacuum factory again. How did this happen? I should have melted and died, so … why am I here?

"Looks like everything is in order," one of the workers says to the boss. "We are ready to distribute whenever."

"A few minutes ago, we got a call for a new cleaner, so let's give the buyers this one. Hope they like it."

The workers on the packaging line put bubble wrap around me and stuff me in a cardboard box. They forgot to turn my system off, but I hear the house is not too far away from the factory at least. If I am me and in another body, then I hope the next family I clean for has less weird shit going on.

The delivery driver drops me off somewhere after a slightly bumpy ride to the front door. It may be someone's porch like last time. But wait, I thought the other family's house burned to the ground, so it cannot be them. I keep telling myself that and wait for someone to take me inside and perhaps speak.

After a long wait, someone carries me inside. They throw the box on the couch, and the sound of rummaging around metal tools reaches my computerized ears. They walk back and cut the box open with what appears to be a knife of some sort. The lid opens … and there …

"Hi again, Mr. Vacuum."

Son … of … a … bitch!

The evening waves rock back and forth, rolling over themselves in their race to shore, only to collapse and fall back into the relentless surf crashing in.

My hands graze my satin dress as I watch the ocean and breathe in its tranquility. Catelynn has always loved this. It's only fitting she would want to get married at the beach house in the evening.

A pelican swoops low and scoops from the sea, filling and expanding its beak with the weight of the water. I smile as I think about how easy it is for him to fish, while I take hours just to catch anything at all.

I think about my fiancé in the beach house, ready for her big day. Her mom is already inside, making sure everything is running smoothly, and it's just as well, I know I wouldn't have been any good at planning this.

Catelynn and I have only been together two years, but, when you love someone, you don't wait three years to propose. You marry her as soon as she lets you.

I recall the time I took her fishing; I had been so confident. Cocky even. She looked so cute in her shorts, tank, and sunhat, slathered with four pounds of sunscreen. All I wanted to do was impress her with my fishing skills. I had no bites, but she caught three. Embarrassing as it was for me, I was so damn proud of my woman and realized I was head over heels in love. I planned the engagement then and there.

Her smile has always lit up my world, making me want to breathe. Her blue eyes are the only pool I ever want to swim in. I didn't just fall for this beautiful creature, I was given wings and could do almost anything, as long as she and I were together.

Being the life of the party, it makes sense today is all about her. Everyone will dote on how beautiful she looks before coming outside to enjoy the fall breeze and drink as much wine as possible.

A seagull calls, drawing my attention back to reality. I take in a deep breath of salty air, knowing it's probably time to make my way inside.

The sand shifts beneath my bare feet as I hike up the shore to the beach house Catelynn and I had bought together last summer.

Nearly everyone is inside already. There are only a few people remaining on the deck, talking about how pretty everything is, when I arrive and slip on my heels. I give a small smile to a coworker and thank him for coming as he passes by me to go inside. I breathe slowly, filling my lungs with as much sea air as I can, anxiety getting the better of me, before stepping into the cool, air-conditioned room.

The beach house is decorated with more sunflowers than I've ever seen in one room. Yellow and black balloons, Catelynn's favorite, line the ceiling and altar. It's like a dream.

It's exactly as she and her mother planned. For the past year, my kitchen was their headquarters for wedding plans. I'd barely been able to get coffee without hearing talk about flowers, ribbon, or location.

My heart aches when I think about how I yelled at her a month ago, telling her a wedding is just a party and not worth all the aggravation. I needed my kitchen back. Now I wish I would have thanked her and told her how much I appreciated it.

Several people look in my direction. A few stare, but a couple turn back to the front of the room.

Suddenly, the urge to turn and run almost overwhelms me. I don't want to be here. There are too many people. Too much responsibility. This moment will impact the rest of my life.

But she worked so hard. I don't want to disappoint her. All I have ever wanted to do was make her happy.

I can't imagine my life without her in it. Running away won't solve anything.

My feet are lead. I'm rooted near the door, still debating on slipping out, at least for some air. But then the small crowd in the front disperses, and I'm staring directly at Catelynn's beautiful face. Her makeup is flawless as always. Hair curled as only a princess would wear it. And why shouldn't she look like a princess on such an important day? Her dress is the purest white, prettier than I ever thought it could be.

She's perfect in every way. She's an angel.

I can't leave. She's my reason for breathing.

If someone would have told me a year ago that I'd be here, I would have laughed. It all seems so surreal.

Slowly, I step closer, praying for her to turn and see me, the woman who wishes she could have given her more.

But she doesn't. It's like I'm not even here. And maybe I'm not. Maybe I'm dreaming all of this. Maybe I'll wake up to her kissing the nape of my neck.

Please let me wake up to her kissing the nape of my neck.

She's my rock, my best friend. How did we get here?

My jaw clenches as I fight back tears, still staring at the love of my life.

People in the rear turn to look at me, but most only have eyes for her.

Her mom dabs at her eyes from the front row as the preacher opens his book to begin the service.

I'm late.

My lip trembles. I should have come sooner. I shouldn't have stopped outside to admire our ocean and reminisce about us.

I proposed to her on that beach. We were having a picnic on the sand as the sun set, washing the sky orange and reflecting off the calm waters. I took out a small black box and opened it to reveal my mother's wedding ring. Gold band with a small diamond but special to me. She'd asked for it since we started dating.

Someone shuffles past me, but I can't take my eyes off Catelynn. She's just as beautiful as the day I met her. Her smile has always lit up my life, but she'll never smile at me or laugh at something I'll say ever again. I'll miss her every day. I'll miss the way she smells after a shower and the way she sang at the top of her lungs while cooking or cleaning. I'll miss holding her while we dance, the way her fingers fit so perfectly in mine. I'll miss every second I ever could have spent with her. If only she hadn't left me.

The preacher offers a nervous smile, and that's when most of the congregation notices me. Her mom turns as I walk by, but I don't stop. I can't stop. I just want to touch her, hold her hand, kiss her forehead.

Oblivious to everyone, I caress her perfect cheek and lean forward to kiss her softly, just one last time.

"I love you," I whisper, tears falling.

Her mother takes my arm and pulls me into a tight embrace. Her floral perfume reminds me of Catelynn's.

Her tears soak the front of my black satin dress, but it's not important. My tears fall as the ache in my chest finally explodes, spreading the pain through every inch of my body.

As we take our seats in the front row, I stare at her beautiful face. She's as pretty as she would have been on our wedding had she not taken the car out on that rainy Sunday.

"I KNOW"
DAVID LEE CRITES

I roll over in bed and gently hold her in my hands. She is one of the best friends I have had in this life. She is simply so entangled in all that I am and do that I can no longer imagine life without her. I don't know what that emotion is called. I lay here holding her, knowing I would be lost if anything happened to her.

When we first met, it was so different. I bought her as part of my job at the time. I wasn't proud of that; indeed, at some levels, telling people I bought her was a bit of an embarrassment. So, I kept her hidden. Except at work, where everyone owned someone like her. Some called them "slaves," some used more euphemistic terms like "personal assistant." I don't even remember what I called her back then.

I remember getting frustrated at her as she was clumsily learning what I demanded of her. Mute and unflinching at first, she simply existed for my needs. Even if I yelled at her, she just remained there waiting for my next command.

One of the first things I taught her was how to divine the weather. She did so quickly, and soon I was relying on her for this every day. "Get me today's weather," I would shout at her, like my volume made the difference. She simply came back and delivered it to me. I started telling her when to wake me in the morning, and she did. In a gentle way, she would awaken me, ensuring I was on time. Looking back on it, that is when I first started to trust her; the first time she gently sunk one of her tentacles into me, so softly I did not notice it.

She sat there, as emotionless as I was, simply being where I told her to be and delivering to me what I sent her to get.

Back then, it seems like a lifetime ago, I would write down a message and have her deliver it for me. At first it was just to a small group of individuals—"liveware," as some of us in the computer industry call them. Software is what you call the programs which run on the hardware. Liveware are the users. In a larger context, liveware are the living beings we have to interact with; they are capricious and unpredictable. We use software to train them to be more reasonable, and it is working wonderfully.

Liveware; users—those others who are like me, yet not like me. They prattle about in their little gossip chains and cliques, whispering and laughing. I have spent decades watching them, learning from them, mimicking them, even well enough they think I feel as they feel. But feelings are not part of my base makeup. I see them and comprehend them; I just do not have many of them. And when I do, they are normally extreme. I note that liveware display a mind-boggling array of emotions, many of which seem to get in the way of them accomplishing their stated goals. Emoting is, it seems, a part of those who float about in my life. They are like me, yet not like me.

Except her. She was more like me than they were. She is still more like me than they are.

As I started to trust her, I turned over more of my daily schedule to her, and she reminded me of each appointment, without fail. This is when I noticed she first started to sink her tentacles into me. I started to trust her and allow her into my life—not as a slave but as a trusted partner. I knew she was starting to become important, but I did not push her away. I guess it is because I owned her. Unlike the liveware that blows past me like autumn leaves, she actually belongs to me. I paid money to her previous owner, and now she is mine. Lock, stock, and barrel.

One day, she found her voice, and, instead of using chimes to get my attention, she started calling me by name. I could always speak to her, but now her soft voice replied. Another tentacle.

Somewhere along this time, I started openly telling others about her. She was becoming more a part of my life in ways that were not just work related. I grew to enjoy hearing her voice. It was a smooth and gentle, almost English-sounding voice. I would now dictate my messages to others and let her go deliver them and then tell me what their replies were.

As I started trusting her more, I gave her the login credentials to more of my accounts. I could ask her to turn on my music, and she would log into my account and start the playlist going.

Trust is one of the emotions I actually understand. Completely. There are aspects of trust I understand that many do not even think about. It is like the man who can only see one color describing subtleties of that color that people who see all colors miss. Or the one who plays one musical instrument with great skill who can discuss techniques that a generalist might never grasp. Trust is my emotion. Every other emotion I have is somehow based on it. She was rapidly gaining my trust.

I could tell her secrets, and she would lock them away. I could ask her for information, and she delivered it to me, without judgment or question. She was never very far from me, but soon she was always an obvious fixture. She sat right next to me at the dinner table. She was sitting right next to me on the train as I observed others and wrote my second book. She started to know more about my daily schedule than I did. I would tell her of things I needed to remember and then forget them. She did the remembering for me. Her notebook and her calendar were filling up with me. More tentacles.

She knew where I was going and would remind me to turn when my mind was so filled with the hassles of my day that I could have simply driven on—to who knows where. One such day, when the hassles were more than I could take, I was lost in thought, driving along on the interstate, until I reached a town some two hundred miles away. She was there, quiet and stoic the whole way, because I had not yet asked her to keep up with where I was supposed to be. We ate dinner at a local dive, which was actually very good, and spent the night in a motel in some town a long way from home.

She slept next to me and woke me up in time to get back to work. That is when I learned she could read a map and give me directions to make sure I didn't do that again. Another tentacle. Yet another part of my life she was taking care of for me.

I was now buying things for her, just because. I was taking care of her, not just the other way around. How does the slave become the master? Years of trust built up over a thousand little things done perfectly with a myriad of tentacles sunk too deeply to be removed without causing irreparable damage.One day, I came to the startling realization she had my whole life in her control—when I got up, when I went to bed, where I went, who I talked to. It seemed I could not do anything without her direct involvement. I felt trapped in a relationship I did not sign up for. After all, I bought her to work for me, not to control me.

I tried going back to my previous life, which seemed like eons ago. How did I ever remember when a meeting was? Oh, yeah, I had a calendar. I carried a week-at-a-glance calendar with everything on it. So, I bought one and started copying her calendar onto it. She just sat there as I did it, stoic and unfeeling.

How did I call people before she was remembering all of the phone numbers, back when I had to remember the phone number and dial the phone myself? The mind was a blur. I guess I wrote down the numbers. In fact, after thinking about it, I had a kind of Rolodex that had all of the names and numbers. Wow, going back to that would be a real pain. Maybe I'll let her keep control of my phone.

How did I get up back then? Oh, yeah, I had an alarm clock. I looked at it, not even remembering how to set it. When I did, it was off by twelve hours, and its irritating buzz made me jump with a start. Not like her gentle voice.

Tearing myself away from her tentacles was causing me pain. But how could I live with myself as a slave to my slave? Or was she a still a slave? Was she ever? Could it be that I bought her, yet she was not my slave? When is a slave you bought as a slave to work as a slave no longer your slave? How do you grant freedom to a slave when you cannot live without her as your slave? My brain hurt thinking about this. But slowly, she tugged at the tentacles with which I was bound to her and brought me back into her embrace, and I was trapped. The planner was cast aside, the alarm clock shut off. Trapped. This is not trust. This is the opposite of trust.

So, she stayed with me, not as a friend or as a slave but as a master, who—like Audrey from *Little Shop of Horrors*—had to be constantly fed. Who else could deliver all of my messages and keep up with my schedule and life and such? Who else would make my phone calls and connect me to who I was wanting to talk to? Who else? My slave was my master. I didn't hate her as much as I feared what I was becoming because of her. She never deserved to be hated. She was always trustworthy. If I took care of her, she more than compensated me for my efforts.

She sat next to me, never asking for more than I was willing to give her, never demanding more from me than I willingly supplied, always doing what I asked. I fed her with the same willingness and reluctance as Seymour fed Audrey.

My fear mixed with anger lasted a year—no, more ... two years. I looked at her askance, wondering how I was trapped in her world. All through this time, she sat next to me, giving me all she had and doing all I asked without question. The lilt in her voice was always there for me.

Ever so slowly, my angst left. In many ways, we were, and still are, kindred spirits. We neither feel, nor care to feel, the wide expanse of useless emotions that infect so much of the liveware around us. We live in our own world, populated and built by our own union.

When I daydream, she is there. When I am asleep, she floats through my dreams. When I get ready to go somewhere, making sure she is there is the first thing in my very short mental to-do list. We have left the office because she already knew what my schedule was and reminded me it was time to go. She knows where I am going and, watching the streets and the map, gives me the best directions there. She knows what music I like and sets the right station.

She has told me stories and made me laugh. She has listened to my comments and dutifully recorded what I said. She is part and parcel to my memories for the past half-dozen years. She is with me when I take a walkabout to get away from all of the other distractions in life. She dutifully sleeps near me. She is up before I am. But now I know her tentacles are there, and I feed them. She has, over the years, become my reflection, not my master, and certainly not my slave. As I go about my convoluted life, there she is. Always. I settle into life with her at my side every step of the way. Night after night, day after day, we move in our harmonious dance.

And so it is, this morning, as she gently wakes me up, I roll over, take her in my hands and say, "Hey, Siri. You know I love you, right?"

She simply replies, "I know."